"Cleverly set in the middle of a civil war reenactment, *The Final Reveille* features a spunky, likeable sleuth and engaging characters. You'll want to visit them in charming Barton Farm again and again. A thoroughly enjoyable mystery with history, humor, and heart!"

—Krista Davis, *New York Times* bestselling author of the Domestic Diva Mystery series

"A spunky heroine in a fast-paced mystery... what a fun book to read!"

—Mary Ellis, author of Civil War H... ...ries

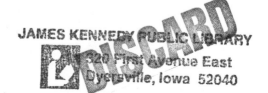

The FINAL
TAP

The

FINAL TAP

A *Living History Museum* Mystery

AMANDA FLOWER

MIDNIGHT INK
WOODBURY, MINNESOTA

FIRST EDITION
First Printing, 2016

Book format by Teresa Pojar
Cover design by Kevin R. Brown
Cover illustration by Tom Jester/Jennifer Vaughn Artist Agency
Map by Llewellyn Art Department

Midnight Ink, an imprint of Llewellyn Worldwide Ltd.

Library of Congress Cataloging-in-Publication Data

Names: Flower, Amanda, author.
Title: The final tap / Amanda Flower.
Description: First edition. | Woodbury, Minnesota : Midnight Ink, [2016] |
   Series: A living history museum mystery ; 2
Identifiers: LCCN 2015049002 (print) | LCCN 2016002421 (ebook) | ISBN
   9780738745138 (softcover) | ISBN 9780738748108 ()
Subjects: LCSH: Murder--Investigation--Fiction. | Maple sugar
   industry--Fiction. | GSAFD: Mystery fiction.
Classification: LCC PS3606.L683 F565 2016 (print) | LCC PS3606.L683 (ebook) |
   DDC 813/.6--dc23
LC record available at http://lccn.loc.gov/2015049002

Midnight Ink
Llewellyn Worldwide Ltd.
2143 Wooddale Drive
Woodbury, MN 55125-2989
www.midnightinkbooks.com
Printed in the United States of America

For Molly and Samantha

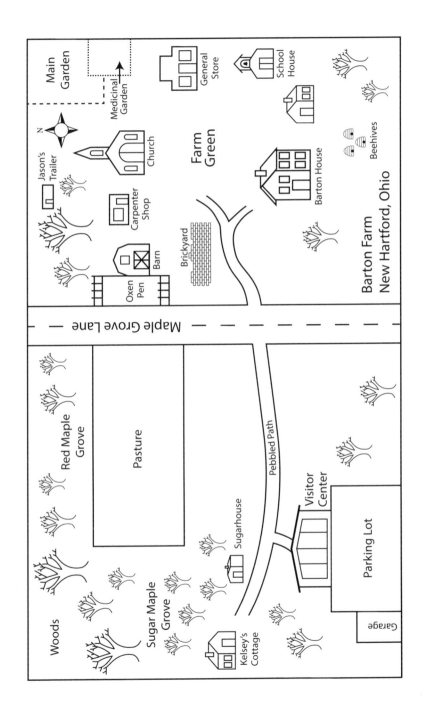

Barton Farm
New Hartford, Ohio

He should be as vigorous as a sugar maple, with sap enough to maintain his own verdure, beside what runs into the troughs, and not like a vine, which being cut in the spring bears no fruit, but bleeds to death in the endeavor to heal its wounds.

–Henry David Thoreau

ONE

Part of my life is stuck in 1863, and I'm starting to realize that might be a dangerous place to live. The thought struck me in the early morning while standing in the sugar maple grove on the west edge of Barton Farm's grounds as my toes curled in from the cold despite two pairs of woolen socks and sturdy snow boots. It wasn't so much the cold that made me question my life; it was the large man standing a few feet in front of me brandishing a hand drill as if it were a bayonet.

I held up my hands. "Dr. Beeson, if you put the drill down, I'm happy to listen to whatever it is you have to say, but if you continue to wave it back and forth, our conversation is over."

He glanced down at the drill in his hand and scowled as if he were seeing it for the first time. With a grunt, he dropped it to his side. "How am I supposed to teach the tree tapping class tomorrow if I cannot tap the trees? They're frozen solid."

It had been an unseasonably cold winter in northeastern Ohio, and even though it was the first week of March, the high temperature still hovered in the twenties. The weatherman had made some murmuring about a break in the weather by midafternoon, but he'd said it with some trepidation. He probably feared for his life if his prediction turned out to be wrong. Staring at Dr. Conrad Beeson and his drill, I could relate. Beeson was a large man, well over six feet and likely to tip the scale at three hundred pounds. He wore black-rimmed glasses and had a full beard that he kept neatly trimmed.

He held the drill up again. "And why on earth do I have to use this antiquated tool? Everyone who taps trees uses a power drill today."

My tan and white corgi, Tiffin, stood at attention, ready to defend me if the need arose. His soulful brown eyes were trained on Beeson's drill.

I took a deep breath. "I understand that, but we would like at least part of the demonstration to be authentic to what tree tapping was like back during the Civil War in Ohio, which our farm and village strives to represent."

He opened his mouth as if he was about to argue the point some more, but I was quicker. "I can understand your frustration, but I have no control over the weather." I did my best to keep my voice even. It was a bit of a struggle. The good doctor was wearing on my last nerve. I sorely regretted including a tapping presentation to kick off Barton Farm's Maple Sugar Festival, a new weekend event on the Farm that I hoped would become an annual tradition and earn some much-needed revenue. During the quiet winter months, the money-making half of Barton Farm—the historical village across Maple Grove Lane—was closed.

"You have to think of something," he protested. "I can't be expected to work under these conditions."

"We could always wrap electric blankets around the tree trunks to heat up the sap. Would that help?" Benji Thorn, my new assistant, asked. She stood beside me with her hands deep inside the pockets of her down coat. Benji was new to the position, but she wasn't new to Barton Farm. Now in her senior year of college, she'd worked at the Farm every summer since high school as a historical interpreter.

I shot Benji a so-not-helping look.

She grinned and, unpocketing a mitten, casually flipped one of her many dark braids over her shoulder.

Beeson glared at her. "I don't appreciate your sarcasm, young lady. This is a serious issue. If there's no sap, there can be no class."

"Now wait," I said, holding up my hands. "We can still have your presentation in the visitor center, and you can still demonstrate how to tap a tree. I'm sure the class will be understanding about the weather. We have thirty people registered, and they're enthusiastic to hear what you have to say about the history of maple sugaring and possible techniques they can use on their own trees."

He scowled. "What is the point of fake-tapping a tree?"

"This is supposed to be educational, Dr. Beeson. I thought that as a college professor, you would recognize that," I said.

"I'm a professor of horticulture and work for the college, but I'm mainly a researcher. I'm not trapped in a classroom all the time with undergraduates who would much rather be twittering each other than learning how to care for plants."

Benji covered a snort with a cough when he said "twittering."

It didn't seem like Beeson missed Benji's snort. The maple sugar expert sniffed. "This is a waste of time, and certainly not worth the measly honorarium you've offered to pay me. I would be better off preparing for my own maple sugar season. Because of the weather, it's going to be late this year. When that happens, the season is usually short. You have to extract the sap from the trees when the trees are ready. When the sap stops running, it stops. There's nothing that can be done about that."

I counted to ten, backward, to stop myself from saying something I might regret or something that would make Beeson quit the Maple Sugar Festival altogether. There wasn't enough time to find a replacement instructor for the tree tapping class; I'd already scrambled to find Beeson when my first expert had backed out. I had things to do—three school buses of third and fourth graders from New Hartford Elementary School were bound for the Farm at that very minute. My director of education had devised a school program to tie in with the Maple Sugar Festival, and I needed to return to the visitor center to greet the children.

"Hey," Benji said, narrowing her dark eyes. "You should be happy Kelsey invited you here to speak. It's a huge event for the Farm, and we already have over a hundred people registered for Saturday and Sunday, not to mention the thirty coming tomorrow for your course. You should be happy with the publicity the Farm is giving you and your book. Kelsey's letting you sell books after the class and during the festival. You can make money off of that."

Benji wasn't a count-to-ten-backward kind of girl.

The book Benji was referring to was *Maple Sugar and the Civil War*, Beeson's scholarly text that had been released a few weeks earlier. During the Civil War, maple sugar was a hot commodity in the north, since after the south ceded from the Union, sugar cane and molasses were hard to come by. In its place, the northerners used maple syrup to sweeten their coffee and to bake with. So when I'd needed to quickly find a new instructor for the tree tapping class, I'd thought Beeson was the ideal candidate—his book fit perfectly with our Maple Sugar Festival, especially since I'd have a small group of Civil War reenactors on the Farm grounds during the festival.

It appeared that I might have been wrong.

Beeson glared at Benji and then at me. "How dare you let your employee talk to me in such a manner!"

I held up my hands again. My fingers stung from the cold despite the two heavy pairs of wool gloves I wore. "Now that we've checked on the trees, I think it would be best if we returned to the visitor center to discuss this further. It's far too cold out here to argue."

"If it's too cold to be outside, it's too cold for sugaring," he said before stomping down the pebbled path in the direction of the visitor center.

After the professor disappeared, Tiffin relaxed and started sniffing the bases of the many maple trees in the grove. The land that became Barton Farm had been purchased by Jebidiah Barton around the turn of the nineteenth century. There were already maple trees there when he arrived, but in 1820 he began planting more, with the intention of starting up a maple syrup business.

It was one of the many farming endeavors the Barton family tried over the years to keep their farm profitable. They were also known for their livestock and their beekeeping. When the trains made it to the northeast corner of Ohio, Jebidiah and his son started shipping their honey and maple syrup back East to their home state of Connecticut. This went on for five generations. Eventually, the last of the Bartons' living relatives willed that the Farm be turned into a museum to preserve local history and teach the community, especially the children, what it was like in pioneer days in Ohio. That happened in 1964; it wasn't until the Cherry Foundation donated the money to renovate the buildings and grounds that the Farm actually became a museum. I was the second director of Barton Farm, and the first one to live on the grounds year-round.

"Can you please try to play nice with Dr. Beeson?" I asked Benji.

She folded her arms. "He's a pompous jerk. Just because he has a doctorate in maple sugar doesn't mean he can speak to you like that."

I hid a smile. "I don't think you can have a PhD in maple sugar. His degree is in horticulture, and we're lucky to have him for this event, especially on such short notice. His book really illustrates the history we're sharing with the community this weekend." After the festival opened on Friday with the tree tapping class, it would get into full swing over the next two days with pancake breakfasts, maple sugaring demonstrations, and the reenactors talking about the importance of maple sugar during the Civil War.

Benji snorted. "He should be thanking you for hiring him at all. We're certainly paying him more than he deserves. I can't believe he questioned his honorarium. It's not like he came from out of state. He's not even coming from out of town. He lives right here in New Hartford."

She had a point. Beeson's speaking fee was higher than I'd expected, but when the original expert was struck down by a mysterious illness and landed in the hospital, I couldn't quibble over details. Of course, I'd thought Beeson was the perfect replacement instructor. And as mentioned, I'd been wrong.

"Can you try to be nice?" I asked. "After Sunday, this will all be over. We can always find a different person to teach the tree tapping class next year if he doesn't work out. We have a whole year to plan."

She grunted. "All right, but it's for you, not for him."

"That's fine with me." I smiled and stomped my numb feet. "Now let's head back to the visitor center. If we stay out here much longer my toes are going to freeze off."

"Mine already have," she said with a sigh.

TWO

Despite her lack of working toes, Benji and I made it to the visitor center without incident. When I walked through the automatic glass doors that led into the building, Tiffin shot across the polished, pine-planked floor and curled up in his dog bed by the hearth. He gave a contented sigh as he rested his chin on his white paws and absorbed the warmth from the crackling fire.

I took a deep breath. The inside of the visitor center smelled like a combination of the fire, pancakes, and maple syrup. The school children who were coming to the Farm would be treated to pancakes, just like our guests would be during the festival.

Benji headed to the kitchen to check that Alice, our head cook, had everything under control for the children's lunch.

Yesterday, the first day of the program, we'd hosted a group of fifteen homeschoolers. We had a few minor maple syrup spills on the dining room floor, but other than that, the day had been a great success. Tomorrow would be the third and final day of the school program, coinciding with the kick-off of the festival.

Because we didn't yet have any maple sugar of our own to turn into syrup, we'd purchased some from a farm in Kentucky, where the sugaring season was already in full swing. I wished that we had our own sugar for the demonstrations, but we carried on with the Kentucky maple sugar because I believed it was important for the kids to see how the syrup was made. I'd sold the program to the local schools not only on the historical aspect the Farm always offered, but on the science too. Temperature control, evaporation, crystallization, and all of those scientific concepts were included in the creation of maple syrup.

As my director of education, Gavin Elliot was great with the kids, probably because he was much like a kid himself. It had been his idea to create the school program as a companion event to the Maple Sugar Festival. I was grateful to see that his idea seemed to be paying off.

Gavin was only a couple of years out of college and constantly being asked by guests what high school he went to. In protest against being mistaken for seventeen, he'd grown a full, dark beard not unlike Beeson's. Now, instead of just looking like a teenager, he looked like a teenager dressed up like a lumberjack for Halloween. He finished the look with a red flannel shirt over his Farm polo and khaki pants.

"Is the sugarhouse ready for the kids?" I asked him.

He glanced over at me. "Hey, Kelsey. The sugarhouse is good to go. I've had the fire going for a couple of hours already and have the batch of maple sugar boiling at the right temperature."

I glanced back through the window. The sugarhouse was an old, whitewashed building, a reconstruction of the sugarhouse the Bartons built on the same spot in 1820. The original building had burned to the ground sometime during the Great Depression.

Smoke rolled out of the sugarhouse's chimney. I hoped to have time to peek inside soon and see Gavin's presentation with the kids, but first I had to find Beeson. "Did Dr. Beeson come in here?" I asked.

"I haven't seen him." Gavin frowned. "I don't know why you picked him as the replacement. I could have done it. I'm the one talking to the kids for the maple sugar program, and the lecture isn't that different. My father taps more trees than anyone else in New Hartford. I've been maple sugaring since I was a kid."

"I know you could have taught it, Gavin, but I didn't want to give you too heavy of a workload. Plus, you'll have a school visit at the same time. Between you and me, though, I'm starting to regret asking Beeson to speak. I thought his new book would be a draw for more guests, but he's turning out to be a bit of a diva."

Gavin barked a laugh. "I could have told you that."

Before I could ask him what he meant by that comment, Judy, who was in charge of our ticket sales, walked over to where we were standing. "I just got a call from one of the schoolteachers. The buses left the elementary school. They should be here inside ten minutes."

I nodded. It didn't take more than ten minutes to drive anywhere in New Hartford.

"I'd better go check the sugarhouse before they arrive," Gavin said, turning to go.

After he exited the visitor center, I asked Judy, "Have you seen Dr. Beeson? He left Benji and me in the maple grove. I expected to find him in here waiting for us. We were going to discuss the class he's teaching tomorrow."

Judy wrung her hands. Before she could answer, Benji approached us from the kitchen. "Alice is good to go," she said.

"Great," I said.

Benji looked from Judy to me and back again. "What's going on?" She stared at Judy's clasped hands and her eyes widened. Judy wasn't the hand-wringing type.

Judy looked down at her hands as if she'd just realized what she was doing. She dropped them to her sides. "Pansy Hooper was just here."

I groaned. "What did she want?"

Judy shook her head. "To complain about all the noise on the Farm."

"Noise?" I asked, even though this came as no surprise.

Pansy Hooper was our closest neighbor to the Farm. Her family owned a little home in the woods about a half mile from the Farm's historical village. Milton Hooper, her father, had lived in that house for decades and never complained about anything. After he died, Pansy and her two teenaged sons had moved into the family home. Since arriving in January, Pansy has done nothing but complain about the Farm. She'd gone as far as to report our noise to the town council. They were shaping up to be the neighbors from hell, something I didn't think I'd have to deal with at Barton Farm. The worst part was, it was the off-season for Barton Farm and she already thought we were too loud. Heaven knew what she would say or do when we started shooting off cannons during the Civil War reenactment in the summer.

I shook my head. "I'll deal with her later. I have to find Dr. Beeson."

Judy wrinkled her nose. Apparently, she was as much a fan of Beeson as Benji was.

"Have you seen Dr. Beeson?" I repeated my original question, looking around the visitor center at the polished floors and exposed wooden beams. Although the center was built to resemble a lodge from nineteenth-century pioneer days in Cuyahoga Valley, it was very much a modern building constructed fifteen years ago. Its Wi-Fi and sliding glass doors gave it away. "I thought he was coming back here to the visitor center."

"He did come in, but he was only here for a few minutes before he stormed off again, mumbling something about the red maples on the other side of the pasture," Judy said.

In unison, the three of us turned around and stared through the sliding glass doors. We could see the wide pasture lands that bordered the woods along the northern edge of Barton Farm. On this side of the Farm, west of Maple Grove Lane, we had my cottage, the sugar maple groves, the visitor center, the pasture for the oxen, and a handful of outbuildings. On the east side of the Farm was the village, where from May to October my first-person historical interpreters acted out nineteenth-century history as if they were living in 1863. I'd arranged to have a few of my top interpreters—including my best friend Laura Fellow, a high school history teacher—on the grounds near the visitor center Saturday and Sunday, dressed in character for the Maple Sugar Festival. Meanwhile, Gavin would be in the sugarhouse, demonstrating how maple sugar is boiled down to maple syrup, and the Civil War reenactors would be on hand to provide their stories about maple sugar during the war to anyone who asked.

"Beeson must have been moving pretty fast if we didn't see him when we walked back here," Benji said. "We were only a few minutes behind him, and I didn't see anyone crossing the field. Did you, Kelsey?"

I shook my head. "Did he say what was so important about the red maples?" I asked Judy.

She brushed her hands on her long khaki skirt. Judy always wore a khaki skirt. I imagined she had an entire closet of them at home.

"He muttered something about the trees being ready," she said.

I frowned. "I guess that's possible. Dr. Beeson was furious that all our sugar maples are frozen solid, so it sounds to me like he thinks the red maples will be ready to tap. He's adamant on the point that he wants to tap a tree that's already running for his class." I frowned. "But those red maples won't do. They're quite a hike from the Visitor Center, and most of the people attending his class are retirees."

"I told you electric blankets will solve everything," Benji said.

"Electric blankets?" Judy asked.

"Ignore her," I said.

"Not to mention that the oxen wouldn't like people tramping back and forth across their pasture," Benji said. "The only person they tolerate is Barn Boy."

"Please call our farmhand Jason," I said automatically.

"I'll try to remember," Benji said. Her tone told me that she would soon forget that promise.

"Should we go after him?" Judy asked.

"You can't," I said. "You need to stay here for when the school children arrive. Benji and I will go. We shouldn't be gone long."

Judy gave me a "yeah right" look.

I frowned and wondered what that was about, but I didn't have time to ask. I needed to be back at the visitor center in time for the school visit.

Benji pulled her hat down over her ears. "Let's get this over with, and just an FYI, I might put in for hazard pay. I've already lost my toes. My fingers may be next."

I rolled my eyes, knowing that she was kidding. Before Benji was my permanent assistant, she was the Farm's brickmaker. If there was any reason to put in for hazard pay it would be that. Making bricks by hand was hot and dangerous work, and Benji had the scars from wasp stings on the soles of her feet to prove it.

Benji and I walked out the sliding glass doors. I looked down at Dr. Beeson's obvious tracks in the snow. "At least the snow is good for something. He'll be easy to find."

Before crossing the pebbled path, we waited for the horse-drawn sleigh to come to a halt in front of the visitor center. It would give the children sleigh rides after the maple sugaring presentation. Since the ground was still frozen, we'd kept the sleigh out, but Jason, the farm-hand, had our large wagon ready to go if the ground started to thaw. The Farm's two draft horses, Scarlett the mare and Rhett the gelding, stood at the front of the sleigh stomping their hooves. Scarlett bumped her head against Rhett. She was the one in charge and everyone knew it.

My master gardener, Shepley, sat in the sleigh's driver seat. Shepley was the resident grouch of Barton Farm—a title I would have assigned to Dr. Beeson, if only by a few points, had Beeson been a full-time employee. Despite the cold, Shepley wasn't wearing a hat. His long gray hair was tied back at the nape of his neck with a piece of leather. He wasn't my first choice to entertain children—actually, to entertain anyone—but he was the one person available. I'd hoped that Jason would step up and drive the sleigh, but he became anxious in a group of more than two people. Four dozen kids would make him run for the woods.

I stepped up to the sleigh. "Shepley, did you see Dr. Beeson walk by here on his way across the pasture? He's the maple sugar expert teaching tomorrow's class," I added for clarity.

Shepley scowled in return. "Did you lose him? I do almost everything on this Farm, but is it my job to keep track of your *experts* too?"

I sighed, not bothering to argue. There was no point in getting Shepley riled up before he faced all those impressionable children. I shivered to think what he would say. I went over to Benji, who was waiting for me at the split-rail fence that surrounded the pasture.

"Just ignore him," she said reasonably. She grunted as she climbed over the fence. I followed. The Farm's two oxen, Betty and Mags, stared at us as we trudged across their pasture in the snow. Steam puffed out of their nostrils and mouths and reminded me of the bison I'd seen in the early morning when I camped in Yellowstone National Park while in college.

"Just so you know, if those two charge you're in trouble," Benji said. "I ran track in high school, and I can outrun you."

I frowned. "Thanks."

On the other side of the field, Benji and I climbed the fence, but that's where Beeson's tracks ended. "Where did his footprints go?" I asked. "It hasn't snowed in the last twenty minutes, so they can't be covered."

She pulled her stocking cap farther down on her ears. "Alien abduction is my theory."

I studied the ground. "This is weird."

"What?" She looked down too.

I pointed. "It looks like brush marks in the snow. It's almost like someone used a pine bough to erase the footprints."

"Why would anyone do that? There isn't anything out here but a bunch of trees."

We followed the brush marks deeper into the trees and found a person lying at the foot of a maple. He wasn't moving, and some of the snow around him was stained red. A sinking feeling washed over me as Benji and I inched forward. Neither of us said a word.

At our feet, Dr. Conrad Beeson lay on his side, the hand drill sticking out of his chest.

THREE

BENJI AND I GAPED at the fallen man for a full minute before either one of us came to our senses.

Benji found her voice first. "Is—is he dead?"

He certainly looked dead.

I shook my head, and then crisis mode kicked in. I knelt next to Dr. Beeson and placed a finger to his neck, leaning close to his face. I felt a pulse. It was faint but there. "He's still alive. Call 911!" I ordered Benji.

She yanked her cell phone from her coat pocket and made the call. I heard her rattle off the address for the Farm.

"They're on their way," she said. She held the phone away from her ear. "They told me to stay on the line."

"Okay, do that and run back to the visitor center and tell them what's going on. You'll have to direct the ambulance here too."

She hesitated. "You want me to leave you here with him?"

"Yes! Go! You have to tell Gavin and Judy what's going on. The school group will be here any minute. It would be best if Gavin took the children to the sugarhouse first to keep them out of the way of the paramedics."

Benji shook her head as if clearing away some cobwebs. "Right!" She took off for the visitor center. She hadn't been kidding when she said she could run fast.

After the sound of her footsteps in the snow faded away, I turned back to the injured man. I wasn't a medical professional, but I knew he didn't have much time if help didn't arrive soon. As much as it pained me to see him lying there with the drill sticking out of his chest, I knew not to remove it. The risk was too great that I would cause more damage by removing the drill bit, and it would only make his bleeding worse. The drill stuck out of the left side of his chest. I hoped that meant it had missed his heart, not that an injured lung was so much better.

I leaned close to his face. "Help's on the way, Dr. Beeson. You're going to be okay." I didn't know he would be okay, and I didn't know if he could hear me. It seemed to be the right thing to say. When my mother had been in hospice before she died, the nurses had told me to talk to her even when she could no longer respond. They said she could hear me, and it would help her. I still didn't know if it helped my mother. I might never know, but talking to her during those last, long—but at the same time fleeting—hours had helped me. It gave me a chance to say everything that I'd needed her to hear.

If Beeson died out here in the freezing snow, his family would never have the chance to do that.

I squeezed his hand. "Help is on the way."

I was so glad my son Hayden was at school, and that he wasn't one of the children who would be visiting the Farm for the field trip. Had he been, he would have insisted on being with me the entire time. I didn't want him to see this. I'd been able to shelter him from what had happened during the Civil War reenactment last summer, and I planned to do that again.

The wail of sirens broke through the frozen air. I let out a breath I hadn't known I was holding, and it came out in a white puff.

"They're almost here," I said in my best upbeat voice.

"Th-they…" the professor whispered. His eyes were still closed.

Maybe I imagined that I heard it. I leaned close, just in case. "They who?"

"Th-they did…"

"Did what? Did someone do this to you? Can you tell me who?"

"Th-they."

There was the sound of people running and crashing through the trees. I ignored the noise of the approaching voices and focused all my attention on the professor. "They who? Please tell me."

"Th-they," he said through parched lips.

"EMS!" someone cried.

"They're over here," I heard Benji shout.

Benji and three EMTs broke through the trees. The first of the EMTs was Chase Wyatt, a sometime–Civil War reenactor who I'd met the previous summer during Barton Farm's reenactment.

Since the reenactment, we'd developed a friendship, but I knew that Chase wanted it to be something more. He'd asked me out on a date more than once since the reenactment ended in July. So far, I'd been able to avoid giving him a direct answer. I wasn't sure that I was ready to bring another adult into Hayden's life. My five-year-old just had his father's engagement to twenty-something Krissie Pumpernickle sprung on him, and the thought of a new stepmother was a lot for a kid to handle. I didn't want to bring up the possibility of a new stepfather—even though Chase and I were nowhere near that—this close to his father telling him about his upcoming wedding. I needed to protect my son from being hurt again.

My best friend, Laura, would argue that I wasn't protecting Hayden. I was protecting myself. I hadn't been on a single date since the divorce was finalized three years ago. A tiny part of me would admit only to myself that I thought she might be right. I'd never tell Laura that. She would hold it over me for the rest of my life and into the hereafter. But I had good reason to want to protect myself. Hayden's father, Eddie, had been unfaithful. I could not go through that again.

Despite all my logical thoughts about why dating Chase was a terrible idea, I felt my cheeks grow hot when he made eye contact with me. If I was asked, I planned to blame my blush on the harsh winter wind.

Chase wore a black hip-length ski jacket over his navy uniform and sturdy snow boots that looked like they were used for hiking or kicking in doors. "Are you okay?" he whispered as he kneeled next to me.

I gave him the slightest of nods. "Dr. Beeson isn't great."

He saw the drill sticking out of the man's chest and winced. As he did so, he checked Beeson's pulse. "He's still alive, but we don't have much time." He waved over his colleagues and they placed a fold-up stretcher on the snow. "Kelsey, I'm going to have to ask you to back up."

I stumbled to my feet and shuffled back to where Benji stood on the edge of the trees. As I did, a young police officer—Officer Sonders, who I'd met the last time someone died on the Farm—broke through the trees. He nodded to me. "What happened? Has there been a crime?"

"I don't know," I managed to say. I nodded to Dr. Beeson and the EMTs kneeling around him.

He shuddered. "I'd better call this in." He stepped away from Benji and me and removed his radio from his belt.

"He's a big guy," one of the other two EMTs said. "How are we going to carry him out? The snow's too deep to pull the ambulance into the woods. It'll get stuck for sure."

"Pull the ambulance around as close as you can get it to the tree line on this side of the pasture, and we will have to carry him that far," Chase said. "Sonders can help."

"Benji and I can help too," I said.

My assistant nodded. Her dark skin had a gray cast to it.

One of the EMTs moved off toward the pasture to move the ambulance into position, and the other knelt beside Chase to stabilize Beeson for transport.

"Are you okay?" I whispered to Benji.

She swallowed. "I've never seen anything like this."

"Me either," I admitted. "Chase and the other EMTs will take care of him. He'll be okay."

Benji twisted her mouth as if she wasn't so sure about that. I had to agree with her. I knew Chase and the others would do everything they could for the professor, but it was hard to believe he would survive his injury.

The EMTs gently rolled Beeson onto the stretcher. Chase placed an oxygen mask over his face and tightened the straps around his body so that he wouldn't fall off the board.

"Are you going to leave that drill sticking out of his chest like that?" Benji's voice was accusing.

Chase's dark eyes glanced at us for half a second. "The surgeons will remove it at the hospital. If we do it here, he might bleed to death."

Benji's face grew a shade grayer.

"He was trying to tell me something," I said. "I think he was trying to tell me what happened."

"There's no time to find out now," Chase said. "We have to get him to the hospital."

I swallowed. "Just tell us what we need to do."

He smiled. "You've done well so far. He's still alive."

That was small comfort. Even I could tell the maple sugar expert was in serious trouble.

The EMT who'd run for the ambulance appeared in the woods. "We're ready to move."

"Good." Chase raised his voice. "Sonders, we need you too."

The officer joined them at the stretcher as Chase signaled Benji and me to come forward. He directed us where to grab the stretcher. "All right, on the count of three, we lift. One … two … three!"

With a Herculean effort, we hoisted Dr. Beeson from the frozen ground. He made the faintest groan. In a small way, I found his protest comforting. It meant he was still alive.

The walk to the road and the waiting ambulance was cumbersome. Even with six of us bearing Beeson's substantial weight, three of whom were paramedics in top shape, my arms shook from the effort to keep my portion of the stretcher level.

Chase directed us as we set the man on a rolling stretcher waiting outside the ambulance. He and his colleagues took over from there.

After the EMTs slid Beeson's gurney into the back of the ambulance, Chase jumped in.

"Let me know how he is!" I called as he shut the door.

Chase gave me the briefest of nods and turned to his patient.

Officer Sonders, Benji, and I watched the ambulance disappear down Maple Grove Lane with its lights flashing.

"I need to secure the scene," the young officer said.

"Do you think it was foul play?" Benji asked.

In other circumstances I would have chuckled at her use of the words "foul play," but not today. I wrapped my arms around my middle as if to hold myself together. Another death on the Farm in less than a year. How was that even possible?

Officer Sonders was neutral. "I don't know. More police are on the way, and you'll probably be hearing from Detective Brandon."

I grimaced. The detective and I weren't the best of friends, or anything close to resembling friends. "Do you need anything else from us?" I asked. "We have a school visit going on, and I should be returning to the visitor center."

"I need your statements about how you found Beeson and why he was here."

I heard sirens and figured it must be the backup Sonders had called. The patrol car pulled up in the space along Maple Grove Lane where the ambulance had been. I was grateful that they parked there, where the school children would not be able to see them.

Officer Sonders spoke to the other policemen for a moment, then returned to Benji and me for our statements, which were brief. Finally, he said we could go but warned again that I would be hearing from the detective. Something to look forward to. Benji and I walked back to the visitor center in silence.

Judy met us at the automatic doors. "I saw the ambulance leave."

"They're taking Dr. Beeson to the hospital. He's going right into surgery."

Judy clicked her tongue. "Godspeed to him then. When Benji came running in here shouting that there was a man with a drill sticking out of his chest in the woods, I almost fainted dead away." She straightened her shoulders. "And I'm not one to faint, Kelsey. I raised six children. I've seen a whole host of disturbing things in my day."

21

I didn't doubt it. "Is Gavin with the school group?"

Judy nodded. "He should be. He wasn't here when Benji came running in, so Jayne ushered the children straight to the sugarhouse like Benji directed her to do. They were already there when the ambulance arrived."

"Good," I said, wondering where Gavin was. I placed a hand on my forehead. I needed to think. I was still reeling from finding Beeson, but I had the Farm to operate at the same time. I couldn't believe this had happened. I'd just been arguing with cantankerous Beeson that morning and now he was at the hospital fighting for his life. Something my mother said to me once came to mind: "If you don't know what to do, do the next thing." My father would have called it shifting in autopilot.

Judy peered at me over her glasses. "Are you sure you're all right?"

I forced a smile. "I should go to the sugarhouse and tell Gavin the coast is clear and he can bring the children back for the program in the visitor center any time."

Judy cleared her throat. "That's a good idea, but you might want to change your coat before you greet those children. You're covered in blood."

I looked down to discover that my light blue ski jacket was blood stained. Immediately, I felt woozy. I had a five-year-old son and I'd seen some pretty unappealing things in my day, just as Judy had, but the sight of Beeson's blood on my coat made me dizzy.

Benji was at my side. She didn't have any blood on her. Then again, she hadn't been kneeling beside Dr. Beeson trying to hear whatever it was he had to say. I was still worried about that. I knew whatever he'd wanted to tell me had been important, or he wouldn't have been so desperate to get it out when he was clearly in tremendous pain.

"Are you going to pass out?" Benji asked.

"Maybe you should sit down," Judy added.

The director of Barton Farm did *not* pass out or sit down in times of crisis. There were school children on the grounds, and it was my responsibility to make sure they had the best visit possible. I took a deep breath through my nose and let it out through my mouth. "I'm fine."

"Sure you are," Benji said, clearly not believing me for a moment.

"I'm fine, and Dr. Beeson will be fine too," I said with as much conviction as I could muster. "I have another coat in my office. I'll go change into it before I go off to the sugarhouse." I glanced around the visitor center. "It looks okay in here, but can the two of you go around and check to make sure there's no sign of what happened?"

"You mean like blood spatter?" Benji asked. Apparently, she'd recovered from her queasiness in the woods.

I blanched. "Just make sure there's no sign of anything related to what happened to Dr. Beeson."

"We'll take care of it," Judy promised.

FOUR

Before Benji could make another comment about my coat, I went down the short hallway beside the cafeteria to my office. As I passed the open and airy dining room, I gave a sigh of relief. Everything was set up for the children's pancake lunch. Little pitchers of maple syrup sat on every table, along with recyclable paper plates and cups. The children would be eating fruit as well as pancakes, and there was milk, orange juice, and water to drink.

Alice had set bud vases with daffodils on each table. I didn't know if the children would appreciate the decoration as much as the pancakes, but I certainly did. The bright yellow blossoms reminded me that spring would be here soon, no matter what the thermometer read on the outside. In my opinion, spring couldn't come soon enough.

All the while, worry over Beeson tickled the back of my mind. I whispered a voiceless prayer for him.

As much as I wanted to go compliment Alice on her work, I put my head down and kept walking. I didn't want to startle her with my bloodied appearance. I made a mental note to tell her how nice it looked the next chance I got. It was my managerial style to praise my employees every chance I had, but I thought under the circumstances this could wait until later.

I unlocked and opened my office door, hanging my blood-spattered coat over the back of the chair. Working on the Farm, I'd been covered with all manner of muck, but this was the first time it was another person's blood. I tried not to think about it. I knew I would throw my coat away before I'd take it to the local dry cleaners. New Hartford was a small town, and a blood-covered coat would certainly make tongues wag. The Farm was already a topic of idle conversation after the events of last summer that led to Maxwell Cherry's death. I grabbed my old black down coat and headed outside.

Instead of leaving through the visitor center's main exit, I slipped out the *Employees Only* exit on the side. My boots crunched as I marched through the layer of snow on my way to the pebbled path that wound through the Farm.

The path was packed down from dozens of feet that had trampled it the last two days during the school visits. I was pleased with how much interest there was in our maple sugar program from the local schools, and I hoped to expand the program by several days next March, although I might schedule everything a week later in order to get warmer temperatures.

As I walked down the snow and ice-encrusted path, I kept making mental lists in my head about how I could make the school visits better next year. I hoped my lists would distract me from what had happened to Beeson. It didn't work. A tiny part of me was afraid the Farm might be sued. It could be even worse if he died. I shook my head. How could I even think about the Farm at a time like this, when the poor man was suffering? What had he been trying to tell me? I wished that I knew.

The smell of hot maple syrup floated out the open door of the sugarhouse. The whitewashed building was small and could only hold twenty tightly packed people at a time, maybe twenty-five if most of them were children. Because there were fifty students from the elementary school at the Farm at the moment, many spilled out into the trees. Jayne was speaking to the teachers and children outside the sugarhouse. I gave a sigh of relief. I was happy to see the members of my staff step up in a time of crisis. Jayne was doing a pretty good job of relating the history of the Farm.

I waved to her before squeezing into the back of the sugarhouse. I watched Gavin run a long wooden paddle back and forth through the maple sugar that was boiling in a long, stainless steel trough. "We heat the sap to a constant temperature between 212 and 219 degrees Fahrenheit to remove the water," he said. "Does anyone know what happens to the water?"

A boy with glasses raised his hand. "It evaporates."

Gavin beamed at the boy. "That's right! The water evaporates and leaves behind the sugar. When enough water evaporates, the sugar becomes maple syrup. To be considered maple syrup in the state of Ohio, the content has to be sixty-six brix or higher. Does anyone know what a brix is?"

No one said a word.

He chuckled. "I didn't know what it was either when I was your age. A brix measures sucrose or sugar content. It's a measuring tool used for soda, fruit juice, and other liquid that contains sugar. For maple sugaring, less than sixty-six brix is not legally maple syrup." He paused. "If it's too diluted, it can't be sold as maple syrup. What does diluted mean?"

"It has too much water," a girl said.

"That's right." Gavin grinned at the class. "Maybe you guys should be teaching me. You know most of the answers already. The brix one was a wringer. I bet your teachers didn't know the answer to that one either." He winked at them.

The kids grinned back. I relaxed. Gavin had everything well in hand. Maybe I could slip away and find out what the police were doing at the crime scene.

Gavin stopped stirring the sap and walked down the metal trough to the part that was closest to his enraptured audience. He pointed to the end section of the trough, which was partitioned from the rest by a metal wall. The space was about a foot across and slowly filling with maple syrup. "The maple syrup moves from the large portion of the trough to this smaller one," he explained. "This way, we can add more sap to the main portion without diluting the syrup we've already made." He held up what looked like a huge coffee filter. "This is what I use to strain the syrup. There are tiny minerals in the sap that are collected by the tree. Even though they're invisible to the human eye, we don't want them in our maple syrup. This filter will strain them out." He set the filter into a bucket, turned on the tap from the trough, and let syrup run from the end of the trough into the filter-lined bucket. "And that, my friend, is how maple syrup is made. Any questions?"

A dozen small hands flew into the air, and kids hopped in place, hoping to catch Gavin's attention.

Spotting me, Gavin nodded to me over their heads. "Why don't we save these questions for the session after lunch in the classroom? Don't forget them! I want to hear every last one you have. Now, I think we can all go back to the visitor center and warm up. I have some great games planned." He paused dramatically. "And I've heard that the Barton Farm cook has some hot pancakes and fresh maple syrup waiting for you."

A cheer went up from the children. The teachers grimaced at each other. I believe the words "sugar rush" flashed in their heads in bright neon letters.

The class filed out, and I waited for Gavin by the door of the sugarhouse. "That seemed to go well," I said.

"They're a great group of kids," he replied.

Jayne led the teachers and students back to the visitor center. I was grateful, because it gave me a chance to talk to Gavin without being overheard.

"Jayne said that professor was hurt. How is he?" Gavin asked.

I sighed. "I'm not sure yet. He was still alive when the paramedics drove away."

"That's something."

"The police are still here," I added.

"They are?" His eyes widened. "Why?"

I frowned. "Because Dr. Beeson was hurt. They have to investigate."

"An accident doesn't need police."

I thought of the hand drill sticking out of Beeson's chest. It hadn't looked like an accident to me. "They don't know it was an accident."

"They think he was attacked?" he yelped.

"I don't know yet," I said.

Gavin didn't say anything as we started walking back to the visitor center. "I hope this doesn't sounds callous, Kelsey, but if you need someone to fill in for Beeson to teach the tree tapping class, I can do it. I'd be happy to."

"I'd love your help, Gavin, but remember, there'll be the school visit at the same time. You can't be in two places at once. I'll have to find an alternative. It's horrible to think about replacing Dr. Beeson already, no matter how difficult he was to get along with. But no matter what happens, he'll be in no condition to teach tomorrow."

Gavin opened his mouth as if he wanted to say something more, but he was interrupted by a teacher waving at him. His face cleared. "I'd better go see what she wants."

I nodded and watched him walk with the teacher to the visitor center. The whole time, I wondered why he was so keen to teach the class, and what he'd been about to say.

FIVE

I RETURNED TO THE lobby of the visitor center. The volume had increased tenfold with the arrival of the kids from the sugarhouse. The teachers tried to control the volume, but it was no use with the excited talk of pancakes. A heavenly aroma filled the entire building.

Gavin whistled to get their attention. The room fell silent. "Who wants pancakes?"

A cheer went up from the students that shook the rafters. After some scrambling, they filed into the dining room.

Officer Sonders stepped through the sliding glass doors. "Ms. Cambridge?" He waved me over.

I followed the officer outside. "How's Dr. Beeson? Is there any news?"

"He's in surgery." He cleared his throat. "Detective Brandon and the chief are at a statewide law enforcement meeting in Columbus today. They're on their way back now."

"Are they hurrying back because you think a crime has been committed?"

He shook his head. "You'll have to ask them that question. The scene is secure. No one should go over there, understood?"

I nodded. "Do you think it's safe to have the children here? Should I send them back to the school?"

Sonders' mouth twisted. "We searched the woods. There's no one there. But to be safe, I'll hang around here until the children are gone, if that's okay with you."

I nodded.

"Any chance I could get some pancakes?"

I smiled. "Sure. Just tell Alice, our cook, that I sent you."

He grinned and went back into the visitor center.

I sighed. As much as I wanted to go check out the scene myself, I wouldn't have the chance with Officer Sonders on the grounds. It would not do if I was caught snooping around. It appeared that I'd have to wait until the detective and police chief arrived.

Two hours later, the school group left, Officer Sonders was called away, and I was in the dining room helping my staff clean up from the pancake lunch. As I scrubbed at a streak of maple syrup on the tabletop with a hot rag, I decided that during the next day's school visit, the pitchers of maple syrup would not be sitting out on the tables. That had turned into a disaster. This was the third major spill I'd cleaned up between making calls trying to line up an instructor for the tree tapping class. At present, I wasn't having much luck at either.

I was scrubbing the table for all I was worth when someone behind me cleared his throat. I turned to find Chief Duffy and Detective Brandon standing there. Chief Duffy was a sixtyish man with a slight paunch hanging over his belt. His most striking feature was a full beard, cut in the style favored by generals during the Civil War. The chief was an avid Civil War reenactor and had even served as a

Confederate general in the reenactment that Barton Farm had held during the summer. The beard gave him a playful teddy bear look that few took seriously. At least, that few took seriously until he threw them into jail.

While I could compare the police chief to a cuddly teddy bear, I doubted that anyone would put Detective Candy Brandon in the cuddly category. As always, the detective's auburn hair was pulled back into a severe bun at the nape of her neck, and her curvy figure was disguised as much as possible with a suit one size too large. Despite her efforts to make herself appear otherwise, she was beautiful in an ice queen sort of way. She was also my favorite paramedic's ex-fiancée. Chase had told me during the summer that they'd broken up because she didn't want children and that was a deal breaker for him. I suspected Detective Brandon still had feelings for Chase by the fact that she'd detested me on sight. She had to know about his pursuit of me. The other EMTs did, teasing Chase relentlessly about it, and those guys liked to talk. Personally, I didn't have anything against the detective other than her suspecting me of murder last summer. That kind of stuff builds a rift between people.

Chief Duffy also knew Chase well because he was Chase's uncle. It seemed like everyone in New Hartford was intertwined in some way. That was the good and bad part about living in a small town.

Detective Brandon's face now rested in a scowl. That wasn't unusual, but the lines of concern on the usually jovial police chief's face were.

I dropped my rag onto the table, and it stuck to the spill. "How's Dr. Beeson?"

Detective Brandon wrinkled her nose at the spilled syrup. Her reaction to the mess was a testament to me that she didn't have any children in her life. Cleaning up syrup was nothing compared to a whole host of other messy things parents and guardians had to deal with on a regular basis.

I wiped my hands on my jeans. "This is about Dr. Beeson, isn't it?"

The chief pulled on his gray beard. "I'm afraid it is."

"He died," I said, as sure as I was of my own name.

Detective Brandon's narrowed eyes focused on me. "And how would you know that?"

I frowned. "I found him with a drill in his chest on the other side of the pasture. I saw his injury."

"Now, ladies," Chief Duffy said. "Let's not start hissing at each other."

Both Detective Brandon and I scowled at the comment. At least we agreed on something.

"You're right that we're here about Conrad Beeson," Chief Duffy said. "Yes, he passed away while in surgery."

My shoulders sagged. When I was in the woods holding Dr. Beeson's hand, I'd told him he would be okay. At the time, I hadn't really believed it, but his passing had turned me into a liar. It was heartbreaking to hear he'd died. I didn't particularly care for the man, but any loss of life was tragic. He must have people in his life who would miss him.

"I'm sorry to hear that," I said sincerely.

Detective Brandon appeared skeptical at my comment. Her reaction made me wonder what she and jovial Chase had talked about when they were together. He must have driven her absolutely insane with his constant banter.

"It's a shame," the police chief said. He hooked his thumbs under his duty belt. "It's even more of a shame now that the county prosecutor has asked for an investigation into the professor's suspicious death."

I swallowed. "He was murdered?"

"Looks that way. It's hard to believe he could fall on a drill like that by accident. The medical examiner will make the official call, but we're treating it as a murder until we hear different. Unfortunately, it might be a tricky call to make since the doctors at the hospital performed surgery on his heart. The medical examiner will have to really look hard to determine where the drill bit entered his chest."

I shivered.

"It's a real miracle that he didn't die right there on the spot," Chief Duffy said.

Maybe it was because of what I'd gone through last summer, but I was willing to bet Barton Farm that Beeson didn't just happen to fall on his drill. I debated whether I should share what he'd said. It would muddy the waters, but I couldn't keep it to myself. I cleared my throat. "Before the EMTs showed up, Dr. Beeson tried to tell me something."

"What was that?" The detective leaned forward. All of her attention was zeroed in on me.

I tried to ignore her close proximity. "He just kept repeating 'they.'"

"They who?" Detective Brandon asked before I could even finish.

I set my irritation aside. "I don't know."

"Did he say anything else? Anything at all?"

I thought for a moment. "He said, 'They did.'"

"They did what?" Detective Brandon snapped.

I glared at the police detective. I knew she had to ask these questions, but she didn't have to have such an attitude about it. "I don't know. That's all he was able to say before the EMTs arrived."

"That's all you got from him?" Detective Brandon's tone was accusatory at best.

I shoved my hands into the pockets of my jeans and frowned at her. "Chase and the other paramedics were trying to save his life. I didn't think it was a good time to give the poor man a twenty question quiz."

Her eyes flashed when I said Chase's name, and maybe I mentioned him just to get a rise out of her. I wasn't above that.

The police chief rocked back on his heels. "Very interesting. Still doesn't mean that he was murdered. 'They did' could be anyone, and in reference to anything."

"There's something else," I said, thinking I'd gone this far and might as well share all I knew about the professor's demise. "There weren't any tracks leading to where Dr. Beeson had fallen."

"What do you mean, there weren't any tracks?" Detective Brandon asked.

"Benji and I followed his footprints across the pasture. On the other side of the pasture, his tracks disappeared into the snow. I mean, completely disappeared. Benji even suggested alien abduction as a possible explanation."

The detective snorted.

"*But*," I said, "on closer inspection, I saw evidence that the footprints might have been wiped away by someone."

"By 'someone,' you mean another person," she said.

I shrugged. "Or Benji's aliens."

The police chief chuckled. The detective did not.

"We need to see the scene," Detective Brandon said.

"I'll finish cleaning up," Alice said from the doorway to the kitchen. I hadn't even realized she was there. I groaned inwardly. As good a cook as Alice was, she was a horrible gossip. Everything I'd just told the police would be common knowledge at Barton Farm before the end of the day.

I thanked her before turning to the police officers. "Let's go." I nodded to their feet. "It's a good thing you're both wearing snow boots. The snow is pretty high in some spots."

Outside, the late afternoon sun had chased away the gray skies, and now the temperature was inching its way above freezing. Water dripped from the visitor center's eaves and gutters in a steady stream, and the breeze held the scent of spring. The weatherman might have been right after all. I crossed my fingers that it would be warm enough for the sap to run for the tree tapping class after all—if there was to be a class. Time was running out to find a replacement for Beeson. It might come down to me teaching the class myself. I was no expert, but I thought I could wing it in a true emergency.

I didn't have any time to relish the coming spring as Detective Brandon said, "You were going to show us the scene."

"Right," I said. "It's this way." I walked straight ahead toward the split-rail fence that surrounded the pasture and climbed over it. Betty and Mags eyed me and went back to chewing their hay.

Chief Duffy climbed over the fence with a grunt. It took some effort for a man that size to cross the four foot fence.

The detective, however, held on to the top rail and stared at the oxen. "What about them?"

"It's perfectly safe," I said. "As long as you don't charge them, they'll leave you alone."

She frowned and climbed over the fence without another word.

The officers followed me across the pasture, Detective Brandon taking care to put either the chief or me between herself and the oxen at all times. As much as I wanted to comment on this, I kept my mouth shut. Provoking the detective over her obvious discomfort around livestock wouldn't win me any brownie points, and I was already in a deep deficit where she was concerned.

On the opposite side of the pasture, we climbed over the split-rail fence again. "I'm going to have to lay off Mrs. Chief's fine home-made cookies if I have any hope of getting back in shape for the re-enactment season," Chief Duffy said as he went over the fence.

Detective Brandon rolled her eyes. I would have loved to know her opinion on her boss's hobby, but then again, I had a pretty good idea what it was.

I pointed at the ground. "Be careful where you step. The brush marks began here."

"Everything here is trampled," Detective Brandon said with a sniff. "There'd be no way to find any tracks even *if* anything was left when you and Benji first arrived."

I ignored the implied insult she'd shot my way. "The EMTs were more focused on getting Dr. Beeson to a hospital than worrying about messing up tracks."

The detective stared at the ground. "So you and Benji were the only ones who saw brush marks. Officer Sonders said nothing about them."

"I forgot to bring them to his attention in all the confusion," I said.

The detective sniffed, as if she doubted my story.

"We need to talk to your assistant," Chief Duffy said. "Is she back at the visitor center?"

I shook my head. "She's a college student, and she had class late this afternoon. She's gone for the day. But I can give you her cell phone number if that would help."

"It would," the police chief said. "Show us where you found the professor."

I led the pair into the forest. It was an easy path to follow with the many footprints left by the EMTs in the snow. Detective Brandon was right—there was no sign of the brush strokes in the snow. I swallowed as we came upon the bloodstained spot where the professor had lain.

Crime scene tape was strung from tree to tree around the blood stain. Officer Sonders' handiwork, I assumed.

Detective Brandon shoved her hands into the pockets of her thick winter coat. "Because of your revelation about the brushstrokes, we're going to have to call some of the officers in to search the scene again while it's still daylight."

The police chief nodded.

As the detective touched the edge of the crime scene tape, Chief Duffy turned to me. "Any idea why Dr. Beeson would be this far from the visitor center?"

I averted my eyes from the scene. "That's a good question. Benji and I met with him this morning in the sugar maple grove on the other side of the pasture, not far from my cottage. He was frustrated with the weather."

"Why's that?"

"I'd hired him to teach a tree tapping class here at the Farm. It's scheduled for tomorrow. He was upset that the trees are still frozen because it's been so cold. It's unlikely the sap would have run enough for him to tap trees and impress his students during the presentation." I cleared my throat. "He was so angry about it that he stomped back to the visitor center without Benji and me. Judy—she runs my ticket office—said he stomped into the building and mumbled something about the red maples on the other side of the pasture before leaving again. My best guess is he came over here to see if these trees were as frozen as the sugar maples in the grove."

"We're going to have to talk to Judy too," Detective Brandon said, removing her hand from the piece of tape.

I nodded. "You can talk to any of my employees. We're all very sorry about what happened to Dr. Beeson and will do whatever we can to help."

She shot me a look. "Just as long as you don't get involved in the investigation."

I frowned. I knew she was referring to last summer, when I'd meddled in the police investigation of Maxwell Cherry's death. But since Detective Brandon had believed that I'd had something to do with that death, she hadn't left me much choice but to meddle.

"I want to talk to Gavin Elliot first," the detective said.

"Gavin?" I asked. "Why him in particular?"

She scowled at me as if it was clear I hadn't listened to her warning about non-involvement. She was right—I hadn't.

"What about this?" the chief asked, breaking into my thoughts. He pointed at the tree where a limb had been broken off.

"I didn't notice that before." The missing pine bough had been ripped from the tree.

Detective Brandon took a small camera from her coat pocket and snapped a picture of the broken limb.

"It looks fresh," I said.

"It is."

"The branch, if we can find it, may have been the one used to wipe away the tracks," I suggested.

"Possibly," she conceded. "Of course, it could have happened any time in the last twelve hours. It doesn't mean that this pine bough is related to Conrad Beeson's death."

I scowled, and Chief Duffy patted my shoulder and smiled.

SIX

Two more police officers joined us in the woods and searched the area under the red maples. One of them was Officer Sonders, who appeared irritated when Detective Brandon questioned how he'd secured the scene that morning.

Chief Duffy cleared his throat. "You have everything well in hand here, Candy. I'm heading back to the station. You give me a holler if you need anything."

The detective nodded and appeared relieved that the chief had turned the investigation over to her.

He nodded to me. "I'll be seeing you at the festival this weekend. The boys and I are looking forward to it." He was one of the Civil War reenactors who would be on the grounds to answer questions. "We should talk next year about having a battle reenactment *during* the festival. There were some battles fought in the winter." His eyes sparkled at the idea.

I suppressed a groan. One Civil War reenactment during the summer was just about as much as I could handle.

Chief Duffy sauntered off. After he'd disappeared into the trees, Detective Brandon turned to me. "I'd like to question your staff that's here today, starting with Gavin Elliot."

I folded my arms. "You still haven't told me why you want to talk to Gavin so badly."

She stared down at me. What I wouldn't give for five more inches, so that we would be looking at each other eye-to-eye.

"Ms. Cambridge," the detective said, "I do not have to tell you anything. This is *my* investigation."

I sighed. I would get the information out of Gavin after she left. "Fine. He should be in the sugarhouse."

She waved me on. "Lead the way."

As Detective Brandon and I crossed the pasture, she continued to keep a wary eye on the oxen. Again, I held my tongue. I was pretty proud of myself that I'd been able to keep my mouth shut twice. Now, if we had to cross the pasture a third time, I couldn't make any promises that I wouldn't crack a joke.

Gavin was in the sugarhouse, as I expected. Part of his job that week, other than running the school visits, was to plan for the Farm's maple syrup production. Since it was the first year we'd done this, we wouldn't be able to make a lot, but once we could tap the trees, the sap we boiled down into syrup would be bottled and sold in the museum shop.

Steam rolled out of the open doorway. I knocked on the frame. Gavin looked up from the sugar he was stirring with his wooden paddle. His smile faded when he saw Detective Brandon standing next to me. He leaned the paddle against the edge of the metal trough. "This is about Conrad, isn't it?"

I frowned. Gavin had said the man's name as if he knew him personally.

41

Detective Brandon nudged me aside and stepped into the sugarhouse. "Yes. I need to talk to you."

I stepped inside the sugarhouse too.

The detective glared at me over her shoulder. "I need to talk to Mr. Elliot alone."

"I'd like Kelsey to stay," Gavin said.

Detective Brandon stepped to the side as if she wanted to have a clear view of both of us. "Mr. Elliot, we can talk about it here alone, or we can talk about it down at the station in a tiny windowless room. You have a right to legal counsel, of course. Ms. Cambridge does not fill in for that."

I rolled my eyes and was glad that my son wasn't there to see it. "Detective, please don't make this more uncomfortable than it has to be. If Gavin wants me here, let me stay. He's going to tell me everything that happened after you leave anyway."

Gavin nodded. "I will."

"Fine. I don't have all day." The detective focused on Gavin. "Is it true that you threatened to kill Dr. Conrad Beeson?"

"Wh—?" I began.

Gavin stared at the top of his work boots. "I did, and I was sorry I said it the moment it came out of my mouth."

The corner of Detective Brandon's mouth turned up. I wouldn't call it even the beginning of a smile. It was more like a twitch, a small indication that she had her prey in her sights. "And why did you threaten him?"

"I wouldn't hurt him." Gavin braced his hand on the rickety table for support. It wobbled but held. "You have to believe that."

"You threatened him. I don't have to 'believe' anything."

Gavin's shoulders drooped. "I'm not proud of that."

She inclined her head. "So please answer my question."

"I said it because Conrad stole from my family. I was angry, and it just came out. I didn't really mean it. I regretted it the moment the words left my mouth."

"If you were angry enough to wish someone dead, maybe you were angry enough to carry out that threat."

Gavin looked from the detective to me. "Conrad is dead?"

We both nodded.

His face paled. "Poor Corrie."

"Who's Corrie?" The detective's voice was sharp.

"Conrad's daughter."

The detective nodded. "I'll need to talk to her too."

Gavin's brow creased. "Corrie would never hurt her father. They didn't have the world's best relationship, but I know she would never do that."

"I need to talk to her because she is probably the next of kin." Detective Brandon studied Gavin. "Are you implying that she might have reason to want her father dead?"

The color drained from Gavin's face. "N—no."

She arched an eyebrow. "Do you know Corrie well?"

He blushed. "Well enough."

So Gavin knew not only Dr. Beeson, but also his daughter, and this was the first time I was hearing about it? Why hadn't he mentioned all this when I'd told the staff that I'd hired Beeson to take over the tree tapping class?

I could almost hear the police detective tuck this latest information into the back of her brain. "So tell me," she said. "What were the circumstances in which you made your threat?"

Gavin's Adam's apple bobbed up and down as he swallowed. "I was at a Sap and Spile meeting, and we had a disagreement."

Both the detective and I blinked at him. "A what?" I asked.

43

He sighed. "A Sap and Spile meeting." Then he blushed. "It's sort of a maple sugaring club. We meet twice a week during February and March in the shelter house in the park."

"What was your disagreement about? You said he stole something. What was it?" the detective asked.

"He stole sugaring rights from my family."

"Sugaring rights?"

Gavin sighed. "My family has been harvesting the maple sugar in the park for generations. My ancestors built the sugarhouse there. Beeson ignored all that history and stole those sugaring rights from us. He swooped in and stole them." His voice became strained.

"How did he do that?" I asked.

The detective shot me a look, but she didn't comment on me asking a question of my own.

Gavin took a deep breath. "Somehow he found out that our lease with New Hartford to tap the park's sugar maples had expired, and he went to them to ask for tapping rights before we had a chance to renew. He had no right to do that. Our family doesn't have maples on our own land. The park was the only place we could tap. Beeson has a big farm with plenty of maples of all varieties. He could have tapped those trees."

"Maybe he didn't think he'd have enough sap to make maple syrup," I said.

Gavin scowled as if he didn't like me trying to find an excuse for the professor. "At the last Sap and Spile meeting, Conrad was going on and on about the modern set-up he was using this year on my family's trees, and I just sort of lost it. I stood up and yelled at him, and I told everyone in the room what he'd done. And do you know what he did?" Gavin's voice shook. "He laughed. He laughed! He'd cheated my father and me—we were both standing right there—

and he laughed. After that I said something like, 'I could kill you over this.'"

I inwardly groaned. This didn't look good for Gavin at all.

Detective Brandon's radio crackled. "That'll be the officers at the scene," she said. "Thank you for answering my questions, Gavin. This was very helpful. I'll want to talk to you again." She gave him a pointed look. "Even though Conrad Beeson's death hasn't officially been ruled a homicide, know that I will be treating it as such until further notice. Don't leave town."

We watched her walk away.

I stared at Gavin, and his shoulders drooped as if he knew what I was thinking. I doubted that he truly knew—because the thought that was bouncing around in my mind had to do with where he'd been when Benji ran back to the visitor center to tell him and Judy about Beeson's accident.

SEVEN

Before I could ask Gavin any questions, Tiffin galloped into the sugarhouse and barked at me sharply. I looked down at my watch and saw that it was almost three fifteen. Hayden's school bus would be rolling up Maple Grove Lane at any moment.

"I've got to go meet Hayden's bus," I told Gavin. "Don't leave until I talk to you." I didn't wait for him to respond as I raced out of the sugarhouse toward the visitor center.

Instead of going inside, though, I headed through the gate in the wooden fence that divided the Farm from the parking lot. As I ran across the lot and started down the long driveway that angled toward Maple Grove Lane, I saw Detective Brandon leaving the grounds in her SUV. Maybe the radio call she'd received hadn't been from the officers at the crime scene after all.

Tiffin and I made it to the stop just as the large yellow school bus rolled down the road. I was grateful the detective had gone. Hayden was naturally curious, just like I was, and if he'd seen the detective on the Farm, he would have had at least a hundred questions I couldn't have answered, or wouldn't have wanted to answer.

The bus rocked to a stop in front of me, and my towheaded son bounced off it. His Lightning McQueen backpack bounced along with him, and his face lit up when he saw me. He looked so joyful that someone might think that I didn't meet his bus at the same spot every day. All the anxiety I'd felt throughout the day since finding Beeson fell away as my son wrapped his arms around my hips.

I waved to the bus driver as she drove away. "Where's your hat?" I asked as I removed mine and put it on Hayden's head.

He pushed it up, as it was way too big for him and drooped into his eyes. "On the playground?" It was more a question than a statement. "I forget."

I sighed. I bought mittens and stocking hats for Hayden by the dozen. This winter alone he'd lost ten hats and countless gloves. I didn't bother to count the gloves and mittens that went MIA; it was too depressing. I folded the bottom of the hat back so that I could see his eyes. "Good thing I have two more stashed at the house. I hope they last through what's left of winter, or I might have to take out a winter gear loan for you."

"Is that a police car?" he asked excitedly as we walked back to the visitor center. There was a lone police cruiser parked in front of the main entrance. One of Chief Duffy's patrol officers must still be in the woods collecting evidence from the scene.

I winced. "It is. The police visited us today," I said, hoping to leave it at that.

Hayden's eyes shined as we drew closer to the car. "We had a police officer come to see us at school today too. He told us all about staying away from strangers."

"I'm glad," I said, holding his hand a little bit tighter.

"Why's there a police officer here? Did you learn about strangers too?"

I smiled. "He's just checking the woods for us to make sure we're ready for the Maple Sugar Festival."

"The police do that? Do the police make maple syrup? That doesn't seem like a very policeman thing to do."

I nodded solemnly. "The police do all sorts of things."

"Can we go help him? Gavin told me all about the maple sugaring. I bet I know even more than that police officer does."

The last thing I wanted was for Hayden to see where the professor had fallen in the snow. I was thankful it was on the on the other side of the pasture and far away from our cottage. "Oh, no. I think he needs to do it all by himself. Protocol, you know."

He wrinkled his nose. "What does protocol mean?"

"It's the certain rules that police have to follow when they work."

Hayden thought on that for a moment. "Like not talking when the teacher is talking is protocol for school?"

I suppressed a smile. "Exactly."

As we walked up to the visitor center, a middle-aged officer was walking to his car. I remembered Detective Brandon calling him "Reynolds" at the scene. He held a large black case about the size of a sewing machine. I wondered if he'd found anything of interest in the woods, but I wasn't about to ask him about it with Hayden standing right there.

Officer Reynolds smiled at my son as he opened the trunk of his cruiser. "Didn't I see you at New Hartford Elementary a few hours ago?"

Hayden straightened up like a cadet in front of his commanding officer. "I'm in kindergarten there. I'm in Mrs. Cooper's class. She wears glasses," Hayden added for clarification.

Officer Reynolds closed his trunk. "Thought so. Did you learn anything today?"

Hayden stood a little straighter. "Stay away from people you don't know, and if you're in trouble, find an adult you know and trust or a police officer."

Officer Reynolds grinned. "Excellent. Now I can rest easy that you and your classmates will be safe."

Hayden grinned as if he'd just received five gold stars for the day.

The officer nodded at me. "I'm all done here. No one should go to that part of the woods. The detective will be in touch."

I nodded.

The officer saluted Hayden. "You stay safe out there."

Hayden saluted back. "Yes, sir."

I placed my hands on both of Hayden's shoulders, and we watched the police cruiser drive away.

"I think I'll be a police officer," Hayden said.

My heart constricted at the thought of my son putting himself at risk like that. But rather than show my fear, I said, "You can be whatever you want to."

He grinned up at me. "I know. You and Dad always tell me that."

At least Eddie and I were on the same page in that respect. Hayden might be the only thing on Earth we agreed on, but it was the most important.

I cleared the lump in my throat. "Let's go inside. My toes are ice cubes."

He giggled and ran for the visitor center's door.

The building was quiet. My staff—except for Gavin, who I'd asked to stay—had long since left, and there wouldn't be any more visitors. By this time of the day Hayden and I had the entire farm to ourselves, except for Jason Smith, who lived across Maple Grove Lane in a small trailer and cared for the animals. He tended to keep to himself. I wondered if Officer Sonders had spoken to him while searching the crime scene. I pulled my ever-present notepad from my coat pocket and added a note to drop by the barn in the morning after I got Hayden off to school. Jason may have seen something. At the very least, he could tell me if he noticed anything unusual going on in the woods over the last few days.

Before heading to my cottage, I walked through the visitor center to make sure all the lights were off and windows and doors were securely locked. Hayden followed behind me, talking a mile a minute about his day at school.

When I'd checked the final window, I interrupted his description of how a boy in his class had gotten a dreaded red card, just about the worst reprimand a child could receive in kindergarten. "Gavin should still be here, working in the sugarhouse. I want to go talk to him."

"I want to see the maple syrup!" Hayden cried at the top of his voice, and he ran out onto the Farm grounds with Tiffin barking at his heels.

I sighed and followed at a much slower pace, only stopping to lock the visitor center's door behind me.

Hayden was already peering into the trough of boiling maple syrup when I stepped into the sugarhouse. Gavin was stirring the syrup he'd made that day, and he would continue the process the next day, which reminded me that I still didn't have a replacement for Beeson's tree tapping lecture. It was too late to cancel the class.

"Hayden, step back from the trough. It's hot," I ordered.

Hayden took a big step back. "Can I taste it?" he asked.

"Not this batch," Gavin said. "It's still too hot. I have some that I made yesterday that you can try." He moved to the rickety table and opened a plastic quart jug filled with amber-colored maple syrup.

Removing a white Dixie cup from a box, he poured a little of the maple syrup into it.

Hayden cocked his head. "You worked all yesterday, and that's all you made?"

Gavin laughed. "Hey, that's not fair. Do you know it takes forty gallons of sap to make one gallon of maple syrup? I'm doing the best I can here."

Hayden giggled.

Gavin handed him the shot of maple syrup, and Hayden tossed it back. "Yum!" he said approvingly.

I cringed. Hayden would be bouncing off of the walls as soon as the sugar hit his bloodstream. Gavin must have realized that too, because he gave me an apologetic look over Hayden's head.

"Hayden, why don't you and Tiffin race around outside some?" I suggested. "I've been so busy today that I haven't spent much time with him. He could use the exercise. Gavin and I will come out too." I glanced at Gavin. "We need to talk."

Hayden took another swig of syrup and pounded the Dixie cup on the table like a seasoned drinker before shouting "Okay!" and running out of the sugarhouse with Tiffin.

I followed, taking care to keep my son in my sights. I felt edgy after the day's events, and my first priority was always Hayden. A moment later, Gavin stepped out of the sugarhouse.

Hayden and Tiffin zoomed around the trees at a dizzying pace. "I might dock your pay for giving him pure maple syrup," I said. "He's going to be bouncing off the walls tonight."

Gavin smiled. He knew I was kidding. Unfortunately, the smile didn't make it to his eyes. I knew he was thinking about Beeson. I was too.

"I think you're in trouble, Gavin," I said.

He held a tiny bottle of maple syrup, no more than an ounce, in his hand and stared at the sugary liquid. "I know I'm in trouble, but I didn't kill him, Kelsey. You have to believe me."

I leaned back against the rough siding of the sugarhouse. "I believe you, but Judy told me that you weren't in the visitor center when the school buses arrived. Where were you?"

He grimaced. "You think I ran out to the red maple grove and stabbed Conrad in the chest with his drill."

"No, but I still need an answer. If Judy told me she didn't know where you were, it won't be long before the police hear it from her or someone else."

"I ran to the john," Gavin said. "Is that a crime?"

I blew out a breath that I hadn't known I was holding. "No, but did you see anyone on your way there? Anyone who can back up your story?"

Gavin's ears turned red. "Who can back up that I went to the restroom?"

I shrugged, thinking of Detective Brandon. I knew she would ask the same questions.

He held the bottle of maple syrup a little more tightly. "And no, I didn't see anyone."

"Why didn't you tell me that you had a problem with Dr. Beeson when I hired him for the tree tapping class?" I asked.

"You'd already hired him. I didn't think it would matter, and my problems with Conrad had nothing to do with the Farm."

I frowned. "Tell me more about Sap and Spile."

"There's not much more to tell other than what you heard me say to the detective. It's a social club of sorts for tree tappers. There's a meeting tonight," he added. "I don't think I'm going to go. All they'll talk about is Conrad's death. Someone there must have told the police about my outburst at him. I really don't want to face them."

"You have to go," I protested. "It shows that you have nothing to hide."

"I don't know…" He trailed off.

"And I'm going with you," I said.

A few feet away, Hayden and Tiffin fell into a heap. Hayden was crashing from his sugar high. The dog barked and the boy giggled.

Gavin looked like he'd drunk the entire quart of maple syrup straight from the bottle. "You can't—"

"No, you can't!" an angry voice interrupted.

EIGHT

I spun around to find a tall man in his sixties, wearing a red-and-black flannel coat and jeans, walking around the back side of the sugarhouse. His rimless glasses sat high on the bridge of his long nose.

"Hayden!" I cried in my sharpest mom voice.

Hayden immediately recognized "the voice" and jumped to his feet. "What's wrong, Mom?"

"Kelsey, it's fine," Gavin said. "This is my father, Webber Elliot."

"Your father?" I asked, then saw the resemblance. They both had the same prominent nose and deep-set eyes.

"Of course I am, and I've been calling you, Gavin, for the last hour, ever since I heard the news. You need to come home."

"Dad." There was a slight whine in Gavin's voice. "I'm at work."

Webber Elliot glanced at me. "I don't care. It's time for you to come home."

"Dad, I'm not a child," Gavin said, sounding like just that.

"Gavin, we'll discuss this at home," his father said.

"I assume you've heard about Dr. Beeson's death?" I asked.

The older man scowled at me. "Yes. This is none of your concern."

I placed my hands on my hips. "It's most definitely my concern. I'm responsible for everything that happens on Barton Farm, and Gavin is my employee."

Gavin scowled at his father. "Don't worry, Kelsey. He was just leaving."

Webber glared at Gavin. "I'll leave when I'm ready."

"Dad, the Farm is closed, and you shouldn't be here. Like you said, we should talk about this when I get home. I'm almost done here, and I can tell you what the police said."

"The police?" Webber barked.

I glanced at Hayden, who was watching the argument with rapt attention.

"Please keep your voices down. I don't want my son to overhear this conversation." I gave them both a stern look. "The police were here today and questioned my employees. We were the last ones to see Beeson alive." I kept a close eye on Webber's reaction.

Webber looked at this son, looking genuinely concerned for the first time. "Did the police talk to you?" he asked.

Gavin sighed. "Yes."

"What did you tell them?"

"What they wanted to know. The detective already knew about the argument I had with Conrad at the last Sap and Spile meeting."

Webber ran his hand through his hair. "You shouldn't have said a word until we spoke to a lawyer."

"A lawyer? Dad, do you think I killed Conrad?"

"No, of course I don't, but a lawyer will stop you from saying anything stupid—like you did at the last meeting when you got into that argument with him."

Even to my ears, Webber's denial that he suspected his son wasn't that convincing. Clearly, Gavin picked up on the doubt because he said, "Dad, I still have work to do. I'll see you at home."

Webber clenched his jaw. "Fine. Come straight home after you're finished here. We have much to discuss before the meeting tonight."

Gavin went back into the sugarhouse without another word.

Webber marched away from the sugarhouse, and I followed him. "Mr. Elliot?"

He turned when he reached the pebbled path but didn't slow down. "What is it?'

"I know you're worried about Gavin. I am too."

"Please, you're just his boss. Don't pretend you know my son."

I stepped back as if he'd slapped me.

As a parting shot, he added, "And don't come to the meeting tonight. You aren't wanted." He stomped down the path.

I let him go, but I was more determined than ever to be at the Sap and Spile meeting.

Gavin stepped out of the sugarhouse, closing and padlocking the door behind him. He waved to Hayden, who was still playing tag with Tiffin in the trees, before walking over to me. "I'm sorry about my dad barging in like that. He's worried. That's all. I wasn't the easiest kid to raise. He did it on his own. My mom walked out when I was in preschool."

"Oh, Gavin, I'm sorry."

He shrugged. "It is what it is. Just don't be angry with my dad for stomping in here, okay?"

"He and I can make up at the Sap and Spile meeting tonight," I said.

Gavin shook his head like I hadn't understood a word he'd just said. "Kelsey, you can't come to the meeting. It's for members only."

"They can make an exception under the circumstances, don't you think?"

"You don't know these people." He zipped up his coat.

"What time is the meeting?" I asked.

He sighed. "Seven, and the only reason I'm telling you is because I know you'll come no matter what. But what are you going to do about Hayden? He can't come. No kids allowed. The men at Sap and Spile take the business of maple sugaring very seriously."

"Let me worry about Hayden," I said, hoping my father could come over to watch him. Dad was a drama professor at the local college. During the summer months when he wasn't teaching, he lived with Hayden and me on the Farm, but during the school year, he stayed in college housing. Now that I thought about it, it wouldn't be a bad thing to talk to my father anyway. He and Beeson worked at the same college. Even though Dad was in the drama department and Beeson was in horticulture, he might have some insight on his colleague. He might even have some suspects for Beeson's murder, if it was murder.

"Kelsey, I really don't think this is a good idea." Gavin still hadn't given up trying to talk me out of the meeting.

"It's the only idea I have, Gavin," I said. "If my hunch is right, Detective Brandon has promoted you to prime suspect in Beeson's death. We have to find other suspects before she gets too stuck on the idea. Trust me, I know how she operates. She's like a dog with a bone when she makes up her mind. You said that your club meets at the shelter house in the park, right?"

He nodded, resigned to the situation.

I decided that Gavin had been through enough interrogations for one afternoon. "I'll meet you there at seven sharp," I said as I headed to the door. "I have to take Hayden and Tiffin home. Seven o'clock. Don't forget."

"How could I possibly forget?" he muttered.

A few feet away, Tiffin lay on the path that led to our cottage, panting softly, and Hayden had flopped into the snow, making a half-hearted snow angel. I gave him my hand and he grabbed it. I pulled him to his feet. "Let's go home. I bet you're ready for a snack."

He perked up. "Can I have ants-on-a-log?"

"Sure." I laughed. My father had taught him to call celery with peanut butter and raisins "ants-on-a-log." It had been one of my favorite snacks as a kid too.

As we walked the snow-covered path that led through the sugar maple grove, I found myself checking the woods more often than I usually did. I didn't know what I expected to see. Some masked man brandishing a hand drill, perhaps? Even though the Farm was isolated, I'd never felt frightened over living in the woods, but now, a tiny bead of fear crept into my brain. Most of that was for Hayden.

Inside our cozy cottage, Frankie, Hayden's one-eyed tabby cat, hissed at us when we entered. Neither of us thought much of it. Hissing is just the way Frankie, named after Benjamin Franklin, chose to communicate. Hayden scooped up the cat and gave him a squeeze. Frankie tolerated this with a scowl and nothing else. Had I picked him up like that, I'd be heading to the emergency room. Frankie and I had an understanding: I left him alone, and he left me alone. It was a good arrangement.

Hayden set his cat on the couch. Tiffin happily yipped at his boy, shaking his tailless rump with everything he had. Hayden rolled on the floor with Tiffin while I made his snack. The pair's earlier fatigue was all but forgotten. Frankie watched them with a curled lip of disdain before dashing up the stairs, most likely to lie in wait under Hayden's bed.

I called my dad, planning to ask him to watch Hayden tonight during the Sap and Spile meeting. There was no answer. I left a message asking him to call me, but I wasn't hopeful that he would get it. As an actor, my father had an artist's temperament and was hard to nail down at times.

I grimaced. The last thing I wanted to do was call my ex-husband, Eddie, and ask him for help. Benji was another babysitting option, but I knew she had class on Thursday nights.

I'd just set my cell phone on the kitchen counter when it beeped. I snatched it up, expecting to see a text from my dad. It wasn't from Dad; it was from Chase: My twenty-four-hour shift ends at 5:30. I will come to the Farm.

Not necessary. I'm fine, I texted back. I wasn't the kind of girl who needed a guy to run to her rescue. I'd been rescuing myself for a long time and was pretty good at it. A memory nagged at the back of my head … maybe that wasn't entirely true. Chase had rescued me from the Barton House cellar last summer when someone had trapped me in there. I frowned. But that was just one time, and I would have made it out on my own eventually. I'd had a plan. He just beat me to it.

The phone chirped again with a new incoming message: See you at 5:45.

I frowned. How typical of Chase not to listen, but this could work to my advantage. Maybe Chase could stay with Hayden while I went to the meeting. That might require a bribe. Food would work. If he was coming straight from the station, I bet he'd be starving. I started gathering ingredients to make a vegetable stew. It sounded good to me on such a cold night, and after spending so much time in the frozen woods.

The stew was made from root vegetables and dried herbs, all from the Farm. Despite his less-than-charming personality, Shepley knew how to care for plants, and the Farm had enjoyed one of its best harvests ever that fall. I was already plotting events we could host around the vegetable harvest next year. We could have gardening and harvesting classes and cooking classes too. Maybe something with "organic" in the title? That would catch people's attention. I wasn't above succumbing to trends to raise the number of visitors to the Farm each year.

The trick would be getting Shepley on board. I frowned. That was no easy feat. Shepley would be much happier if no one came to the Farm and he was left alone with his plants. But if that happened, there would be no Farm at all and Shepley would be out of a job. We'd received a nice endowment and trust from the Cherry Foundation last November, upon the death of Cynthia Cherry, the Farm's original benefactress, but that alone wouldn't be enough to sustain the Farm. We had to be self-sufficient to keep our doors open. It was something I was determined to do, especially since I had committed the next fifteen years of my life to Barton Farm. One of the stipulations of the trust was that I had to agree to stay on as the Farm's director and live in the cottage for the next fifteen years. It's one thing to have job security, but it's quite another to be tied to your job with iron chains.

Yet I knew Cynthia had set it up this way not only to protect the Farm, but to protect me. She'd cared about Hayden and me and had spent thousands to renovate the old caretaker's cottage into a home for us. The cottage was small, and the kitchen, living room, and dining room spaces were all one room. Behind the kitchen, there was a large pantry that we'd converted into a spare room for my father during the summer. There was one full bathroom on the lower level, and a half bath and Hayden and my bedrooms upstairs. That was it.

I hadn't asked for much, but everything I requested, Cynthia made sure happened. By tying me to the trust, she'd ensured my job until Hayden was well into his college years. I blinked away tears. Cynthia had been like a much-beloved aunt to me. I teared up every time I thought of her, even this many months later.

I wiped a tear from my eye and set Hayden's snack on the coffee table, along with a cup of apple juice. He sat on his knees in front of the couch, zooming his favorite Matchbox cars back and forth over the cushions. Seeing him there, so happy in our home, made me all the more grateful to Cynthia for what she'd done—and even more determined not to let her down. She'd believed in the Farm and in me. Barton Farm had to thrive.

I told Hayden about his snack and went back to the kitchen to work on the stew.

My son jumped to his feet, grabbing two ants-on-a-log with the motion, and walked into the kitchen. He watched me chop carrots and toss them into a large stew pot. I already had butter, onions, and herbs melding together at the bottom of the pot.

"Is that for me?" Hayden sounded like he'd much rather eat real ants than whatever I was cooking.

"I thought you liked vegetable stew," I teased.

"Yuck!"

"The stew is for Chase. He's stopping by after work. Since I doubt he'll have eaten by the time he gets here, I thought I would make him something."

Hayden wrinkled his nose. "And you're feeding him that?" He acted like serving Chase vegetable stew was the greatest insult I could think of bestowing on the paramedic.

I laughed. "Adults like this kind of stuff. It's perfect for a cold winter's night."

He didn't look convinced and popped a raisin in his mouth.

"Don't worry. You're eating mac and cheese."

He pumped his fist. "Yes!"

NINE

HAYDEN WAS FINISHING HIS mac and cheese when there was a knock on the cottage's front door, promptly at 5:45. I gave the stew pot one final stir before I replaced the lid and caught myself checking my reflection in it. I dropped the lid onto the pot and told myself to snap out of it before marching across the living room to the front door.

I opened the door to find snow falling all around Chase, giving him an ethereal look. If a faceless man could be considered ethereal, that is. His scarf was wrapped so tightly around his head that all I could see were his warm chocolate brown eyes, which seemed to be in a constant state of amusement.

I broke eye contact and stepped back. "Come in before you freeze to death." The temperature had dropped with the setting of the sun.

He stomped the snow off his boots onto the front porch as best as he could before stepping over the threshold. I shut the door behind him, and he started the long process of removing his winter gear: scarf, hat, gloves, coat, and down vest. I held out my arms and he piled them on.

He placed his hands on his flat stomach. "Do I smell dinner cooking?"

Hayden looked up from his mac and cheese. "I got mac and cheese. Mom made stew for you." He wrinkled his nose. "You can't have my mac and cheese."

Chase's laughing brown eyes met mine. "You made dinner for me?" He lowered his voice so that Hayden couldn't overhear. "May I consider this a *date?*"

I hung his coat and winter gear over the back of the sofa. "I thought you might be hungry if you just got off work. I would do it for any *friend.*"

He grinned and stepped out of his boots, leaving them by the front door. "Your friendship is a start." He winked at me.

I turned away to hide my blush. "Hayden, if you're finished eating, you and Tiffin can watch TV on my bed until Chase and I finish dinner."

My son's eyes sparkled, and he gulped down the last of his milk. It wasn't often that I let him watch television on a school night. As much as I wanted Chase not to get the wrong idea and think this was a date, I still wanted to talk to him about Beeson before bringing up babysitting, and I couldn't do that with Hayden in the room.

As if he was afraid I would change my mind, Hayden shouted for Tiffin, and the pair galloped up the stairs. I listened until I heard the bedroom door slam.

"He must really like TV," Chase said.

"It's a special treat. I don't let him watch much." I shrugged.

"Why doesn't that surprise me? I can tell you're one of *those* kinds of moms," he teased.

I put my hands on my hips. "What does that mean?"

He held up his hands as if in surrender. "It was a compliment. You're one of those moms who are all about your kid. I respect that and find it very attractive."

I rolled my eyes, and for the second time that day, I was glad that Hayden wasn't there to see me do it. It wasn't a habit I wanted my son to pick up. I wished I could break it myself. "Have a seat." I pointed to the kitchen table.

Chase did as he was told. I felt him watch me as I dished out two hearty portions of stew. My stomach grumbled as I did. I'd only had a granola bar for lunch.

I set the bowls on the table and went back for a loaf of bread that Alice had made the day before in the Farm's breadmaking machine, plus two glasses of water.

"Can I help?" Chase asked. "I'm very good in the kitchen. I do a lot of the cooking at the firehouse during my shifts."

"I'm fine," I said as I took the seat across from him. I pointedly ignored his comment about being good in the kitchen. He was a terrible flirt, and I had to remind myself of that. "Do you have to go back to the firehouse?" I asked as I set everything on the table and took a seat.

He blew on a spoonful of stew. "Nope. Since I just came off of a twenty-four-hour shift, I have forty-eight hours free. I thought I could help you out."

I picked up my spoon. "Help me with what?"

"The maple sugar professor's death. I assume you want to find out how he died, since it happened on your watch and on the Farm."

Chase was right. I did want to know what happened, mostly because of Gavin's situation. I couldn't believe that my staffer could kill anyone. Had it been Shepley, I wouldn't have been that surprised. But Gavin? It just didn't fit into what I knew about him.

"You've gotten involved with a police investigation before," Chase said when I didn't respond right away.

I didn't need him to remind me of that. Beeson's death was the third suspicious death related to Barton Farm in less than a year. It wasn't true that any publicity was good publicity. These events were not good publicity for the Farm.

Chase set his water glass on the table. "I've been thinking that you could use these unfortunate events to your advantage. If this keeps up, you could always start giving ghost tours of the Farm. It might be a real moneymaker for you."

"Not funny," I said. "Barton Farm isn't haunted."

"That's not what I've heard. There have always been rumors about one of Barton's daughters wandering the Farm grounds at night." He wiggled his fingers near his face in a spooky gesture that made me think he'd been a *Scooby Doo* fan as a child. "I heard about her when I was a kid."

"There is that story," I admitted. "But Barton Farm is not haunted by any twenty-first-century ghosts. Nineteenth-century ghosts are fine."

He grinned. "I can tell you're giving the haunted ghost tours some real thought."

I frowned because he was right. The future of a nonprofit like Barton Farm was never certain—one bad storm or tornado coming through the grounds would take us out permanently. I really hoped that wouldn't happen. I loved the Farm so much, I'd married myself to it for fifteen years. I couldn't let it go down on my watch.

Chase wiped his mouth with his napkin and leaned back into his chair. His stew bowl was empty, and I hadn't even taken a bite of mine yet. "So, what do you plan to do?"

"I have a proposition for you."

He grinned from ear to ear. "And what's that?"

"It's not what you're thinking."

"What do you think I was thinking?" The corner of his mouth twitched.

I told him what I'd learned about Gavin's history with Conrad Beeson, and Detective Brandon zeroing in on Gavin as her number one suspect. "I need to go to the Sap and Spile meeting tonight to see if anyone else might have had a reason to kill Beeson," I finished. "I was wondering if you could stay with Hayden while I'm gone."

Chase frowned. "I thought they didn't even know for sure if he was murdered."

"They don't. At least, not officially, but it looks that way. That's what the chief said."

"Wait a second." Chase removed his cell phone from his pocket and placed a call. "Hey, Uncle Duff," he said. "How's it going?" He listened for a moment and laughed at something his uncle said. "I'm calling because I was wondering if you had any news about Conrad Beeson. I was one of the EMTs on the scene, and I heard he died. Do you know how?" There was another pause. "Oh." Chase sounded disappointed, and he met my gaze across the table.

My heart sank. I knew what Chief Duffy was telling his nephew. He was telling him that Conrad Beeson had been murdered.

"And it's certain?" Chase asked. He was quiet for a few minutes as he listened to his uncle. "All right then. I'll see you Saturday." He hung up and slipped his phone back into his pocket.

"He was murdered?" I asked.

Chase nodded. "My uncle said that the medical examiner believes that he had a heart attack."

"That's not murder," I said.

Chase held up his hand. "True. But someone stabbed him in the chest with the drill while he was still alive, and that's what killed him."

I covered my mouth with my hand. "Who could do such a thing? Is the medical examiner sure?"

Chase nodded. "The angle of the wound indicates that it came from above when Beeson was lying on his back. There's no way he would have gotten that injury from accidentally landing on the drill."

"It's a miracle he stayed alive as long as he did."

Chase met my gaze. "Your friend Gavin is in some serious trouble."

"Did your uncle mention Gavin?" I asked anxiously.

He shook his head and sipped from his water glass. "Not specifically, but he did say Candy was certain it would be a quick case."

I rubbed my forehead. "Then it's even more important that I go tonight. Tomorrow, I plan to go to the college. My dad and Dr. Beeson both work there. I thought I'd drop by in the morning to find out what Dad knows. I tried to call him, but he didn't answer. I'm not sure how much interaction he and Beeson had, since they were in different departments. I don't even know if they knew each other."

"It's kind of hard for me to believe anyone in the vicinity of your father doesn't know who he is. His presence"—Chase paused as if searching for the right word—"is commanding."

"Anyways, if you can't stay tonight to watch Hayden, I can call Eddie," I said. "I've been thinking about asking Eddie to take Hayden after school tomorrow. It's his weekend with Hayden as it is. It would only be an extra day." I frowned, hating the idea of losing any time with my son, but I had to do what was right for Hayden.

"Why would you do that?" Chase's face had gone blank when I'd mentioned my ex-husband. He didn't care for Eddie, and I was afraid the feeling was mutual. Then again, I wasn't a huge fan of Eddie's fiancée, Krissie, either. I supposed that it came with the territory. Eddie and I were high school sweethearts and got married right after college. I knew now we'd married more because that's what was expected rather than what either of us had really wanted. Even so, I'd never regret my relationship with Eddie. It gave me Hayden, who was my greatest joy. An annoying ex-husband and his ditzy fiancée were a small price to pay for such a stellar kid.

"Now that we know it's"—I lowered my voice and shot a quick look at the stairs—"*murder*, the police will be coming and going on the Farm. I don't want Hayden exposed to that."

Chase wiped his mouth with a napkin. "I can understand, but won't this give Eddie more ammunition for joint custody?"

I gripped my spoon like it was dagger. Chase noticed because he held up his hands in mock surrender. "You look like you're ready to gouge my eyes out with that."

Slowly, I uncurled my fingers from the spoon and set it next to my half-eaten bowl of stew. My appetite was suddenly nonexistent.

Chase frowned and some of the characteristic humor went out of his eyes. "I'm sorry. I shouldn't have brought the custody battle up."

"There's no custody battle yet." I took a deep breath. "But yes, Eddie wants to change the terms of our custody arrangements after his wedding so that he and Krissie can spend more time with Hayden." I took a deep breath. "I can't say I blame them. If our roles were reversed, I'd want more time with Hayden too. It's not unreasonable for them to ask. And don't worry about it. It's always in the back of my mind, ever since Eddie mentioned the idea last summer. It's always there." I forced a laugh. "I suppose it always will be, until Hayden turns eighteen."

"If Eddie and Krissie have kids of their own, maybe they won't want to fight for custody anymore."

I scowled at him. Clearly Chase didn't have children. What he suggested wasn't any better—I didn't want Eddie to cast Hayden aside if or when he and Krissie had children. It would be as if Eddie had replacement children for Hayden. My son loved his father and Eddie was a great dad, I had to give him that. Hayden would be heartbroken if he thought he'd been replaced. If my son was heartbroken, then so was I.

I stood up and started clearing the table.

"Uh-oh," Chase said. "I can tell by your face that I said something wrong. What was it?"

I set the bowls in the kitchen sink. "You just showed me that you aren't ready for all the baggage that comes with being my b—friend." I almost said "boyfriend" but saved myself at the last moment.

"What's that supposed to mean?" Chase stood up.

I shook my head. It would be too difficult to explain, and I didn't know if I could or even wanted to. "If I'm going to make the Sap and Spile meeting, I'd better get going. Can you stay with Hayden?"

He smiled. "You still want me to?"

"I'm kind of desperate."

He laughed. "Well, sure. Since you put it that way."

My shoulders drooped. "I'm sorry. It's been a long day."

He flashed me his thousand-watt smile. "It's no problem. Hayden and I will read a story, and I'll tuck him into bed. Easy as pie."

"If you're sure," I said, suddenly getting second thoughts.

"Go." Chase walked across the room and set his empty water glass in the sink next to the bowls.

"All right. I'll just go tell him." I headed up the stairs.

I found my son and dog in the middle of my bed watching a Spider-Man cartoon. I ruffled Hayden's hair. "Hey, Bud, I have to go to a meeting in town, but Chase is going to stay here with you. Why don't you get on your PJs and get ready for bed?"

"It's not bedtime yet," he complained.

"I know, but if you get all ready, you can hang out with Chase downstairs until I get home. I should be back for bedtime."

He cocked his head and considered this. "Why is Chase staying with me? He's never babysat me before."

I sat beside him on my bed. "There wasn't anyone else to stay. I couldn't get ahold of Grandpa, and Benji has class."

"Is he your Krissie? Are you going to marry him like Dad is marrying Krissie?"

I bit the inside of my lip.

"Because if you want a Krissie, that's okay with me. Dad got one. It's only fair that you can have one too. It doesn't have to be Chase. Whatever Krissie you want is okay. I know you'll make a good choice. You're good at picking out things. You always do a good job picking out my clothes, and this morning Mrs. Cooper told me I was a snappy dresser."

I laughed with tears in my eyes and wrapped my son up in a bear hug. He yelped and struggled to wriggle away. "You have no idea what an exceptional person you are, Hayden Cambridge."

Fifteen minutes later, Hayden and I came down the stairs with Tiffin on our heels. Chase was sitting on the couch reading a novel from my bookshelf. He set the book aside. "Are you ready to party while your mom is gone?"

My son's face lit up. "Yeah!"

Oh boy. "Try not to wake up any of the neighbors during your wild party," I said.

Hayden wrinkled his brow. "Mom, the closest neighbor is far away."

"Exactly," I said pointedly to Chase.

He grinned in return.

I went to the door and got ready for a trek across the frozen tundra. Chase joined me at the door while I pulled on my gloves. "Thanks again for doing this," I said. "I really do appreciate it. I know there must be things you'd rather do on your night off than hang out with a five-year-old."

"Not really," he said.

I searched his face to gauge whether or not he was teasing me again, but all I saw was sincerity. My conversation with Hayden upstairs flashed across my memory, and I broke eye contact. "I should be back by nine. Hayden's bedtime is eight, but it's okay for him to stay up a little later until I get back."

Chase nodded. "Got it." He opened the door for me but didn't step out of my way.

I pulled down the scarf covering my mouth so that he could hear me. "Is something wrong?"

He looked as if he wanted to say something but had changed his mind. "Nope. Nothing's wrong. Go catch a killer. Hayden and I will be fine."

I left, wondering what else he'd wanted to say.

TEN

I KNEW WHERE THE shelter house was located in the large, wooded park surrounding Barton Farm. It was a popular location for children's birthday parties, and I'd been to my share there. It was about a fifteen-minute walk from my cottage, but considering the dark and the cold temperatures, I opted to drive. Plus, I was running late and didn't have enough time to find my way there in the dark.

By the time I arrived, the parking lot was half full. The red pickup truck I parked next to had a maple leaf decal in the back window. I recognized Gavin's white truck by the front door. He was perched on the bumper. He jumped off of it when I got out of my car. "You found someone to watch Hayden?" He sounded slightly disappointed.

"I told you I would. Chase is watching him," I said.

Gavin's eyes widened, but he knew better than to comment on that. He cleared his throat. "I still don't think this is a great idea."

"I disagree." I lowered my voice as an elderly man with a cane shuffled through the shelter house's door. It banged closed after him.

"Gavin, Dr. Beeson's death has been ruled a murder. He did have a heart attack, but someone stabbed him in the chest."

In the yellow security light over the shelter house's door, Gavin paled. "Oh no. And the detective thinks I did it?"

"Exactly. That's why it's even more important that we see who else might have a motive."

He glanced at the closed door. "You're going to find an entire room of suspects here. No one in Sap and Spile liked him." He paused. "Before we go in there, I just have to warn you. They might not be too excited to see you. My father knows you're coming, of course. He's not happy about it, and the other men won't be either."

I eyed him. "Is this a secret club like the Masons or something?"

Gavin shook his head. "We don't do anything in secret. It's just that you'll be the only woman there."

I arched my brow. "Women don't tap trees?"

Another elderly man climbed out of his car and gave me the once-over as he shuffled into the shelter house.

Gavin lowered his voice. "It's a men's club."

My mouth fell open. "You could have shared that little fact with me this afternoon."

"I just was so shocked by your insistence on coming that I didn't think to mention it. Maybe they won't make a big deal out of it. They're all very interested in Dr. Beeson's death. He was the president of Sap and Spile. Now they'll be scrambling for position."

I pulled at my gloves. It was warmer than it had been the night before, but it was still below freezing. "Scrambling for position? Don't you have a vice president who could step in and take over until someone else is elected?"

"Yes," was his tentative answer.

I frowned.

He waved away the next question forming on my lips. "Let's go in. We can spend all night talking about the crazy way that Sap and Spile is run. I think when you meet everyone it'll make more sense."

As soon as Gavin opened the door, I could hear the rumble of many male voices coming from a meeting room to our left.

I followed Gavin inside and removed my stocking cap but not my coat. The shelter house didn't have any central heating and was sparsely furnished with a half dozen wooden picnic tables. It was warmer than outside, though, because there was an enormous hearth, big enough to hold two full-grown men, on the far side of the room. A huge fire raged in the middle of the hearth, giving off heat. Most of the men were close to that end of the room.

"Brace yourself," Gavin said under his breath.

"Brace myself for what?" I asked, but he was headed toward the fire.

I squared my shoulders and walked across the room after him. Slowly, I became aware that all conversation had ceased when I'd entered the shelter house.

The men who stood around in small groups or sat at the tables stared at me. There were roughly twenty men in total. Gavin was definitely the youngest. The rest looked like retirees, or just a few years shy of that. There was a mixture of confusion and outrage on the men's faces. I was now beginning to understand why Gavin had told me to brace myself.

To the right of the fireplace there was a small round table that held a photograph of Dr. Beeson. In the photo, he was in the woods holding up a tree spile—the hollow metal peg that's drilled into the maple tree to begin the run of sap. He wore a plaid coat and beamed at the camera. Beside the photograph was a stack of *Maple Sugar and the Civil War*. A small sign said that cash and checks were accepted.

Checks could be made out to Conrad Beeson. I hoped that his family had some way to cash those checks now that he was dead. I wondered if he had children other than Corrie, the daughter Gavin had mentioned to the detective.

Gavin was speaking to his father, who scowled at me. Nevertheless, I was about to join them when a small man approached me. He was just a little over five feet tall and bald. I was only five two, so it wasn't often that I met a man who was shorter than me.

"We're so glad that you came," the man said. "We're hoping you can shed some light on Conrad's death. Gavin tells us you were the one who found him."

"I was one of the people. My assistant Benji was with me."

"Is Benji a dog?" he asked.

"No, she's a girl." I was glad that Benji wasn't there to hear this comment. She was pretty sensitive when it came to the canine she'd been named after, and when Benji was sensitive, she threw things. I examined the man and felt like I'd seen him before, but I couldn't place him. "Have we met?"

He shook his head. "Not formally. I was at the Civil War reenactment at Barton Farm this summer."

It was possible that's where I'd seen him. But there had been several hundred reenactors on the Farm that weekend, and I'd been dealing with another murder.

He held out his hand to me. "I'm Robert Stroud."

"Oh," I said, immediately recognizing the name of the maple sugar expert who'd bowed out before I hired Conrad Beeson to take his place. "I'm so glad that you're feeling better."

He blinked at me from behind his glasses. "Better?"

I nodded. "You've been sick. I'm happy to see you out of the hospital so soon."

He sniffed as if I'd offended him. "Hospital? I was never in a hospital."

"You *were* in the hospital," I argued, not sure why he would deny it. "That's why you couldn't teach the tree tapping class at the Farm."

"Whatever gave you that idea? I was looking forward to teaching the course. I was sorely disappointed when I got your call telling me that the course was canceled."

I blinked at him. "My call? I never called you. The course isn't canceled."

He glared at me. His friendly demeanor had completely vanished. "Yes, you did. You called me just two days ago and told me that you were sorry, but there weren't enough participants signed up for the course, so it was canceled. I offered to teach free of charge to those who'd signed up. It didn't seem right to me to leave those who wanted to learn about tree tapping with nothing. You said that you thought it was better just to cancel the course and try again next year."

"Robert," I said, becoming aware that the other men in the room were now watching us as the conversation became more heated. "The class wasn't canceled. I never called to tell you that. Someone claiming to be your daughter called me and said that you were in the hospital."

"Daughter?" He stepped back. "I don't have any children. Why would you take some woman's word for it? You could easily have called me to confirm."

"And you could just as easily have called me back to double-check on the cancellation. It seems to me that we both were played."

"Who would do that?"

I shook my head. Who would call me and pretend to be Stroud's daughter? And more importantly, *why* would they do that?

"I'm sorry for the confusion," I said finally.

"Do you still want me to teach the class?" Stroud asked eagerly.

I hesitated, given his extreme reaction to the mix-up, but the tree tapping class was at ten the next morning. I was running out of time to find a replacement, and if I didn't want to be stuck teaching it myself, I really didn't have any other options. "Actually, yes. Dr. Beeson was going to teach the class in your place, so—"

"Beeson!" he snapped. "You told me the course was canceled, and you hired *him* of all people?"

"Like I said, *I* never called you," I said through gritted teeth. "Just like it wasn't really your daughter who called me to tell me you were sick."

"Robert." A severe-looking man with a mane of gray hair approached us. "It's time to bring the meeting to order. Since you're the vice president, that would be your responsibility." He didn't add *now that Beeson is dead*, but it was implied.

"Oh, right, thank you, John. If you could excuse me, Ms. Cambridge," Stroud said politely.

I blinked at the sudden shift in his demeanor.

He shuffled to the front of the room, where there was a long table. The huge fire snapped and crackled behind him, giving the proceedings an almost medieval feel. In the middle of the table there was a gavel, and he picked it up and stared at it as if he was surprised to have it in his hand. He whacked it on the tabletop. "Gentlemen." He nodded to me. "And lady. This meeting of the Sap and Spile Club is now called to order. May your trees produce sap."

"Long live the syrup," the men in the room said in return.

I wondered which alternative universe I'd landed in, one where maple sugar was treated like a deity of some sort.

Stroud cleared his throat. "As you all know, our president, Conrad Beeson passed away quite suddenly this afternoon. Gavin has brought Kelsey Cambridge here to talk to us about the incident."

I shot Gavin a look. That wasn't what I signed up for. I was there to size up the suspects, not give a show-and-tell.

Gavin stepped forward. "I asked Kelsey to come here tonight because she can tell us about where and how she discovered the professor."

"Was he murdered?" a man in the back of the room asked.

"If anyone deserved it, it was Conrad. Insufferable man," another voice added.

I spun around, searching for the comment's origin, but I just met the hostile gaze of irritated tree tappers. Gavin had said that I would find an entire room of people at Sap and Spile that wanted Beeson dead. It appeared he'd been right about that.

Stroud smacked his gavel on the tabletop again. "Order, please!"

The room grew quiet.

Stroud took a deep breath. "I know that we're all upset over Conrad's passing, but we can't allow our emotions to run away with us."

A man snorted in the back.

This time I managed to see who it was. He was tall, with thick black hair, and I would place him in his forties—which with the exception of Gavin was young for this crowd.

"Don't be ridiculous, Robert," the man said. "No one here is broken up over Conrad's death. He was an absolute parasite."

I could have been wrong, but I thought the man's voice sounded like the voice that had said Conrad deserved to die. I inspected him with interest. It appeared I had my first real suspect.

"Now, Buckley, you know that Conrad made a huge contribution to the maple sugar community in New Hartford and the entire state of Ohio."

Buckley moved to the front of the room. The other members of Sap and Spile quickly stepped out of his way. I guessed he was someone who was accustomed to having others move for him. He marched to the front of the room and plucked one of Beeson's books off of the pile. "I, for one, am glad that I won't have to hear about this anymore. Ever since it was released, all Conrad could talk about was his book and what a great work it was. This is what I think of it." He tossed the paperback into the fire behind Stroud's table.

ELEVEN

I STOOD THERE STUNNED as the flames ate away at the paper. Had he really just done that?

The room was completely silent, and then someone in the back started to clap. Before I knew it, everyone in the room was clapping, even Gavin and Stroud.

Buckley picked up another copy of the book and made a move as if he was going to toss that one in the fire too. I ran forward and ripped it from his hand. "You can't burn books!"

He looked down at me. "I'm not burning just any book, I'm burning *his* book."

Stroud smacked his gavel on the table repeatedly. If he wasn't careful he was going to throw out his shoulder from hitting the table so many times. "Please, everyone, can we please calm down. If everyone would take a seat, we can discuss this more calmly."

Buckley didn't move for a full five seconds, and then he shrugged and sat at one of the tables at the front of the room.

Stroud let out a breath. "Thank you." He licked his lips. "Kelsey, what can you tell us about Conrad's death?"

I turned around to face the crowd so that I could watch their reactions as I spoke—especially the reaction of Buckley, who was now my prime suspect. In my opinion, anyone who could burn a book was capable of murder. "There's not much to tell. Dr. Beeson was visiting Barton Farm this morning in preparation for the tree tapping class that he was to teach on the Farm tomorrow morning."

Out of the corner of my eye, I noticed Stroud stiffen when I mentioned the class. I waited a beat to see if he would say anything. When he remained silent, I went on. "Beeson went off by himself to check another group of trees and presumably had a heart attack. My assistant and I found him and called 911."

"So he wasn't murdered?" someone asked.

"The police haven't made a formal announcement," I said, hoping that Gavin wouldn't share what I told him earlier.

That hope went unanswered, because Gavin stepped forward. "The police say he was murdered, and they think it was me."

Conversation erupted as the men discussed this latest bit of information.

"That's ridiculous," Webber said. "My son wouldn't do this."

I found his denial of Gavin's guilt interesting, especially after the argument they'd had by the sugarhouse just a few hours ago.

"We all know they think it was him," said a man in the back smugly. He had a short blond ponytail and a goatee.

Gavin's father glowered at him.

The other man seemed unfazed. "And we all know that both you and Gavin have a reason to want Conrad Beeson dead. With him gone, you'll be able to retain your rights to tap the trees in the park."

Gavin stepped forward. "Were you the one who told the police what I said to him, Daniel?"

Daniel rocked back on his heels.

82

I was beginning to wonder if the Sap and Spile club should be billed as a fight club. I'd only been there for a half hour and all I'd witnessed so far was a litany of arguments among the members. I supposed that I could cut them some slack, considering their club president had just been killed, but I had a feeling that many of their meetings went like this, murder or no murder.

Daniel glared at me. "Tonight's meeting is a joke. We should have canceled it the moment we heard about Conrad's death. It's gotten so bad that we're even allowing women into our meetings. Oh, how swiftly we have fallen."

What was it, 1908?

"Now, Daniel," Buckley said. "Gavin asked Ms. Cambridge to come to shed some light what happened to Conrad. We can make an exception for such an important matter, can't we?"

A white-haired man at the front of the room spoke up. "I agree. And I also agree with Ms. Cambridge that burning books is not something we should do. We should return these copies here to Conrad's family, and they'll decide what to do with them." He shook his head. "It just seems such a shame that Conrad would drop dead like that right after his book was released. He said he's been working on it for years."

Stroud gripped his gavel so tightly his knuckles turned white.

"Is something wrong, Robert?" Buckley asked.

The smaller man released the gavel as if it caused him pain to do so. "I—I was just thinking of the injustice of what happened to Conrad. It's terrible." He cleared his throat. "But Daniel's right. I think we should end the meeting early tonight. We're not doing any good here fighting about Conrad and his book." He smacked his gavel on the tabletop. "Meeting adjourned."

The men in the room muttered to each other as they shuffled to the door to leave. I watched them go. I'd come to the meeting looking for an alternative suspect to Gavin, and it appeared I had more than I could handle. I wondered if Detective Brandon knew about this group, because she needed to talk to them. I would put Buckley and Daniel at the top of the list.

Stroud walked up to me. "I'm so sorry you had to witness that. As you can imagine, Conrad's death has taken everyone by surprise."

"I can see that," I said diplomatically.

He cleared his throat. "I also would like to apologize for my own behavior earlier. I overreacted about Conrad teaching the tree tapping course. That was all."

I nodded.

"So, if you're still in need of a lecturer for tomorrow morning, I'm happy to do it."

I sighed. I wasn't really enthused about spending any more time with any of the members of Sap and Spile, but I did need an instructor. "Yes, I would appreciate that," I said. "The class begins at ten, so if you could arrive around nine thirty, that should be plenty of time for you to set up."

"I'll do that." He gathered up his gavel and walked away.

I hadn't realized, when I was talking to Stroud, how quickly the shelter house had cleared out. The only people left now were Gavin, his father, and me.

Webber was breaking up what was left of the fire with a poker and dousing the last ashes with water from a metal bucket. A plume of smoke filled the room. He set the bucket back onto the floor. "I told you not to come. Look what's happened because you didn't listen. We couldn't even have a real meeting."

"Dad," Gavin said.

Webber frowned. "Go home. Both of you. I have to do the final check of the building and lock up."

Gavin and I agreed and walked outside into the cold together. After the door closed behind us, I said, "I need to see where your old sugarhouse is in the park, that you were fighting with Beeson over."

"Why?" he asked, a slight whine in his voice.

"Because I want to see what the big deal is." I put on my stocking hat and tucked my long brown braid up into it.

"Can't you take my word for it?"

I shook my head. "I think I need to see it."

"I have a school visit to lead tomorrow," he complained.

"I know that, and I have a busy morning planned. We'll go later, in the afternoon, so plan on it."

Before he could say another word, I climbed into my car and drove back to the Farm.

Ten minutes later, as I opened the door leading into my cottage, I heard the television. Chase sat in the middle of the couch. Tiffin lay on his right side, and Hayden lay curled up under his left arm, asleep. Even Frankie was in the room. True, he was perched on the dining room table looking like he was about to strike, but for Frankie that was very social. My heart did a little flip-flop. It was a feeling I hadn't had in a very long time.

Chase placed a finger to his lips and was careful not to disturb my son as he turned off the TV with the remote. Gingerly he slipped out from under Hayden on the couch and gently laid my son's head on a pillow before tiptoeing over to me by the door. "How did your meeting go?" he asked in a whisper. "You're back sooner than I expected."

"The meeting ended early, but it was fine. Interesting," I said in the same hushed tones. "I now have more suspects than I know what to do with."

He raised his eyebrows in question as he shrugged into his coat.

"I'll tell you later. I should get Hayden to bed. He's going to be so tired in the morning, and it's a school night."

Chase nodded. "He's a great kid. We had a lot of fun. I'd like to hang out with him more, if you're up to it." He wrapped his scarf around his throat in a practiced move. "I'd like to hang out with you both more."

"Chase," I began, but I didn't know what I was going to say, so I stopped.

"Have you reconsidered our date?" he asked.

"Our date? We've never had a date," I said.

He gave me a sideways grin. "That's what I was hoping you would reconsider."

Before I could answer, he leaned forward and kissed me on the cheek. "I'll see you tomorrow, Kelsey."

I closed the door behind him and told the butterflies doing backflips in my stomach to knock it off.

TWELVE

THE NEXT MORNING AT seven thirty, Hayden and I stood at the end of Barton Farm's long driveway and watched as the elementary school's lumbering old school bus crested the hill. Hayden jumped in place. He loved school, and I was so grateful for that.

The bus stopped in front of us, and Hayden turned and threw his little arms around my waist, giving me a mighty hug. I hugged him back. I relished every squeeze and felt heartsick when I thought of the day when he would no longer want to hug me in public.

"I love you," I said. "Have a good day."

"Love you, Mom," he said and galloped to the bus door.

The bus driver greeted him by name with a great big smile and waved at me.

I watched as Hayden made his way to the back of the bus and fell into a seat next to one of his classmates. I waved until the bus disappeared. Then I crossed the street into the village.

The village was closed up tight for the winter and wouldn't officially reopen until mid-May. However, many of my seasonal workers would return in early April to begin the long process of cleaning and repair needed to make the village ready for another season.

A striking red cardinal bounced on a maple limb beside the pebbled path and cocked its head to look at me, as if asking why I was coming into the village at this time of year. What the cardinal didn't know was that I walked through the village every day, sun, rain, or snow. As the live-in director of the Farm, I felt it was my duty to keep an eye on every aspect of it. That included Jason.

As I walked to the two-hundred-year-old barn just on the other side of the street, the two oxen, Betty and Mags, stared at me from the pen beside the barn. Jason hadn't yet walked them across Maple Grove Lane to the large pasture. In the cold, they were the only two animals tough enough to be outside. I saw that the Farm's milking cow didn't even bother to stick her nose out the open barn door.

"Jason?" I called as I stepped inside the dim barn. I didn't want to startle my farmhand. He could be as skittish as a colt.

There was no answer. I hadn't really expected one. Jason was a nineteen-year-old young man of few words.

I found him in the middle of the barn measuring feed into pails. The three sheep baaed when I walked by. I suppose they expected me to feed them. They would have to wait for Jason.

Miss Muffins, the barn's calico cat, jumped onto a hay bale and held out her neck asking to be petted. I gave her a good scratch. "Hey Jason," I said. "How are the animals today? I know winter can be hard on them, and we've had a bad one this year."

He didn't look up from his measuring. "Everyone is fine. Some of the sheep had a tough couple days, but they've snapped out of it now that the weather is warming up."

"Glad to hear it." I picked up Miss Muffins and cuddled the calico under my chin. How much I wished that Hayden had wanted a cat like her to bring home instead of Frankie the Destroyer. "And how's your trailer?"

"Good." Jason looked up from the feed pail that he was filling. "I'm grateful to have it."

Last summer, I'd learned that Jason was sleeping in the barn most nights. He claimed that he wanted to be close to the animals. I'd tried to convince him to move off the grounds, but I continued to find him on Farm property at all hours. After some prying, I learned that he had nowhere else to go. He was a former foster kid with social anxiety who'd put himself through two years of college to earn an associate's degree in animal husbandry, with the plan to work with animals. I was impressed that he'd managed this feat. It seemed that living around other people was something he could not handle, and I didn't have the heart to kick him out on the street.

Finally, I'd taken a little of the money from the trust and bought a small trailer for Jason to live in on the village side of the Farm. The trailer was tucked back into the trees a few hundred yards from the barn, out of the view of the tourists who would visit the village in the summer months. I took his minuscule rent out of his paycheck.

Not all my employees, namely Shepley, were pleased with my decision, but I'd found it was helpful to have another person living on the grounds when I needed help, especially during the winter when no one else was there other than Hayden and me. In fact, Jason had come to my rescue in January when a frozen pipe had burst in the visitor center in the middle of the night.

"Are you planning on coming to the pancake breakfasts this weekend?" I asked.

He gave me a look. Jason hated the crowds. He wouldn't even face them for hot pancakes with maple syrup.

"You're more than welcome to come." I knew he wouldn't. I sat on the hay bale with Miss Muffins on my lap. "I stopped by because I wondered if you saw all the commotion across the street yesterday."

"I saw the ambulance," Jason said as he poured the measured feed into the trough just inside the sheep pen.

I nodded. "The maple sugar expert I hired had an accident in the woods." I paused. "He died."

Jason pressed the lid down on the plastic container of feed until it clicked into place. He made no comment. Most of my conversations with him were one-sided.

"Did you see anything unusual going on? I mean, before the ambulance and police came?"

He gave me a strange look.

"The thing is, the police say that Beeson was murdered."

"Murdered," Jason murmured.

I stroked Miss Muffins' back. I couldn't get the memory out of my head of Beeson trying to tell me something before he died. Part of me—and it was a big part—thought that he'd been trying to tell me who his attackers were. "Did you see anyone on the grounds?" I asked. "What about a hiker who may have been wandering in the woods?"

Jason poured feed into the food trough for the dairy cow and shook his head. "I saw the police, the ambulance, and the school bus come and go. Nothing else. No one walked over to this side of the road. If they did, I would have spotted them. All the trees are bare, and I can see from the barn all the way across the green, and to Shepley's gardens."

I sighed. It had been a long-shot at best that Jason might have seen something. Although he had a clear view of all the happenings on this side of the Farm, he certainly couldn't have seen across the pasture into the cluster of red maples where Dr. Beeson had fallen. "Have you noticed *anything* strange over the last few days, anything at all?"

He started to shake his head, and then stopped.

"What is it?" I asked.

He looked down. "I've seen the Hooper boys cutting through the village now and again."

I frowned, remembering Judy saying that Pansy had stopped by the visitor center yesterday less than an hour before Benji and I had found Beeson in the woods. It seemed like I needed to drop in on my neighbors. It wasn't a social call I looked forward to, so I'd decided to take Benji with me.

"Did the boys do anything other than cut through the village?" I asked.

Jason swallowed. "Not that I saw."

I couldn't exactly take that as a no, but I didn't want to push my farmhand too far. It had taken me months building trust to convince him to talk to me this much. I didn't want to ruin what I'd achieved.

I noticed his employee radio sitting on the edge of a barn stall. The green light wasn't on. "Your radio isn't on, is it?" I asked him.

"I don't know," he said, seemingly baffled by my question and by the radio all together.

I stood up and got the radio from the stall door. I turned it on.

"I was trying to save the batteries." He swallowed.

"Don't worry about the batteries," I said. "I need to be able to reach you if something comes up. You need to have this on and with you at all times. That was part of our agreement."

He nodded and clipped the radio to his belt.

THIRTEEN

After leaving Jason to his animals in the barn, I headed for the visitor center. I still had over an hour before Stroud arrived for the tree tapping class. Two buses of school children would arrive at about the same time, and I needed to have my wits about me to make sure everyone went in the right direction.

It was still hard for me to believe that the Maple Sugar Festival was finally here, kicking off with the tree tapping class. It had taken months of planning. By late Sunday afternoon, it would all be over. I sighed. Or would it? With Beeson's death, I felt like I would be talking about maple sugar for many weeks to come.

My radio crackled at my hip. "Kelsey, are you there? Over," Benji said. She loved to end radio conversations with "over."

I removed the radio from my hip. "I'm here, Benji. What's up?"

There was a pause, and I waited and waited. Finally, I said, "Benji, what is up?"

"You didn't say 'over,'" she complained. "How do I know you've finished speaking if you don't say 'over'?"

I groaned. "Can you just tell me what's going on?"

There was a pronounced pause when Benji didn't say a word.

"Over," I said grudgingly.

"Sure!" she said as if she'd won the lottery. "Shepley's here at the visitor center. He had a few choice words to say about the Maple Sugar Festival."

"Of course he did," I muttered.

"And he wants to talk to you."

"What about?" I asked, wrinkling my nose at the thought. "Over."

"I don't know. He refused to tell me," she said. There was a little bit of hurt in her voice. Before I'd promoted her to my assistant, Benji had had a good relationship with the ornery gardener. More than anyone, she'd been able to carry on a normal conversation with him. That had seemed to change when she was promoted. It was almost as if Shepley felt that she'd sold out by leaving her post at the brick pit and taking a job in Farm management. I knew that Benji would never admit it, but it hurt her that Shepley now treated her like he did the rest of us.

"Okay, I'm on my way." I clipped the radio back onto my belt and increased my pace.

When I stepped into the visitor center, I found Shepley pacing back and forth near the door. I knew something was up right away. He never came into the visitor center, not even for mandatory staff meetings. He thought that the rules and directions I gave the rest of the staff didn't apply to him.

Judy nodded in his direction when she met my gaze. She was in the process of counting out tickets for the pancake breakfasts. Pre-sales had been strong, so much so that I'd hired a few extra cooks from a temp agency so that we would be able to keep up with the demand for pancakes.

Shepley tapped his foot. "What took you so long?" he snapped.

"Hello to you too, Shepley."

He curled his lip into a sneer. The gardener was a small man, close to my own height of five two. His long gray ponytail was tied back with a piece of garden twine. The white scar cutting across his left cheek, which had never been explained, stood out more than usual with his face beet-red in anger. "You shouldn't keep me waiting when such a violation has happened."

"I didn't know a violation was part of the story," I said. "You didn't tell Benji your reason for wanting to talk to me this morning. I don't have much time before our maple sugar expert arrives, but you can tell me now."

"You're going to want to make time for this. It's a top priority."

I removed my hat and could feel the aura of static electricity floating around my head as hair escaped from my standard long French braid. "Please just get on with it, Shepley."

He glared at me and said, "I want to know what you're going to do about the damage to my garden."

"Damage?" I asked. Now he had my full attention. "What damage? I walk the grounds every day and haven't seen anything out of the ordinary on the village side."

"Then your observation skills are severely lacking. Someone has broken into my garden and trampled it. Trampled it!" He shook with anger.

"What?" I cried.

He nodded as if I'd finally given him the reaction that he'd been looking for. "Yes. Someone has broken into the garden and stomped every bed I have."

"At least it's winter and nothing is in bloom," I said to myself.

Shepley heard me. "It's still no good for the plants. The crocuses are sprouting."

"Will they be all right?" I asked.

"I think so, but this makes me very uneasy as spring approaches. I will not have all the bulbs that I planted one by one last fall be trampled to death this spring. We have that fence around the garden to keep the deer out, but it seems that some two-legged cretin has broken in instead."

"Are you sure it wasn't a deer? Perhaps the gate was left open." Even as I said this, I knew that Shepley would take offense to it, but it was a question that had to be asked.

"I would never leave the gate open." He eyed me. "Did you leave it open? You and I are the only ones with a key."

"No. I peek through the fence on my daily rounds, but I never go in." Maybe the damage was in the back, which would be why I hadn't noticed it. "Why don't you show me now."

Benji slid into the lobby and saw me standing with Shepley. She pulled up short.

"Do you need something, Benji? Shepley and I are headed to the gardens. It appears there was some damage overnight."

"What kind of damage?" she asked.

Shepley pointedly ignored her, and I suppressed a sigh at his childishness. "Someone stomped through the garden. Would you like to come along?"

She looked at Shepley's stony face and shook her head. "I'll stay here. There are just a few things that I need to mark off our list for the weekend and we'll be good to go. The classroom is all set up for the tree tapping class."

"Thanks, Benji. I don't know what I would do without you."

She gave me a small smile, but she watched Shepley, who refused to meet her eyes. I sighed. I would have to deal with the rift between them at some point, but it would have to wait. The Maple Sugar

Festival and a murder were about my quota of what I could handle at the moment. I motioned to the door. "Let's go, Shepley."

Shepley and I walked in silence down the pebbled path. As the snow melted, the path became muddy. I hoped that it would be mostly dried out by Saturday morning when the festival was in full swing. If not, mud would be tracked into all of the buildings.

I was just happy for the silence. It gave me time to wonder what I was going to do about Dr. Beeson's death. I knew Detective Brandon wanted me to leave it be, but I wasn't sure I could do that. Who would stab a man like that with a drill? It was just too gruesome for words.

As we crossed Maple Grove Lane, Shepley pointed at the barn. "I wouldn't be surprised if it wasn't that boy you allow to live on Farm property who trampled my plants."

"Jason would never do that. Barton Farm is his home," I said, coming to my farmhand's defense.

"Oh, I know it's his home." Shepley picked up his pace as we entered the green, and I had to increase my speed to keep up with him.

The gardener looked over his shoulder. "If there was decent oversight of the Farm by the Cherry Foundation, he would never have been allowed to live on the grounds in the first place."

I came up alongside of him. "Shepley, if that were the case, you would have been fired a long time ago. The Cherry Foundation would never put up with you for as long as I have."

He scowled but didn't argue with me. Maybe because he knew it was the truth.

The gardens came into view. A five-foot-high split-rail fence lined with chicken wire surrounded the main garden. Even at a distance, I could see that the damage was extensive. As upsetting as that was, I was happy to see that the much smaller medicinal garden next to it appeared untouched. A seven-foot-high iron fence surrounded that garden to keep intruders out. Many of the plants inside were poisonous. We grew them on the Farm because the Barton family had had a similar garden to treat aliments on the same spot. Mrs. Barton used many plants and herbs from that garden to treat ill children and neighbors. However, because of the contents, it needed to be under lock and key. We had an incident last summer when someone with malicious intent broke into the medicinal garden. Because of that, it was padlocked twice. I wasn't going to allow anyone to use the Farm's plants to hurt anyone else again.

Shepley unlocked the gate to the main garden, and it swung open.

"Was the gate locked when you found the mess?" I asked as we stepped inside.

He nodded. "It was locked up tight."

I frowned. That could mean that someone from the Farm had gone in. Shepley and I had keys, yet there was also a spare key in my office. I kept my office locked, but Benji had a key to my office and could access all of the keys ... but she would never have done this.

I examined the damage. It looked like someone had done the Irish jig up and down the rows of plants, twice. I again felt relief that it was in the middle of winter. Had someone walked in the garden like that in the middle of the summer, it would be truly devastating to the Farm. Our heirloom gardens, which only had plants in keeping with what could readily be available and used in gardens during the Civil War, were one of the Farm's great showpieces. Shepley's gifted hand with plants was the only reason I kept him around.

Shepley watched me. "What are you going to do about this?" he shouted. "No one, absolutely no one, should come into my garden without my permission."

"Shepley, I don't know who may have entered the garden, but I need to remind you that the garden is technically the property of Barton Farm. It's not your personal space."

He ignored my last comment. As far as he was concerned, the garden was his and there was nothing I could say that would convince him otherwise.

"Listen, I can see why you're upset," I said. "This is upsetting to me too. You've put a lot of hard work into the garden to make it the envy of the county."

He nodded, as if mollified. "And see the crocuses. Some of them won't recover their spring growth because of this." He pointed to thin green leaves peeking out of the snow. Some were stomped beyond recognition.

I shook my head. "The first thing we need to do is secure the garden. Go to the hardware store and buy a new padlock for the gate. Then, if someone has a key, at least it will give them pause." I sighed. "This could just be a practical joke by local kids with no plans to return. The fence is only five feet high." The Hooper boys immediately came to mind.

"We should put barbed wire on the top. That'll keep the cretins out."

I frowned. I didn't like that suggestion. There were too many children on the grounds during the summer. I didn't want any of them getting hurt by a barbed-wire fence. There were enough ways to get hurt on the Farm as it was without adding to the list. "I don't think that's a good idea."

"And you think a new padlock is?" Shepley asked. "Is that all you're going to do about it? It's vandalism. Someone should be held responsible."

I didn't argue with him on that point.

"Are you going to call the authorities?" he continued.

I wondered about calling Chief Duffy. He would brush it off as kids, just like I'd tried to. But I thought Detective Brandon might take it a little more seriously, especially if it could be tied to Dr. Beeson's death. "I'll talk to Detective Brandon about it."

"When?" he asked.

I wasn't sure. "As soon as I can. The tree tapping class is today, and I really should get back to the visitor center so I can meet with the new instructor." It was the best answer I could give him. My eyes swept over the garden again. "Shepley, do you see that?"

"What?" he barked.

"There's a clear footprint in the snow." I took a couple of steps closer to it. "You're right. This definitely wasn't done by any deer."

Shepley walked over to me and stared at the spot. It was a boot print, and the shoe size was much larger than mine. It was most likely from a man, but I couldn't completely rule out a tall woman either.

"Now will you call the police?"

I sighed and removed my cell phone from my pocket.

FOURTEEN

The dispatcher said Detective Brandon was already on her way to the Farm for her current investigation, and in fact she was walking across the muddy village green five minutes later. Officer Sonders followed behind her at a much slower pace.

The detective joined us inside the garden and took a moment to take in every detail of the scene. "You said there was a print."

Shepley scowled at her. He liked the police detective just about as much as I did.

"It's over here," I said quickly, before Shepley could voice a rude comment.

She stared at the boot print while Officer Sonders snapped photo after photo of it. She waved him away. "That's enough, Sonders. It's one measly print. You don't need four hundred shots of it."

The officer put his camera away.

"Do you think this could be related to Dr. Beeson's death?" I said. It was a question I'd been dreading to ask ever since the officers arrived, but I knew it had to be considered.

"Not likely. Nine times out of ten, vandalism like this is committed by a group of bored teenagers. My advice would be to change the locks to the garden gate and consider getting some type of extra security."

"The gate wasn't unlocked," I said.

"That could mean one of two things. It was someone with a key—"

I started to protest, but she held up her hand. "Or someone climbed over the fence. It's only five feet high. That wouldn't be a huge deterrent for someone determined to get in." She walked to the fence and pointed to an overturned wheelbarrow on the other side of the fence. "In fact, I think that's exactly how they got in. They climbed onto the wheelbarrow and jumped the fence. The person would have to be agile, but it wouldn't even be a challenge for a teenager."

I frowned, upset with myself that I hadn't noticed the overturned wheelbarrow first.

"I suggested barbed wire to keep the cretins out," Shepley said.

"That certainly would be a deterrent." Detective Brandon nodded as if she liked Shepley's thought process. I didn't think it was a good sign that the two of them were like-minded. "I'd say this was a case of random vandalism," she added.

I didn't like the sound of "random vandalism," and I debated telling her about the Hooper teenagers, but I stopped myself. I still wanted to talk to Pansy Hooper and her sons before turning their names over to the police.

Even if the Hoopers were innocent, the trampling of the garden was upsetting. Yet it could have been much worse—what if some rowdy teens decided to damage one of the historic buildings in the village? Not for the first time, I wondered if I should install security cameras on Farm grounds. I had the money from the Cherry Foundation's trust to do it. However, a security system wasn't in keeping with the nineteenth century integrity of the village. Not to mention there was no electricity on this side of Maple Grove Lane. Jason's trailer ran on a small generator. I would either have to ask the electric company to run some wires or purchase a much larger, much more expensive generator. Both options would cost more than I could imagine.

"I think Sonders and I are done here," Detective Brandon said. "We have everything we need." She nodded to Sonders and the two of them headed out the gate.

I left Shepley standing in the frozen garden alone and jogged after them. "Detective, doesn't it seem strange that you had to come out here twice in as many days? I think you shouldn't automatically assume the vandalism in the garden was done by teens. It may be related to Dr. Beeson's death. You have to entertain that idea."

"Ms. Cambridge, rest assured that I entertain every idea when it comes to solving my cases."

I almost cracked and told her of my suspicions about the Hoopers, but the radio on my belt crackled. "Kelsey, come in? Over."

"Yes, Benji?" I said into the radio.

There was a pause, during which Detective Brandon and Officer Sonders took the opportunity to walk away. The paused stretched a few seconds longer. I sighed. "Over."

"Robert Stroud is here to set up for the tree tapping class. I thought you'd want to know."

"I'm on my way," I said and headed for the crosswalk on Maple Grove Lane.

When I stepped into the visitor center, I found Stroud holding a briefcase and standing with Judy at the ticket counter.

"Mr. Stroud," I said as I approached him. "Thanks again for filling in on such short notice."

"Please call me Robert," he said.

"And you can call me Kelsey."

He nodded and examined the visitor center's main room. "It's impressive what you've accomplished with the Farm in such a short time. I remember coming here when my nephews were small and enjoying it, and it wasn't half the establishment it is now."

"Thank you," I said. "I wouldn't be able to do it without the generosity of the Cherry Foundation."

"It was a great loss to the community when Cynthia Cherry passed."

I simply nodded. Thinking about Cynthia always brought tears to my eyes. I cleared my throat. "Let me show you where you'll be."

He adjusted his grip on his briefcase and followed me across the visitor center to the classroom on the opposite side of the building from the dining room.

When I stepped inside, I found Gavin checking the equipment. On a long table there was everything that Stroud would need for his presentation: spiles, filters, and a hydrometer that would measure the sugar content of the maple syrup. The hand drill was missing—it was in the evidence room at the police station. Gavin had replaced it with a battery-operated drill. That would have to do.

Gavin stepped around the table. "Everything you need for the class should be here."

Stroud walked forward and examined the table's contents. "This should do nicely. Thank you, Gavin." He straightened up. "And I'm sorry about how last night's meeting went. Rest assured that no one at Sap and Spile thinks you had anything to do with Conrad's death."

Gavin nodded curtly. "I'd better go get ready for my school visit." He walked out of the door.

I pointed to the laptop and projector in the corner of the room. "I wasn't sure if you would be showing a PowerPoint as part of your talk, so I had Benji bring that in. I can set it up for you if you need it."

He shook his head. "I'm a little old fashioned in that way. I'll pass out some handouts, and I see you have a whiteboard in the front of the room if I have to write something down for the class to remember."

I nodded.

At the back of the room there was a table holding thirty copies of Beeson's book, along with a sign listing a price. Stroud noticed it and frowned. "What are those doing here?"

"I bought them," I said. "So that Dr. Beeson could have a book signing after the class. Even though he's gone, I'd still like to get them sold. I think the students in your class will be interested in it."

Stroud pursed his lips.

Thankfully, any further discussion about the books was interrupted with the arrival of the first students for the course. An elderly couple walked in and beamed. "Is this the tree tapping class?" the woman asked.

"It sure is," I said.

"Wonderful! I've been looking forward to this class for a week. Ken and I have wanted to tap our trees for years. We have six sugar maples on our property. This will be the year that we're going to do it." She walked over to the book table in the back of the room. "Oh, I've been so looking forward to reading this." She picked up a copy and looked at Stroud. "Are you the instructor?"

He nodded.

"Can you sign my book before the rest of the class arrives? Ken and I might have to sneak out early to pick up our granddaughter from school. She goes to half-day preschool." She moved toward Stroud with the book held out in her hand.

Stroud stepped back from her as if she offered him a snake. "I'm so sorry. You're mistaken. It's ..." His voice caught. "That book is not mine. My name is not on it."

The woman dropped the book to her side. "But the confirmation email I got said the author of *Maple Sugar and the Civil War* would be teaching the class."

"I'm so sorry for the confusion," I said in my best cruise director voice. "Conrad Beeson, who was going to teach the course and wrote that book, wasn't available today."

I winced internally. That was one way to put it.

"Why not?" she asked.

The man, who I assumed was her husband, Ken, put a hand on her shoulder. "You remember, Carol—that's the professor who died yesterday. I read about it in this morning's paper. It said that he'd had a heart attack right here on the Farm."

I bit the inside of my lip and waited to see if Ken would mention anything about murder. I hadn't been able to check the paper yet to see what the media coverage of Beeson's death was. I was disappointed that the Farm was mentioned. More bad publicity for my beloved museum. But when Ken didn't say anything more, I knew the fact that Beeson had been murdered hadn't been made public. I had a feeling that Ken and Carol would have shared that little fact if they knew about it.

Carol drooped. "What a terrible shame. I really wanted him to sign my book." She looked to me. "I collect signed copies from authors, you see, and then sell them online. I've done very well at it. It's amazing what people will pay for a bestselling author's signature."

Her husband nodded. "It's a shame. If we'd been able to have it signed before he died, then it might be worth more now that he's dead."

Five or six more adults filed into the classroom, and as the sound of children's voices could be heard in the lobby, I took that as my chance to escape the awkward moment. "If you will excuse me." I fled the room.

Three dozen children milled around the visitor center, whooping and laughing. Their teachers asked in vain for them to quiet down. I wove through the children and reached Gavin's side at the doors to the Farm grounds. He looked up from the clipboard that he held. "Looks like I'll have my hands full today."

I scanned the room. "I think so." I glanced outside. The sun was shining and the temp would be in the mid-forties. That was Ohio for you—one day it was the tundra and the next spring was knocking on the door. "The sap might be running today after all."

He nodded. "I tapped a tree this morning in the sugar grove to test, and it's running."

"Great. I'll let Robert know, so he and the class can tap some trees." Gavin nodded.

"Don't forget, after your school visit we have to check out the sugarhouse in the park," I added.

His shoulders sagged. "I was hoping you'd forgotten."

"I don't forget anything."

"I know. It's annoying," he said.

I laughed. "You'd better start the program." I inclined my head toward the children in the room. "They're plotting mutiny."

He nodded and then put his fingers in his mouth and whistled. The shrill sound brought all conversation in the room to a complete halt.

I rubbed my ear. Sheesh, he could have warned me. I'd need to get my hearing checked after that blast.

I returned to the classroom while Gavin told the kids to line up for a tour of the maple grove. I peeked into the back of the room. The class was full and Stroud was in the middle of his introduction.

"I've been maple sugaring since I was a child. It's a long-running tradition in northeast Ohio, and one that early settlers like the Bartons did in order to make sugar to sweeten their coffee and tea, and to bake with. Since there are so many varieties of sugar today, maple sugar is not as popular for baking as it once was."

A man with a bald patch on the back of his head spoke up. Since I was in the back of the room, I couldn't see his face. "So the early settlers discovered maple sugar?"

"Oh, no." Stroud shook his head and seemed to relax as he warmed up to his subject matter. "The Native Americans were tapping trees long before any white settlers arrived in the Cuyahoga Valley. They would use a hatchet to make a small V-shaped cut into the tree, and then they would take a sturdy piece of bark to make a spile. To boil the water out of the sap to create syrup, they used hot rocks. As you can imagine, that took a lot of time, up to three days of constantly heating and changing the rocks. Many of the Native Americans couldn't wait that long, so they made hard discs out of the maple sugar, and they even used that as currency."

I slipped out of the room, happy to see Stroud had the class well in hand. I found Benji in the dining room, helping Jayne set the table for the children's pancake lunch. I was happy to see that the containers of maple syrup were sitting on the counter between the dining room and kitchen and would be distributed by an adult. The less maple syrup spills, the better.

"Benji," I said.

"What's up?" she asked.

"Everything seems to be going smoothly with the school visit and the tree tapping class. I'm going to run an errand."

She set a fork on a placemat. "An errand?" She glanced over at Judy, who was on the opposite side of the room, and lowered her voice as if she didn't want Judy to overhear. "This wouldn't have anything to do with Dr. Beeson, would it?"

"Maybe," I said.

"Kelsey." Benji stretched my name out into three syllables. She glanced at Judy again. "Gavin told me that the police confirmed Dr. Beeson was murdered."

I nodded.

She blew out a breath. "Then don't you think you should stay out of it? Wasn't what happened last summer enough for you?"

"It was more than enough, but the police think Gavin is behind his death."

Benji looked as if I'd slapped her. "They do?" she squeaked.

"What's wrong?" I asked.

She set the container of silverware she was holding on the cafeteria table. "Then I think I made it worse for him."

I wrinkled my brow.

"Detective Brandon was waiting for me outside my apartment last night when I got home from class. She asked me if I knew where Gavin was when Dr. Beeson was killed. I told her that I didn't." She sighed. "And I told her that I couldn't find him when you sent me back to the visitor center to tell him and Judy that we found Dr. Beeson in the woods." She chewed on her lip. "I shouldn't have done that."

I patted her shoulder. "You didn't do anything wrong. You were honest with the police. I would never ask you to lie." I paused. "But you can see how it looks bad for Gavin, can't you? And why I have to help him?"

She nodded. "All right. I'll handle things while you're out."

I thanked her and headed for the exit.

FIFTEEN

AFTER STOPPING IN MY office for my coat, I jumped in my car and drove to New Hartford College, the small technical college where my father was a drama professor. The college specialized in courses that dealt with costume, makeup, and set design. They also had a few classes in acting and playwriting, and those were the ones my father had taught for the last thirty years.

It was the middle of the spring semester, and students and faculty made their way across campus. Since the thermometer was approaching forty, a few hardy male students wore shorts. I parked my car as close as I could to the theater building, where crocuses were just beginning to sprout by the front door. Another sign of spring.

I hurried inside and peeked into the large auditorium to make sure I wasn't interrupting play practice or a class. Dad taught most of his classes in the auditorium itself. He said that actors learned better on the stage than in the classroom.

My boots made an eerie shuffling sound on the brushed velvet carpet. The house lights were down, and only the lights that told me of the many exits were illuminated.

The auditorium was used for college events, but they allowed the town of New Hartford to use the space for town meetings and community events; at a price, of course. The vast open space gave me the creeps much more than the cramped old buildings on Barton Farm ever did.

I hurried down the long aisle and up the steps onto the stage. My father's office was backstage, tucked away in what was meant to be a dressing room. Office space was a premium on the tiny campus, and that small, windowless room was the best the college could offer him, not that he minded. I couldn't imagine his office being anywhere else. Whereas it would make me crazy to be isolated from the rest of the campus, it never bothered Dad. He said it made him feel close to his dramatic kindred spirits.

Dad's office door was open, and yellow light poured out onto the dark backstage area. I knocked on the doorframe.

"Well, hello," he bellowed. He always spoke as if he were projecting his booming stage voice. As well as being a professor, Dad was also an active participant in local community theater, a regular scene stealer on the New Hartford community stage. "I have to say I'm surprised to see you here. I thought you would be back at the Farm preparing for the weekend." He rested his hands on his round belly as if it were a shelf. "I'm looking forward to my stack of pancakes doused in maple syrup. I hope you'll save your father a few extra servings."

"There'll be plenty for everyone," I said with a smile, stepping into the cramped space. "Alice bought enough pancake fixings to serve the Roman army."

He grinned. "Good to know."

I sat in an uncomfortable wooden chair across from him. Piles of books, notebooks, and papers stood in precarious stacks on his desk.

There was also a pile of plays that he was reading. My office back at Barton Farm didn't look much better. Like father, like daughter. We had no grasp on organizing paper. Thankfully most of my files were digital now, which was so much easier. "What are you working on?"

"I was just doing a little grading. I have a great crop of student players this year. I hope several of them go on to four-year colleges for their BFAs. I was thinking of putting on a showcase at the end of the semester. I just have to convince my department chair and the academic dean." He wrinkled his nose at the thought. Dad had never been one for college politics. He set the student play he was reading aside. "But I always have time for my favorite child."

"I'm your only child," I said with a smile.

"I know. What a blessing that is, so I don't have to choose a favorite. That must be awkward for a parent."

I leaned back in the chair. "Parents are supposed to love all their children equally."

He shrugged. "So they say."

I shifted in my chair.

Dad pulled the pillow out from behind him. "Here. It might make it a little more tolerable. I've been asking the college for new office furniture for years. Now they're just waiting for me to retire."

"You'll never retire."

He grinned. "You're right. That's one of the perks of tenure. I don't leave until I say so. I wish they'd just accept that and give me a new desk." He leaned back in his own chair. "You never just drop in for a visit. What's going on?" His eyebrows knit together. "Is Hayden all right?"

"Hayden's perfectly fine." I paused. "There was an incident on the Farm yesterday."

He perked up. "Oh?"

"With Dr. Beeson."

He blinked. "The horticulture professor?"

I nodded. "He was hurt. Well, more than hurt."

Dad scratched his chin. "I suppose I should come out of my cave more often to know what the news is on campus. How is he?"

I frowned. "That's the problem. He died."

Dad's eyes grew two sizes behind his glasses. "Died? How?"

I went on to tell him everything that happened since the moment Dr. Beeson left Benji and me alone in the woods. "The police believe he had a heart attack and then someone stabbed him with his drill after he fell. He was trying to tell me something before the paramedics arrived."

"Did you ask them to find out what he was trying to say?" Dad leaned across the desk.

I shook my head. "No. I wish I had. He was in so much pain, and the EMTs had to help him if they could. There was a chance they might have been able to save his life, even if it was a slim one at best."

Dad fell back in his chair. "How sad. I didn't know Conrad well. We'd see each other occasionally at meetings and campus-wide events, but the horticulture and animal husbandry departments are sort of off by themselves. You can't even walk to their offices. You have to drive." He paused. "Was Chase one of the paramedics that came out?"

"He was." I tried to keep my voice as even as possible. There was no way I was going to tell my father that Chase came to the cottage last night, even though his visit had been completely innocent and related to the murder. Laura and my father were both in the same camp to find me a new boyfriend. The pair of them had redoubled their efforts to set me up with a guy ever since Eddie had announced his engagement to Krissie. I was perfectly happy with my life. I had

Hayden and the Farm. I didn't have much time for anything or any-one else. If I chose to date again, it would be up to me, not them.

"Chase is such a nice young man, and he admires you," Dad said, confirming my suspicions.

I frowned. "Can we talk about the dead man?"

Dad sighed. "All right. So you plan to find out what happened?"

I nodded and told him about Gavin's involvement in the case.

Dad clicked his tongue. "That's too bad. Gavin is a nice young man too. I've always liked him."

"I know, and I have to help him. I'm certain he didn't do any-thing wrong." I paused. "I mean, announcing to an entire room of Sap and Spile members that he wanted Beeson dead wasn't the best idea in the world. But he'd never go through with it. I just have to convince Detective Brandon that that's true."

"That's your mother in you talking," Dad said. "She was a cru-sader too." His face drooped and for the first time since I'd arrived, he looked his full sixty-seven years. "God rest her soul."

My mother had been the love of my father's life. He hadn't even looked at another woman since she died, although he had a long list of widowed admirers. There was no one who could take mom's place in his heart. If I admitted it, it was something I'd wanted in my own life. I thought I had found it when I married Eddie, but I'd been wrong. Now I didn't know if I would ever find it. I knew Chase had a crush on me, but as flattering as that was, it wasn't the same as undying love.

"What do you want me to do to help?" Dad asked.

I shook the morose thoughts from my head. "Maybe poke around campus and find out whatever you can about Dr. Beeson from your colleagues. I have a *long* list of suspects from the Sap and Spile Club, but I don't want to ignore other possibilities."

Dad perked up. He loved playing detective. "I'll ask around and see if anyone on campus knows about him, or about who might want him dead."

"Thanks. I should head back to the Farm. We have a school visit today and a tree tapping class."

"You have a lot going on at the Farm this year."

I nodded. "I have to. I want it to succeed for Cynthia's sake."

He smiled. "She cared about you like a beloved niece. She would be very proud of what you've accomplished, and so would your mother."

I looked down so he couldn't see the tears in my eyes.

Dad perked up. "Before you go back, you should check out the horticulture building where Beeson worked. You might learn a thing or two about Conrad while you're at it. *And* you might always meet someone who didn't care for him."

I realized Dad was right. "Why didn't I think of that?"

He grinned. "You just need a detecting consultation from your old man. I'd love to go with you." He peered at his watch. "But I have class in a half hour."

"Where's the horticulture building? You said I have to drive there."

He nodded. "It's not physically connected to the main campus at all. It's a series of barns on the outskirts of New Hartford, on the opposite side of the park from the Farm."

I frowned. "Could someone walk from the college's barns to Barton Farm?"

He pursed his lips. "I suppose so. It would be a three-mile hike. I wouldn't want to do it in the snow and mud."

But a person intent on killing Dr. Beeson might just think it was worth the trip.

Somehow, from the stacks of papers on his desk, Dad was able to immediately put his hands on a campus map. He circled the horticulture building with a fountain pen. "It's a short drive." He slid the map across his desk to me.

I stood up. "I'll tell you everything that happens," I promised.

"You'd better," he said. "Be careful."

SIXTEEN

Blustery wind shook my car as I drove the short distance from the main campus to the horticulture and animal husbandry campus. To reach the cluster of buildings, I drove up a long, bumpy gravel driveway. The harsh winter had left it torn up with deep ruts.

I parked in a small lot, which was half full, beside the first barn. After consulting the map my father had given me, I noted that the horticulture department was located in an enormous greenhouse behind the large horse barn.

I grabbed my purse and dropped the map into it before exiting the car. My boots sloshed through slush as I came around the side of the barn and headed for the greenhouse beyond.

I opened the glass greenhouse door, and the humid air hit me like a tropical breeze. It felt lovely against my dried-out and tired winter skin, like an instant facial, and it was hot. Within seconds of letting the door close behind me, I was roasting in my heavy down coat. I unzipped my coat and removed my scarf as I scanned the room.

The greenhouse smelled like fertilizer and dirt. There were rows and rows of seedlings. The plants were waiting for it to be warm enough for them to be sold and put in someone's garden. That wouldn't be until mid-May in this part of the country. I wondered if my master gardener Shepley had ever been in this greenhouse to purchase plants. I thought he would enjoy seeing it. Then again, that would be a very bad idea. He would tell anyone who would listen everything they were doing wrong in caring for the plants.

A young woman wearing bib overalls and holding a hose nozzle stared at me. Her long, chestnut-colored hair was tied back in a ponytail on the top of her head, and it waved back and forth when she moved. "May I help you?"

I cleared my throat. "I hope so. I'm Kelsey Cambridge. I'm the director of Barton Farm, and I came to—"

She cut me off. "Are you here about Dr. Beeson?"

I blinked. "Why yes, I am. How would you know that?"

"Because he died at Barton Farm yesterday." She gave me an accusing look, as if I'd stabbed the professor with the hand drill myself.

And technically, he'd died at the hospital, but I didn't think it was wise to correct her. "I know. Everyone at the Farm feels terrible over what happened." I swallowed as images of Beeson trying to tell me who *they* were came back to me again.

Her face fell. "We're all upset about Dr. Beeson."

Considering Beeson's rudeness to Benji and me at the Farm, I was surprised to hear this.

"It was a terrible way to die, to keel over in the woods all alone," she said, giving me that accusing glare again.

My brows shot up, and I felt my curiosity perk up as I wondered what this girl knew. "The police said he had a heart attack. That's what caused him to fall." I didn't add that someone had finished the job by stabbing him in the chest with the hand drill.

She gripped her nozzle a little tighter. "Were you with him? Did you see what happened?"

I frowned, hoping that she wouldn't turn the hose on me to run me out of the greenhouse. Something told me she was considering it. "No."

"Then you don't know," she said, as if that ended the conversation. She turned on the hose. Much to my relief, she directed the water onto the seedlings and not me.

There was an awkward silence between us as I watched her water. I cleared my throat and spoke loudly enough to be heard over the drone of the water spray. "I'm very sorry. I know this must be difficult, but I was wondering if I could talk to someone about him." I paused, thinking quickly of an excuse to be there. "He was to teach a class to aspiring tree tappers today. I wondered if he'd left any notes here that were meant for the talk. Perhaps with a coworker?" I didn't mention that the talk was already in progress and that Stroud seemed to be doing just fine.

The girl turned off the hose, and, to my surprise, tears sprang to her eyes. "Don't you think you're moving on very quickly?"

I gave her a sympathetic smile. "I understand that it does seem a little callous, and I'm sorry about Dr. Beeson's passing. Unfortunately, the tree tapping class can't be canceled."

She studied me with watery dark eyes. Perhaps Benji and I had misjudged Beeson. It was clear that this girl cared deeply for him.

"Are you all right?" I asked.

Gruffly, she wiped a tear from her cheek. "You'll have to ask Buck. Maybe he can help you."

"Buck?" I asked.

She pointed to the glass door at the back of the greenhouse. There were large windows that stood on either side of it that looked into a large classroom. She dropped her arm and went back to watering. I had been dismissed, and our conversation was over.

After a beat, I followed the girl's directions and wove through the rows of seedlings to the back. I stepped through the door, and the temperature changed dramatically again. I wondered how many people working here suffered from a chronic cold, given the constant change of temperature as they moved from room to room and building to building.

The classroom was brightly lit but empty. I was debating whether or not to step through the door across the room to see where it led when Buckley, the bald man from Sap and Spile, walked in. Buckley. Buck. Great.

He pulled up short. "You're not in my class. Are you lost? Can I assist you in some way?"

I relaxed. Maybe he didn't recognize me from the meeting last night. That hope was short-lived.

He pointed his finger at me. "You're the woman from the Sap and Spile meeting, aren't you?"

I nodded. "I'm Kelsey Cambridge. I'm the director—"

"Of Barton Farm. I know." He set his laptop on the desk at the front of the room. "That still doesn't explain what you're doing in my classroom."

I had a feeling that Buckley wouldn't buy my story about wanting to see Beeson's tree tapping lecture notes. "I was visiting my father at the college. Roy Renard—he's a professor of drama."

"I know who he is."

"Yes, well, I thought I would swing by and share my condolences with Dr. Beeson's colleagues."

He folded his arms. "I'm not buying what you're selling. If you were on the main campus visiting your father, you had to make an effort to come all the way out to the barns."

Busted.

I went on the offensive. "I don't care if you believe it or not. It's the truth. To be honest, I'm just as surprised as you are to find you here. I didn't know you worked with Dr. Beeson when I saw you at Sap and Spile."

"I don't know why you would, or why you would care." Buckley opened his laptop. "Even though I don't believe your story, I'll accept your condolences on behalf of the entire department."

I nodded. "Thank you. I see you're getting ready for class, so I'll leave you to it."

He grunted but didn't look up from his computer.

I slipped out through the door back into the main part of the greenhouse. The girl who I'd met earlier was gone. I debated searching for her. Of all the people I'd met in Beeson's life since he died, she was the only one to shed a tear over his death. I glanced over my shoulder into the classroom and found Buckley watching me through the window. I wiggled my fingers at him and headed outside. It seemed that my search for the young woman would have to wait.

I left the greenhouse, welcoming the cool air for the first time. And I'd only been in the stifling environment for a few minutes.

"I didn't do anything wrong!" a high-pitched female voice yelled from the other side of the building.

As usual, curiosity got the best of me and I followed the sound.

I came around the corner and saw the young woman I'd met leaning against the greenhouse wall and talking on the phone. She didn't have a coat, but her face was flushed as if she were experiencing the onset of a hot flash.

"I did what I was told. That was it. It was my job," she said sharply to someone on the other end of the phone line. "Are you insane? There's no way that I'm going to the police." She looked in my direction and her eyes widened. "I have to go." She hung up. "What are you doing?" she demanded.

"Are you okay?" I asked.

She burst into tears.

SEVENTEEN

I TOOK A TENTATIVE step toward the crying girl. "Hey, it's okay. Can I get someone for you? It can't be as bad as that?"

"It is. Dr. Beeson is dead, and it's my fault." She covered her eyes with her hands.

I froze. "Come again?"

She dropped her hands, and her mouth fell open as if she'd just realized what she'd said. "I have to go." She raced around the side of the greenhouse.

Without pausing to think that I might be chasing a killer, I ran after her. As I came around the corner, I saw a door slam open on the back of the building. I raced for it and caught it before it closed. Stepping inside, I had to blink a few times as my eyes adjusted to the dark.

Three long black counters cut across the room, surrounded by stools. Equipment filled the space, and dozens of tropical plants bent toward the sunlight pouring in the bank of large windows on the far side. It was a lab.

"Hello?" I called out.

There was no answer. I remained quiet for a full minute, listening hard for any snuffling sounds from the upset girl. Nothing. Clearly she was a very quiet breather, or she wasn't there. There was another door at the end of the room. I suspected it led to the hallway and she was long gone.

I removed my cell phone from the back pocket of my jeans. It was almost noon. The school children would be filing into the cafeteria by now for their pancake lunch, and the members of Stroud's class would be in the maple grove drilling holes into the trees and setting the spiles for sap. I should return to the Farm and help out. That was my real job, not chasing after some emotional college student or catching a potential killer.

Then I heard a sneeze.

She was in the lab. I inched forward, trying to make as little noise as possible. Then I ran into a rolling cart with my hip and sent it careening into the closest lab table.

There was a scream, and the girl popped out from under one of the tables and bolted for the door on the other side of the room.

"Wait!" I cried.

To my surprise, this time she stopped and spun around. "Why? What do you want?"

I held up my hands as if to show her that I meant no harm, which was the truth. "I want to make sure you're okay. You seemed pretty upset outside." Who was I kidding? She was still upset.

She rubbed her eyes and smudged her eye makeup. Although the eye shadow smeared a little, the mascara remained perfectly in place. She must have been wearing a heavy-duty waterproof brand. "Who are you?"

"I told you that back in the greenhouse. I'm from Barton Farm."

She blinked her wide eyes at me, reminding me of one of the many deer that I startled on my early morning walkabouts on the Farm. "I know that, but why are you following me?"

I decided to play it straight with the girl because clearly I wasn't getting anywhere being evasive. "I overheard you mention going to the police. Do you know something about how Dr. Beeson died?"

She flopped onto a stool, buried her face in her hands, and bawled.

I walked across the room and slid another lab stool close to her. "Shh, shh, calm down. You'll make yourself sick." I heard myself repeating my mother's words. Many times she would use the sick card when I was an inconsolable child in order to make me stop crying. I can't say that it ever worked on me, but it seemed to do the trick on the girl.

There was a roll of paper towels on the neighboring lab table and I ripped off a half dozen sheets and handed them to the girl.

She took the entire wad and rubbed them across her face. After she gave her face a thorough scrub-down, she crumbed the paper towels into a tight ball in her fist and took a shuddering breath. "This is his lab. It's even harder to think about his death in this room."

I glanced around the lab, noticing Beeson's nameplate on the teacher's desk for the first time. "What did you mean when you said that Dr. Beeson's death was your fault?"

She looked at me with a confused expression.

"I'm not the police," I said reassuringly.

She nodded. "I know that. If it hadn't been for me, he wouldn't have even been on the Farm yesterday."

"Why do you say that?"

She swallowed, and an idea struck me. "Were you the one who called me and told me you were Robert Stroud's daughter and that he had gone to the hospital, so he couldn't teach the tree tapping class today?"

She didn't meet my eyes. At least one mystery was solved.

"And you called Stroud and told him that I'd canceled the class because of low attendance, which was also a lie."

She pressed the paper towels to the corner of her eye. "Dr. Beeson asked me to. He was a tough professor, and not tough in a nice way. Everyone knew that he enjoyed failing students. I wasn't failing, but I was getting a C in his lab. He said that if I did it, he'd give me an A. I have a 4.0 GPA, and Dr. Beeson was the only one who was going to give me a lower grade. I'm hoping to go to a four-year school next year, and I need the best grades possible to get the most scholarship money." Her eyes pleaded with me as if begging me to understand.

Her reason for making the calls for Beeson hadn't been what I'd expected, and I was relieved about that. I'd had an employee the year before who got tangled up in a love affair with an older man, so automatically my mind had gone there. It hadn't ended well for anyone, especially for the man.

"Why did he want you to do this? Did he give a reason?"

"He said that he should have been the one teaching the class anyway, since he wrote a book about it."

"*Maple Sugar and the Civil War*?"

She nodded.

"Let me get this straight. He asked you to lie to two people because he wanted to teach my class at the Farm." I frowned, remembering how obsessed Beeson seemed with the idea of teaching the class, especially when the trees were frozen.

She chewed on her lip. "So you see, it is my fault. If I hadn't made those calls, he wouldn't have been at the Farm that day. He would still be alive."

"Dr. Beeson had a heart attack. It seems to me that he would have had one eventually. You can't be blamed for that."

She stared at me. "But I heard he was stabbed in the chest with a drill."

There was that. It appeared the news about the stabbing had gotten out after all. The question was whether it was just a rumor on the college campus or if it had reached the rest of the town.

"What's your name?" I asked her.

"Why?" She shrank back.

I waited and didn't say anything. After a beat she said, "Landon." However, by the way she said it, I suspected it wasn't her real name. But it didn't matter. Detective Brandon would figure out who she was; I had to share this information with the cops. It might help Gavin, or it might not. If Landon said that Gavin knew about Dr. Beeson plotting to take over the tree tapping class, then it might look even worse for him.

I decided to cut the girl not-named-Landon a break. "This isn't your fault. If you hadn't agreed to make the call for Beeson, he would have found someone else who would. He seemed like a determined man to me."

"You think so?"

I nodded.

"Are you going to tell the police about this conversation?"

There was no point in lying to her. "Yes, and if you answer their questions honestly, as you did mine, I'm sure that there won't be any repercussions for you."

She stood up from her stool. "I should get back to work. I need to finish watering."

I stood too.

She gave me a worried smile, but she still didn't tell me her real name. "Thanks for talking to me."

"You're welcome, *Landon*." I said her name in a way that told her I knew it wasn't real.

She grimaced and left the lab. I waited a beat and headed for the door after her. Then I paused. Hadn't Landon said this was Beeson's lab? I glanced around the room. There might be something here that would give me a clue as to why he was killed and who may have done it.

There was a filing cabinet in the far corner of the room with a potted ivy plant on top of it. The ivy's vine spilled over the sides of the filing cabinet and hovered just inches above the floor. It seemed as good a place to start as any.

The drawers were unlocked, and the first drawer listed what looked like scientific names of plants. Had Beeson been poisoned, I would have found this drawer much more interesting.

I realized that although this was Beeson's lab, he wouldn't keep anything important, like his research or his student files, out in the open like this where students or pesky museum directors could poke their noses into it. His office would be the best place for that information, but I was short on time and had to return to the Farm if I didn't want to completely miss the school visit and what remained of the tree tapping class.

I was just closing the bottom drawer of the filing cabinet when the lab door, which Landon had exited through, swung open. I expected to see her, or maybe Buckley—being caught snooping by either one of them was problematic. In reality, the person who came through the door was ten times worse.

"What do we have here?" Detective Brandon asked in her deceptively smooth voice. "Ms. Cambridge, I wish I could say you were the last person I expected to see in the deceased's lab, but then I would be lying."

"I—I—" I couldn't think of a good excuse for being there, because I didn't have one.

She flicked on the lights, and I was momentarily blinded by a fluorescent glow. She stepped into the room like a cheetah stalking her prey. I bet I could outrun her about as well as I could outrun a cheetah. "I'm interested in hearing your reason for being here," she said.

I straightened my shoulders and got ahold of myself. "I followed a student in here. She was distraught over Dr. Beeson's death. I thought I could help."

"How kind of you." Her voice dripped with sarcasm. "Where is the student now?"

"She left just a little while ago, through that door. I'm surprised you didn't run into her."

"Did she run out before or after you started opening Beeson's filing cabinets?"

"Before," I admitted. "I was just looking to see if there were any notes here that could be used for the tree tapping class at the Farm," I explained, sticking to my original story.

"And what did you find?"

"Nothing," I said, heading to the door that led outside. "I'll just be going now and leave you to it. I'm sure you have some detecting to do."

She jumped in front of me and blocked my way to the door. "Not so fast. Do you know that I could take you in for tampering with a crime scene?"

I gritted my teeth. "This isn't a crime scene."

She took a step backward, closer to my escape door. Drat. "No, but it's a place of interest because of its relation to the murder victim, and you have no reason for being here."

"I told you about the student," I said. "If you choose not to believe my story, there's nothing that I can do to change your mind."

"What was her name?"

"She told me it was Landon, but I'm certain that wasn't her real name. I think she didn't give it to me because she was afraid that the police would want to talk with her."

"And why would we want to do that?" Detective Brandon asked.

I told her what faux-Landon had told me.

The detective wrinkled her flawless brow. "So Beeson wanted to be on your Farm to teach? Why?"

"I have no idea. Maybe he wanted some more publicity for his book—we're selling it this weekend. It seems like a very extreme course of action to take to sell a few copies of his book, but…" I trailed off.

"Interesting theory."

I made a gesture of looking at my watch. I didn't wear a watch. "Gosh, look at the time. I really need to get back to the Farm or I'm going to miss the school visit that we have there today."

She stared at me and finally stepped aside. "I know where to find you."

I sidestepped around her and put my hand on the doorknob.

"I will find out what happened, Ms. Cambridge. Don't get in my way. You might think you're protecting your friend Gavin, but in truth, you're only making it worse for him."

I slipped through the door without a word. She wanted me to argue with her, but I refused to take the bait. Detective Brandon hadn't liked me since the moment she'd met me last summer at the

Civil War reenactment. It didn't help that she was Chase's former fiancée.

Outside, I let out a breath I hadn't even known I was holding. I knew that the detective let me off easy. I could have gotten into some serious trouble snooping in Beeson's lab. In fact, it made me even more nervous that she'd gone so easy on me. I wondered what her game plan was. The only thing I knew for sure was that I wouldn't like it.

EIGHTEEN

A MAN CAME AROUND the side of the building wearing coveralls and pushing an empty wheelbarrow. He stopped in front of me. "I didn't expect to see you here."

It took me a second to place him, but his blond ponytail and goatee were the giveaway. "Daniel?"

He nodded. "That's right. And you're Kelsey. You crashed our Sap and Spile meeting last night."

I frowned. "I hadn't meant to crash it." I pointed to the wheelbarrow. "You work here?"

He eyed me suspiciously. "I do. I'm on the maintenance crew. That means I have a reason for being here. Do you?" He arched an eyebrow.

I told him my lame story—which was becoming lamer every time that I repeated it—about needing Beeson's notes for the tree tapping class, which at this point was all but over.

"Did you find them?"

I shook my head.

"I've known Conrad a long time. We joined Sap and Spile just about the same time. I doubt he would keep anything as important as his notes on campus. He didn't trust anyone."

That was interesting. "What do you mean?"

"He was a suspicious man, to the point it made a person uncomfortable to speak to him. It was almost as if he hoped to catch a person doing something wrong. He was always on the lookout for someone to screw up, and when you did, Conrad was there, ready to pounce." He said this last part as if he was a man speaking from experience.

"Was he waiting for anyone to mess up recently?"

Daniel scowled. "I need to get back to work." He adjusted his grip on the wheelbarrow "But let me tell you this—Beeson won't be missed on campus. I can tell you that."

As I considered following him, my cell phone rang. I fished it out of my coat pocket. The number was the main office of the Cherry Foundation. This couldn't be good. Ever since I'd been initially told about the trust from the Cherry Foundation, they'd left me to my own devices. The board didn't seem to be interested in the daily operations of Barton Farm, and that was just fine with me. But now the Foundation was calling. There had to be a reason. I doubted it was about another windfall of money for the Farm.

I started down the path that led back to the small parking lot and answered. "Hello."

"Ms. Cambridge. This is Henry Ratcliffe," the hoarse-sounding older gentleman said.

I slowed my pace. Henry was the head of the board of trustees for the Foundation. I'd only met him once, and it was in passing when I'd been to the office to sign the papers, agreeing to my part in the trust. This could not be good if he was calling. I played it cool. "Hello, Mr. Ratcliffe. How may I help you?"

"The board has heard about the unfortunate incident that happened at Barton Farm yesterday morning, and we would like you to come in and meet with us to discuss what impact this may have on the Farm." He paused. "Today."

"Today?" I squeaked.

"Yes, today," he said with an air of irritation, as if he were surprised that anyone would dare to question one of his summons. "As you can imagine, after the events of last summer when we lost Maxwell Cherry on the Farm, the board is very sensitive to anything like that happening again."

"Dr. Beeson didn't die on the Farm."

"We know this," he said coolly. "But he had his heart attack there, and his injury was inflicted on Farm grounds. I take it you'd hired him for your Maple Sugar Festival to teach a course in tree tapping, as it were."

I took a sharp breath. Henry was well informed, much better informed than I'd expected him or anyone from the Cherry Foundation to be about the happenings on Barton Farm. I frowned at the phone. "What time?"

"Our meeting convenes at two thirty. We will see you at three sharp. I know that we haven't had much interaction with each other since Cynthia Cherry's passing, and I want to keep the lines of communication open. It was most unpleasant to hear about these unfortunate occurrences at Barton Farm from someone other than the director herself."

"Who did you hear them from?" I paused beside my car.

"It's no matter," he said in that same cool tone.

It mattered to me. If I had a mole on my staff, I wanted to know about it. I stopped myself from saying that. I didn't think Henry would appreciate it. Then again, Alice had overheard my conversation with the police chief and the detective, and there was that article, however brief, in the newspaper. The news about Barton Farm could be all over town by now. It didn't have to be one of my employees.

"That's a bad time for me," I began. "My son will be home from school, and—"

"Ms. Cambridge, need I remind you how important Barton Farm's relationship is with the Cherry Foundation's board?"

I ground my teeth. "No, you don't."

"Good. Please leave your son at home." He hung up.

I glared at the phone. What a jerk. There were other names I called him in my head, but they don't bear repeating.

Now I needed to figure out where to send Hayden until I got back from the board meeting. Part of me wanted to take him along just to defy Henry, but Hayden would be bored out of his skull waiting for me outside of the meeting. I couldn't put my son through that, no matter how amusing it would be to see the head of the board of trustees fume.

Eddie would be at work, so I couldn't ask him. He was a physical therapist. The school where Laura taught let out later than Hayden's, and Dad had play practice. Krissie was an option, but I'd rather jump through a plate-glass window than ask my ex-husband's fiancée for help. Judy, Gavin, Benji, or any one of my staff would be willing to babysit, but I hated to ask them to stay after working a long day at the Farm. Plus, Gavin still needed to show me his family's old sugarhouse.

I was about to call Judy when another name came to mind: Chase. He had the day off, and he *had* offered to help me if I needed it. I knew he'd meant with the investigation, but childcare was a major part of my life too. Maybe taking care of Hayden would give him an idea of what it's like to have a child. It could be a good test.

I jumped into my car, started it, and called Chase. He answered on the first ring. "Did you miss me already?" he asked in his usual jovial tone.

I wasn't sure how to answer that, so I said, "I'm sorry to be bothering you on your day off, but—"

"You're never bothering me. You can call me any time, day or night."

"Good to know," I said, glossing over those implications. "I need a favor."

"And you came to me for once?" There was a smile in his voice. "It gives me hope for us after all."

Again, I ignored his flirty comments and told him about my afternoon meeting at the Cherry Foundation and needing someone to watch Hayden for an hour or two.

"Say no more. I'll be there at two."

"You really don't need to come that early. Hayden's bus doesn't arrive until three fifteen."

"I'll see you at two," he said and hung up.

I inwardly groaned. I didn't want to be "that girl" that led a kind man like Chase on. Because despite his crazy flirting, he was a very nice guy.

My phone rang almost immediately, and Laura's face appeared on my screen.

As soon as I put the phone to my ear, she shouted, "You have another dead guy at the Farm and you didn't tell me? I had to hear it from Benji! Benji!"

I winced. "Shouldn't you be teaching?" I asked.

"It's my free period, so you have exactly forty-two minutes to tell me everything about the dead guy. I mean everything. You owe me details, Kel. As my best friend, you have a moral obligation to tell me everything going on in your life. That also includes finding dead people."

"I didn't find a dead person this time." I shifted the car into drive. I put the phone on speaker and told her everything as I drove back to the Farm. As I was turning into the parking lot, I made the mistake of mentioning the meeting with the Foundation's board that afternoon.

"Who's taking care of Hayden while you're there? You know I would, but I have school until three fifteen."

"It's no problem," I said. "I have it all taken care of."

"Is it your dad?" she asked.

I hesitated. "No."

"What's going on?" She sounded suspicious. "Why aren't you telling me?"

"Chase is watching Hayden," I said, resigned. I didn't want her to accuse me of keeping secrets from her again.

"Chase!" she screeched.

When my ear stopped ringing, I said, "Ow. I think you permanently damaged my hearing."

"You'll live," she said dryly. "I find it quite interesting that you're calling Chase in your time of need. Quite interesting."

"Stop it. I knew he was off today, so I gave him a call. No one else was available. It wasn't like the Foundation gave me any warning about this meeting."

"Uh-huh," she mused. "And no one on the Farm could meet Hayden's bus?"

I gritted my teeth.

"And how did you happen to know Chase's work schedule?"

There was no way I was telling Laura that Chase had dropped by the cottage last night. She would immediately get the wrong idea, and I would never hear the end of it. Knowing my friend, she was already picking out her maid of honor dress for the wedding.

I blew out a breath. "He was one of the EMTs that came to the Farm when Benji and I found Dr. Beeson."

"Ah," she said, letting me know that she thought there was more to it than that. "Clearly, you have some explaining to do. I'm coming over later."

"You don't have to," I began.

"I know I don't have to, but a best friend's duty is to race to your side in your time of need. I hope Chase is still there by the time I arrive."

Great. That sounded like a disaster waiting to happen. I'd better beat Laura to the Farm, because if I left her and Chase alone too long, they'd have the wedding planned before Chase and I even went out on our first date.

I was about to argue with her more when she said, "A student just stepped into my classroom. I gotta go. See you tonight." She hung up.

NINETEEN

When I walked into the visitor center, the sound of children's laughter greeted me, and I immediately felt some of the tension in my body release. The sound of children having fun while learning the history of the Cuyahoga Valley was what I lived for. I didn't know what Henry and the other members of the Foundation board had in mind for me, but I knew that I wouldn't let them jeopardize that.

Judy hurried over to me. "Thank goodness you're back." Her face had a pinched expression.

I was immediately alarmed, because Judy was one of the most even-keeled people I had on staff. "What's wrong?"

She sighed. "It seems that one of the people in the tree tapping class was injured."

"What?" I yelped. "How badly?"

"I don't know. Benji just left to check it out."

"Where is the injured person?"

"In the sugar maple grove." She chewed on her lip.

I ran out of the visitor center onto the Farm grounds. Tiffin, who was pacing on the other side of the automatic doors as if he were waiting for me, barked and raced down the pebbled path toward the sugar maple grove. The corgi was herding me to the injured visitor.

I heard the tree tapping class before I reached them. Benji's voice carried through the trees. She sounded calm and in charge. I felt a wave of relief wash over me and slowed my pace from a run to a fast walk.

Tiffin ran ahead, and I found the group in the part of the woods where Benji and I had been with Beeson before he ran off and died. The class was clustered in a circle around something. I scanned their faces for any signs of horror or alarm. At this rate, I wouldn't be surprised if I ran into another dead body.

"Is everything okay?" I asked.

Benji pushed through the crowd. "Hey, Kelsey. We're fine. One of the class members twisted his ankle on a root."

The class parted so that I could see the injured person. The elderly man, who was wearing a safari hat and heavy wool coat, sat on an overturned log and rubbed his ankle. He wore loafers, which was not the best footwear choice for tramping in the woods. I made no comment on this. He winced and rubbed his ankle again.

Lawsuits flashed across my mind. The Farm was insured for such an incident, like any museum would be, but it would still be a nightmare, a nightmare that I didn't need. I was already being called in by the Cherry Foundation board as it was. I didn't need a reason for a repeat visit.

I walked over to the man. "Are you all right? Would you like us to call the paramedics?"

He grimaced, as if the thought of the EMTs coming out was worse than the pain in his twisted ankle. "Not necessary, but I do think you need to do something about all these roots around the trees. Someone could get killed. I'm lucky that it was only a twisted ankle."

I just stared at him. He wanted me to do something about the roots in a forest?

A woman, wearing a red hat and matching gloves, patted my arm. "It was a wonderful class, and not to worry, my husband will be fine. Russ is a bit of a big baby."

Stroud helped the man to his feet. Russ tentatively put weight on his foot.

"Nothing a little ice won't fix," Russ's wife said.

I glanced at Benji, and as if she knew what I was thinking, she held up her clipboard. There was an incident report clipped to the front. Good girl.

"I'm so sorry that you were hurt," I said to Russ. "Please let us know how we can help."

His wife patted my arm again. "We'll be fine." She lowered her voice. "And you don't need to worry about us suing the Farm. My Russ hates paperwork."

That was a relief, I supposed.

Stroud cleared his throat. "Class is just about over, but I want to thank you all for coming out today. I hope that you'll try tapping the maples on your own land. You have my contact information if you have any questions during the process."

The class members clapped, and Stroud beamed. It almost appeared as if he grew an inch or two with their appreciation.

The class broke up. Russ and his wife were some of the first to leave. I pulled Benji to the side. "Good job on the incident report."

Benji beamed. "Thanks. I know how the Foundation has been on your case about filing the small incidents on the Farm."

I glanced around to see if anyone was listening. There were only five class members left in the woods, and they surrounded Stroud, peppering him with questions. He seemed to be in his element as he told them the best methods for running a small maple sugaring operation.

"About the Foundation—I've been summoned."

Her dark eyes widened. "Summoned? Why?"

I took the incident report from her hand and skimmed it. All the pertinent information was there. "They want me to come in and brief them about Dr. Beeson's death."

Benji swore. "Kelsey, what are you going to do? Do you need me to watch Hayden? I can skip class."

I shook my head. "I don't want you to do that. You miss enough classes as it is because of your job here." I paused. "Chase is coming, and he'll meet Hayden's bus."

Her eyes grew even wider. "Chase Wyatt?"

I cocked my head and tried my best to appear neutral. "Do you know another Chase?"

"I just think it's weird, that's all. You've been insisting for months that you guys are just friends, but now he's coming here to watch Hayden…" She trailed off.

"We're friends. I would have asked you or Laura if you'd been available. In fact, Laura will be here later. She just can't be here in time to meet Hayden's bus."

Benji opened her mouth. I knew it was to offer skipping class again.

I held up my hand to stop her. "I don't want you skipping class. I'm sure it won't be long, and Chase is available. Don't worry about it."

She frowned as if she wanted to say something more. I walked over to join Stroud and the students.

"Thank you so much," one of the men said. "This was very helpful. I plan to go home and tap my tree this very afternoon."

Stroud nodded. "Remember, don't over-tap. One or two spiles, depending on the size of the tree, should do the trick. With this turn toward warmer weather, you might even get some sap today."

The last members of the class headed for the path back to the visitor center. Through the forest, I could just see the tip of my cottage. When summer came and all the trees in the grove were leafed out, the cottage would be completely hidden from view. "Thanks again for taking over this class on very short notice," I said to Stroud.

He nodded sagely. "Yes. Except for that small incident of the man's turned ankle, everything went very well. I appreciate you inviting me to teach."

"While I was out, I stopped by the college where Dr. Beeson worked," I told him. I watched for his reaction and wasn't disappointed.

He gave a sharp intake of breath. "Why on earth would you go there?"

I frowned. "It's the same college where my father teaches. I was there to see my dad."

"Oh." Stroud relaxed just a little. It was an abrupt change from the man who'd just been teaching the tree tapping course with so much self-assurance. It seemed to me that the maple sugar expert was nervous when speaking about anything other than tree tapping or making maple syrup.

I paused, wondering if I should say what happened next, but Stroud had a right to know as much as I did. I took a breath. "While I was there, I ran into a student of Dr. Beeson's."

His body went full-on guitar string tense again. "I don't know why that concerns me."

"She said Dr. Beeson asked her to call you and me, separately, to cancel your involvement in the tree tapping class. She pretended to be me when she called you, and pretended to be your daughter when she called me."

His mouth fell open. After a half second, he snapped it shut. "Beeson was behind it?" His voice was sharp.

Behind Stroud, I saw Benji surveying the ground around the trees, looking for anything that the class members may have dropped. She carried a cordless drill in her hand. Just seeing it gave me the chills.

"Why would she do that?" Stroud asked, bringing me back to the present.

"Dr. Beeson asked her to, and promised to raise her grade for his class if she did." I stepped back. "He didn't tell her why he wanted her to make those calls. She didn't know. I really don't believe she understood what she was doing."

"What's her name?" he asked.

There was no way that I was telling Stroud her name, even her fake one. She was going to have enough trouble when she went to the police and told them what she did. I shook my head.

His face turned beet red. "You won't tell me?"

I shook my head again.

He spun around and marched away, splashing in the mud as he went.

TWENTY

BACK AT THE VISITOR center, the children were filing out to the waiting school buses. My shoulders drooped. This was the second day in a row that I'd missed participating in the school visits. Both times were because of Beeson. I shook off the uncharitable thoughts. The man was dead, so I had no reason to feel sorry for myself.

Gavin high-fived each child who walked out the door. One of the boys smacked him hard, and Gavin winced and shook out his hand as if the impact smarted. He was laughing though, and the kids were eating up his antics. Seeing Gavin and how great he was with the kids, it was hard for me to believe that anyone could think he was a killer, threat or no threat.

Gavin caught me watching him and handed out the required high fives to the last three kids in line at a run before coming over to me.

"How did it go?" I asked.

"Great. They're great kids."

"And I can see they love you too." I smiled.

He shrugged, but there was a slight blush to his cheeks.

"Listen, Gavin," I said, turning serious. "I want to go to your family's sugarhouse in the park. How long do you think it would take to get there and back?"

He thought for a moment. "Maybe fifteen minutes if we hike there."

I pulled my cell phone out of the back pocket of my jeans. "It's one thirty. That should give us enough time. I have to be back before three." I paused. "I have a meeting with the Cherry Foundation."

"Was this meeting planned?"

I sighed. "Not by me. Let's go to the sugarhouse now, before my meeting."

He slumped against the ticket counter. "Are you sure you want to do this? There doesn't seem much point."

"If Beeson was tapping the trees in the park, I want to see that sugarhouse and who might be there. It's within walking distance of where he died. Someone from the sugarhouse could have run over to the Farm, stabbed Beeson with the drill, and run back like nothing happened."

Gavin winced at my theory of events. "Beeson usually did his sugaring alone. I can't imagine anyone else was there."

I thought for a moment. "Maybe the sugarhouse was where he was headed all along. Maybe he wasn't interested as much in the red maples as in returning to his sugarhouse."

Gavin frowned. "It wasn't his sugarhouse."

I gave him a sideways look. "Okay, the park's sugarhouse."

His frown deepened but he didn't argue with me about the ownership of the sugarhouse anymore. Then he nodded. "All right. I hope you have on comfortable boots, because it's a bit of a hike. With all the melting snow and slush, the trail might be hard to find."

I followed Gavin outside and whistled for Tiffin as I went. He galloped after us and slid under the fence around the pasture. Betty and Mags didn't seem to be fazed anymore with people walking through their land—there had been so much of it in the last few days.

The day was warmer than it had been in weeks. I removed my stocking hat and shoved it inside my coat pocket. The temps were supposed climb into the forties, and it seemed like they had.

"The sap has been running," Gavin said as we walked. "It should be fine for the festival tomorrow."

I frowned as the irony of the situation hit me.

"Is something wrong?" he asked, shortening his long strides to match mine.

"It's just that Dr. Beeson stomped away from Benji and me when he thought our trees couldn't be tapped because the sap wasn't running yet. Now they are. It seems like such as waste. He might still be alive if he hadn't stomped off in a tantrum about it being so cold."

"Beeson was a hot-head."

I arched an eyebrow at him. "And you're not? Threatening to kill him was a bad idea."

Gavin climbed over the split-rail fence on the other side of the pasture. "I know. That was stupid, but I was just so furious."

I climbed over the fence too. When my feet hit the ground, I said, "Tell me how the land rights work."

"Well, even though the park technically belongs to the state, for the most part New Hartford manages it, including the sugaring rights," Gavin explained. "My family has been maple sugaring there for fifty-some years. When the state decided to turn the woods into a park, New Hartford gave my grandfather the rights to continue tapping the trees for twenty more years. They said it was renewable when that time was up. It was a peace offering, so that my grandfather would stop complaining to them about the woods becoming a park. Dad and I knew about the time limits on the tapping rights expiring, and we went to the town council to extend them. That's when we found out Beeson had beat us to it. I don't know when I've ever been so mad." His face turned red. "When I said in that meeting that I wanted to kill him, I did. I could have."

I stopped in the middle of the woods, and for the first time I wondered if I'd made some terrible mistake and Gavin was guilty. I waited.

Tiffin barked and circled us, as if he could herd us on to the sugarhouse.

"I could have killed him, but I didn't." There were tears in Gavin's dark eyes. "Do you believe me?"

I gave a sigh of relief and patted his arm. "Of course I believe you, Gavin. And you may think you could have killed, but I don't. You don't have it in you. I've seen you with the kids on the Farm and with Hayden. You wouldn't hurt a fly."

He gave me a half smile, but his eyes were worried. "Are you saying I'm not tough?"

"I'm saying that you have more compassion than you give yourself credit for. There's nothing wrong with that. How did you get involved in Sap and Spile anyway?"

Gavin sighed. "I did it for my dad. Our families have been members for generations and he wanted me to continue the tradition. I know it's what my dad wants, but it hasn't been easy. The guys in the group can be Neanderthals and no one wants to use any of the new methods for tree tapping. They're doing it the same way they have for fifty years. Conrad was the only one of them who wanted to find new ways to operate. I guess I can give him that much." His shoulders drooped, and he changed the subject. "It shouldn't be too much farther now. I can smell maple syrup boiling." He frowned. "Someone must be here."

"I thought you said Beeson worked alone."

"I thought he did." Gavin lowered his voice to just above a whisper. "He always has before."

I sniffed. There was the faint smell of maple syrup on the light breeze. My brow furrowed. "Who could it—"

"Don't move!" a husky voice shouted, accompanied by the whirl of a power drill just behind me.

I didn't get to finish my sentence.

TWENTY-ONE

FOR THE PAST TWENTY-FOUR hours, I hadn't been a big fan of drills, power or otherwise. I considered all drills to be enemies, especially those so close to running me through. Slowly, I turned around.

"What are you doing here?" A girl close to Gavin's age held the drill in the air like it was a gun. I didn't know if she planned to drill Gavin and me or just throw it at us. I guessed that she hadn't made up her mind yet, and we'd need to start talking before she did.

Gavin held up his hands. "Corrie, calm down."

The girl looked to be on the chubby side, but that could have been her heavy down coat. She had a full face and piercing green eyes lined in black eyeliner. Those eyes were currently glaring at Gavin for all they were worth. "What are you doing here, Gavin?"

"What are *you* doing here, Corrie?" he countered. "I've never known you to take any interest in maple sugaring."

"What do you know about my interests, Gavin Elliot?" She scowled.

Gavin glared. "Put the drill down before you hurt yourself. You're the last person on earth who should have access to power tools."

She lowered the drill. "I can boil maple sugar as easily as you or anyone in Sap and Spile can. It's not brain surgery. Are you here to collect the park's sap now that my father is dead?"

I lowered my hands. "You're Dr. Beeson's daughter?"

She dropped the drill to her side, but I noticed that her finger stayed on the trigger. I would continue to keep my distance. "So what if I am?" she spat. "Who is this with you, Gavin? Your new girlfriend? It's nice to know that you can move on so quickly."

The top of Gavin's ears turned bright red. "She's my boss, Cor. Kelsey Cambridge, the director of Barton Farm. You've heard me talk about her before."

I glanced from Gavin to Corrie and back again. Slowly, my maple-sugar-filled brain put the pieces together. They were a couple, or at least they had been. But given the tone of the conversation, they weren't anymore, and the breakup was still fresh for both of them. "You two know each other?" I asked.

Corrie redirected her glare from Gavin's face to mine. I had to say, I wasn't one hundred percent comfortable under her inspection. "We've known each other since we were children."

Gavin cleared his throat. "We dated for a little while."

Corrie lifted her drill into attack position. "Since when is four years 'a little while'? You always have to qualify everything. Like you qualified why you dumped me."

I took two tiny steps backward.

"I couldn't stay with you after you sided with your father," Gavin said. "You know how much he hurt my family. We've been maple sugaring here on this land for generations, and he swooped in and stole it out from under us. Do you agree with what he did?"

Corrie shook her drill at him. "You can't ask me to choose between you and my father."

She had a point. I'd refuse to do that too. Now it was starting to make sense why Gavin had been so reluctant to come over and check out his old sugaring site. I gave my director of education a sideways glance. He could have warned me about this possible complication, just as he could have warned me that Sap and Spile was a men-only club. I wondered what else my employee wasn't telling me.

Gavin's ears turned that much redder. "I didn't expect you to be here, Corrie. What are you doing here?"

She scowled at him. "What does it look like I'm doing? I'm finishing what my father started."

Gavin looked as if he wanted to say something but stopped himself.

This conversation wasn't going well with Gavin in the lead. "Corrie," I began. "I asked Gavin to bring me here to see your father's sugaring operation. I hadn't realized it was so close to the Farm. I wondered if maybe he was heading this direction when he fell."

She turned her attention to me again but didn't lower her drill. "I wondered the same thing. That's why I came here to check it out. I found it in full sugaring operation—his sap barrel was already collecting sap. He set things up so that the moment the sap began to run, he could start syrup production right away. I knew if I didn't boil it, all his hard work of tapping and piping the trees would go to waste."

"Did you find anything unusual when you arrived? Other than the fact that the trees had started to run?" I asked.

She shook her head. "No. Everything was in order. It's as if Dad stepped out for an hour or two and fully intended to return." Her voice caught.

Gavin folded his arms across his chest, as if he didn't trust them to be loose.

151

It was like the Capulets and the Montagues of maple syrup. All it needed was a dramatic death scene. Seeing how Corrie had yet to relinquish the drill, that still might happen.

"Corrie," I said. "Do you care if I take a look around the sugarhouse? There might be something here that will tell us what your father was up to before he came to Barton Farm."

"That lady detective was here with another officer early this morning. She searched the entire place and asked me, like, a hundred questions, like I was a suspect. I'm the one whose father just died. You'd think she would remember that and show some compassion."

"Detective Brandon can come off a little brusque, but she's just doing her job," I said, surprising myself by coming to the detective's defense.

Corrie scowled as if she didn't agree. "If you promise not to touch anything, I can show you around." She narrowed her gaze at Gavin. "That goes especially for you." She pointed a finger at him. "And I don't want to hear a word out of you that this used to be your place. It belongs to the state, and New Hartford can grant the new maple sugaring rights to whoever they want."

Gavin opened and closed his mouth as if he wanted to say something. In the end, he remained silent.

Gavin and I followed Corrie off of the path and into the trees. Ahead I could see a gray and weathered sugarhouse. The smell of maple syrup was strong, and white smoke billowed out of the chimney. Plastic tubing ran from tree to tree, causing a spiderweb effect in the forest. I knew the tubing was more efficient than the old galvanized metal pails that we used at the Farm, but it certainly took the charm out of maple sugaring.

"Hey!" Corrie yelled. "Hey!" Then she took off at a run.

Gavin raced after her, and Tiffin and I followed too. I had an image of a masked killer running through the trees.

Corrie waved her arms and shook her fist at a tree. "You do that again, I'm going to barbecue you."

I looked up. It was a squirrel. The creature peered over the tree limb and I could have sworn I saw a smile on his whiskered face.

Gavin held up a piece of tubing. It was bitten all the way through.

"I just replaced this length of tubing this morning, in this very same spot." Corrie looked like she was close to tears.

"I can fix it for you," Gavin said. "It won't take long."

"I don't want your help," she snapped.

Gavin dropped the piece of gnawed tubing like it was an electric wire.

Overhead, the squirrel chattered. I looked up. He'd brought friends. Two other squirrels on neighboring limbs stared at the tubing below with a glint in their eyes. I didn't hold out much hope that Corrie's maple sugaring operation would stay intact.

She flopped onto the forest floor in tears, then sat crossed-legged and cried.

Gavin and I looked at each other.

"Help her," I mouthed at him.

"You help her," he mouthed back. "She hates me, and you're a mom."

It seemed kind of low for Gavin to play the mom card on me.

I knelt beside Corrie and wrapped my arm around her. She turned and buried her face into my shoulder. Gavin hovered a few feet away.

"Gavin," I said. "Why don't you get whatever it is that you need to fix the tubing?"

Corrie looked up. "I said that I don't want his help."

"I know, but I have a feeling that you're fighting a losing battle with those squirrels. You might as well have Gavin replace the tubing at least once."

"Fine," she murmured and wiped at her eyes.

I nodded at Gavin. He hesitated for just a moment and then melted into the trees without a word. Tiffin galloped after him.

Corrie straightened up and wiped at her nose with the back of her hand. "I'm sorry. I shouldn't have lost my head over that stupid squirrel. It's not like it doesn't happen all the time. One of the biggest problems in tree tapping is squirrels eating through the tubing. It comes with the territory."

I scooted a few inches away from her to better see her face. "Have you always helped your father with maple sugaring?"

"No, I didn't want anything to do with it." She paused. "My dad wasn't the easiest person in the world to get along with. He was super critical and selfish and generally a terrible guy." She covered her mouth. "I shouldn't say that about him now that he's dead."

I dropped my arm from her shoulders and sat back on my heels. The damp earth seeped through my jeans, but I ignored it. "Then why are you here?"

"I don't know exactly. I came to the sugarhouse after the police told me what happened. I'm not sure why I did. When I got here, I saw that sugaring was going on and felt like I had to finish it. It was like I owed that to him. I don't think it was for him as much as for me. I wanted to close the book on the sugaring and never think about it again." She glanced into the limbs of the maple tree above. "I just didn't know that I would have so many complications."

"Is Gavin a complication?"

She sighed. "Yes. I never should have been dating him in the first place. I didn't even like him when we started going out, but I knew my father would hate it…"

"So you agreed to date Gavin to make your father mad."

She nodded. "At least at first. But then I started to really like him— until he dumped me over the stupid maple sugar. I hate maple sugar."

"Why did you side with your father over it, if you were estranged?"

"Gavin and his father were blowing it way out of proportion. Gavin's dad went crazy after he lost the tapping rights to the park. He filed all sorts of injunctions with the town and even took his case to the county." She paused. "Gavin didn't think for a moment how much worse he was making it for my family. Everything Gavin and his father did to stop my father only made him more furious and determined to fight them. You can't know how obsessed my father was with sugaring. It was like his religion."

I thought back to the pledge to syrup that the Sap and Spile members had made when I was there. The same thought had struck me at the time.

"What happened when Webber Elliot filed all those injunctions?" I asked. "Did the town government do anything to stop your father's sugaring operation?"

"They did nothing. Mr. Elliot just ended up wasting his time. I told Gavin that, and he dumped me. He told me I had to pick a side. When I told him that I couldn't betray my father no matter how awful he is, he dumped me."

I winced. I remembered being that young and passionate about a conviction. Some of that mellows away with age, but I had a feeling this wouldn't be the case when it came to Gavin and his family's sugaring heritage. Instead of sharing these dark thoughts, though, I sighed and said, "Gavin might come around."

"I don't care if he does. I'm done with all of it." Corrie stood up and brushed leaves from her clothes. "It's just maple sugar. It's not worth killing over, right?"

"Right," I said, but apparently at least one person disagreed.

TWENTY-TWO

I stood. "You know what I think?" I asked her.

Corrie looked at me. "No, what?"

"I think you should let all of this go. It's not your job to worry about your father's maple sugar. If it goes bad, so be it."

She bit her lip. "You think so? It was his life's work. Should I just let it spoil in the barrel? That's what my mother would have done."

"Where's your mother now?"

"Kentucky, I think. I'm not sure. My parents divorced a long time ago."

My heart went out to the girl.

"I don't think I can let it go. I don't think I can do that," she said.

Gavin came back just then with a new length of fresh tubing. "You can't do what?" he asked her.

Corrie cleared her throat. "Gavin, you win. It's all yours. I'm *done.*" She said "done" with so much force that I knew she was speaking about more than the maple sugar. She turned and headed to the path that led out of the park.

"You're leaving now?" Gavin called after her.

She didn't even break her stride.

Gavin turned to me. "What did you say to her?"

I folded my arm. "I told her that she didn't have to take care of the sugarhouse if she didn't want to."

Gavin held up the piece of plastic tubing. "And now I have to do it."

I shook my head. "No, not if you don't want to either. No one has to do any of it. No one will die if the trees aren't tapped." I winced. "Sorry. Poor choice of words, but you know what I mean."

Gavin threw up his hands. "We can't let all this maple sugar go to waste. That would be a tragedy."

"If you're so worried about it, I'm sure someone from Sap and Spile would jump at the chance to do it," I said in my most reasonable tone.

Gavin sighed. "Of course I'll do it."

"Great!" I smiled and headed toward the sugarhouse.

He walked after me, still holding the piece of tubing. "Where are you going?"

"To do what I came here to do."

I stepped into the sugarhouse. The ceiling was low, like the ceilings in many of the buildings back on the Farm. The floor was concrete, and there wasn't much to the room. Most of it was taken up with a long boiling trough. Steam rolled off the top as water from the maple sugar evaporated. At the other end of the trough there was a brick chimney. A black cast iron door was closed over the fire. A pile of firewood sat nearby at the ready to keep the fire going.

As the maple syrup was created, it fed into the end of the trough and was kept separate from the sap, just like at the sugarhouse on Barton Farm. In fact, I could see that this sugarhouse's set-up was identical to ours, with the exception of the use of tubing on the trees—which wouldn't be historically accurate on the Farm. It made sense, of course, since this operation had been set up by Gavin's family, and Gavin had designed the sugarhouse on the Farm.

A large wooden paddle sat on the only piece of furniture in the room, a table that looked like it had been in use since the nineteenth century. Beside the paddle was a hydrometer. That was it. This was a small, labor-intensive operation.

Gavin stepped into the doorway, blocking the light. "What are you looking for?"

I let my shoulders droop. "I was hoping that I'd know when I saw it, but I don't spot anything out of the ordinary here, do you?"

He shook his head. "Other than Corrie, but now she's gone." His voice held an accusatory tone.

"I think you could mend that relationship, Gavin." I paused. "If you wanted to."

He pressed his mouth into a thin line.

I patted his arm as I walked out of the sugarhouse. "I need to return to the Farm to get ready for my meeting with the Foundation."

"I'm going to stay here and check the rest of the tubing." He sighed as if he found the task daunting.

I nodded and whistled for Tiffin. I headed back to the Farm, more confused about Beeson's death than ever.

I made a quick stop at my cottage to change for the meeting at the Foundation; the board frowned on Farm-appropriate clothing like jeans, polo shirts, and work boots. By the time I reached the visitor center, Judy was locking up.

She turned her key in the door that led to the gift shop and moved to secure the front doors. "Tomorrow will be a big day for the Farm."

I sighed. "I hope so. To be honest, I'm starting to regret the Maple Sugar Festival. The main events haven't even started and it's already a disaster."

She dropped her keys into the pocket of her khaki skirt. "It's not your fault if Dr. Beeson got himself killed. From everything I've heard about him, he was an unlikable man and a prime candidate to be murdered."

I blinked at her. "Everything that you've heard about him? Have you been talking to Gavin?"

She frowned. "Did Gavin know Dr. Beeson?"

"They were in the same maple sugar club."

She blinked. "They have clubs for maple sugar?"

"It appears so. Who were you talking to?"

"Dr. Beeson's wife, of course. She and I used to work at the same accounting firm. We're both doing other things now, but I called her yesterday after the news. I wanted to offer my condolences.

"Beeson's wife?" I blinked. Hadn't Corrie said that her parents were divorced? "I thought he was divorced."

"Almost. They were in the middle of it when Beeson died."

"But doesn't his wife live in Kentucky?"

"Oh, you must be thinking of his first wife. I think Sybil mentioned that Conrad's first wife lived near Louisville or Lexington. I don't know. I get those two cities confused."

"Sybil is his second wife?"

She nodded and lowered her voice even though it was clear we were the only two people in the visitor center. "Sybil lives right here in New Hartford. In fact, she and Dr. Beeson were still living in the same house even though they were barely speaking to each other. It has been a very contentious divorce, or at least that was the impression I got when I called."

"She told you all that over the phone?"

"Oh yes," Judy said. "She was quite chatty and told me all about it. To be honest, her frankness caught me by surprise, but I think I caught her right after she heard the news from the police and she was just dying to talk to someone."

I wondered if Sybil would still be as forthcoming with me. "Do you know where I can find her?"

Judy smoothed her khaki skirt. "Oh, I thought you would know her since she works for the Cherry Foundation."

Chase knocked on the visitor center's locked front door and peered in through the glass.

Judy frowned. "What's he doing here?"

"I asked him to come. He's going to watch Hayden." I paused. "I've been summoned to a meeting at the Cherry Foundation."

"That sounds ominous," Judy said, but she was watching Chase.

"Very," I agreed.

There was a pause, and Chase knocked again. She headed to the front door, I knew with the intention of letting Chase into the building.

I placed a hand on her arm to stop her. "Can you tell me what Sybil does for the Cherry Foundation?"

Judy shook her head. "I don't know exactly. She works in the office."

I was no longer dreading my meeting at the Foundation. In fact, it might just be the visit that would lead me to Beeson's killer.

Chase knocked on the door's glass window this time, and Judy hurried away from me. "I should let him in. You know I would have been willing to wait for Hayden's bus if I didn't have to pick up my grandchildren in Akron."

I smiled. "I know, Judy. Hayden and Chase will be fine."

She looked at me with raised eyebrows. Great, it appeared everyone on the Farm was getting the wrong idea about Chase and me.

She hurried over to the door and opened it.

Chase waltzed into the visitor center. "I thought you were going to leave me out in the cold all day." He directed his comment at me, but his characteristic smile took a bite out of his words.

"Chase, I'm glad you're here," I said. "All I need you to do is meet Hayden's bus at the driveway entrance on Maple Grove Lane. I've already called the school and told them you'll be meeting him in my place."

"I'm happy to be of service in any way that I can," Chase said, still with the grin on his face.

Judy looked back and forth between us like she was trying to sort out our dynamic in her head. "Oh!" she yelped as she looked down at her watch. "Is that the time? I'd better go pick up my grandkids."

After Judy ran out the door, I said, "Please don't give my staff the wrong impression."

Chase grinned. "What impression would that be?"

TWENTY-THREE

BEFORE CYNTHIA CHERRY PASSED away last fall, the Foundation's offices were in downtown New Hartford, in a historic brick building that was almost as old as the Barton House on the Farm. Since Cynthia didn't have any living heirs, she bequeathed everything to the Foundation; after her death, to save money, the Foundation moved its operations to her estate until it could decide what to do with the expansive house and grounds. The estate was ten acres, surrounded on three sides by the park. It was premium land, and if the Foundation sold it, it would be for an optimal price. The only hindrance was that Cynthia Cherry was very specific regarding who the land could not be sold to. Land developers with plans to tear down the house and subdivide the property were off her list.

I opted to ring the doorbell instead of using the impressive knocker in the shape of an owl. Then I stepped back and stared up at the imposing Tudor replica. It rose four stories high and was constructed with red brick and dark wood. Less than a second after I rang, the door opened and I came face-to-face with Cynthia's old butler, Miles. Miles and I had never been pals, but I was happy to see that the Foundation had kept him on. He was seventy if he was a day and devoted to Cynthia. There wasn't much call for butlers in Ohio, so it was unlikely that he would find another position had he been let go or asked to retire.

"Ms. Cambridge, we've been expecting you." He spoke in a dull tone that I swear he picked up from British television. No one in New Hartford spoke like that. He stepped back to let me inside. "They're in the library. You may go right in."

I pulled my cell phone out of my purse and saw I was twenty minutes early. I'd been right in thinking the meeting would be running ahead of schedule.

I thanked Miles again. I wanted to say I was glad to see him, but I was sure such a statement would only embarrass him. I walked along the polished marble hallway toward the library. The décor of the estate had not changed since Cynthia died. It was an eclectic mix of cultures and colors. Each room was dedicated to Cynthia's many travels. The kitchen was South American, the solarium was the Caribbean, and the entryway was Grecian. The mix of conflicting styles was another hindrance to the board selling the estate. Who would find this décor appealing? When Cynthia was alive, the mix of cultures and colors had worked because her vibrant personality filled up the place and was the glue that held everything together. Without her, it was just a very expensive hodgepodge of antiques that no one really wanted. If anything, seeing all her treasures—such as the marble bust of some Ancient Greek on a pedestal—only made me miss her more.

Not surprisingly, the library where the board waited for me was done in a sedate British style. The colors were dark, the furniture made of heavy wood and leather. It reminded me of my imaginings of the professor's house in *The Lion, the Witch and the Wardrobe*, where the Pevensie children stayed. I remembered that in years past, Maxwell Cherry, Cynthia's late nephew and heir, had considered it his favorite room in the house. It fit his tastes.

I stepped into the room and found the six board members sitting in a circle of leather straight-back chairs around an enormous round table. A seventh chair in the circle was empty, presumably for me.

The only one of them to smile at me was Denise Compton. She'd been one of Cynthia's closest friends, and Cynthia had insisted that she be on the board. I wasn't sure how Henry Ratcliffe and the others felt about this nepotism. I wouldn't say that Cynthia didn't trust the board; she just didn't leave anything up to chance. She was cautious. I was certain the many stipulations in her will drove Henry nuts. He could walk away if he chose, but that meant that he'd have to leave all of Cynthia's money behind. He wasn't going to do that.

A retired lawyer, Henry had had a very successful practice in New Hartford for nearly forty years before retiring and accepting his position on the Cherry Foundation board of trustees. He'd been handpicked by Maxwell Cherry to be the head of the board, which immediately made me more wary of him. He had to be closing in on seventy years old himself, but he kept his youth intact by spending countless hours on the tennis courts. It showed. He had luxurious silver hair brushed back from his forehead in an elaborate wave that would be absolutely impossible for me to achieve with my own hair even if I wanted to.

"Ms. Cambridge, please take a seat." Henry gestured to the other side of the round table. The table looked like it had been pulled out of central casting for a *Camelot* remake. I glanced at the suit of armor in the corner of the room in case it was Lancelot come to life. It appeared to be antique. It must have cost Cynthia a small fortune.

Henry folded his hands on the table. "We appreciate you coming here today."

"We do," Denise interjected with a smile.

Henry pursed his lips and continued. "Ms. Cambridge," he said in a slight drawl that made me wonder if he affected that accent because he found it to be more lawyerly. "By the goodwill of Cynthia Cherry and her foundation, you have the gift of continuing the good work of Barton Farm with little interruption from the Foundation's trustees, but you must know that if something unseemly occurs—such as another person dying on the Farm grounds—it has an impact not just on the Farm, but on the Foundation as a whole."

"Understood. But technically, Dr. Beeson died at the hospital." I folded my hands on the table, mimicking his posture.

"That's neither here nor there. He was there because he was hired by you with Foundation money. That makes it a Foundation problem. We cannot have another dead person as part of the Foundation's reputation. We're still dealing with the after-effects of the death of Maxwell Cherry. We cannot add to that. It would sully the reputation of the entire institution."

"I understand that," I said through gritted teeth. "But I'm afraid I must remind you that the Farm received its money from the Cherry Foundation with no strings attached, except for my agreement to stay on as the director for the next fifteen years."

Henry gave me a small smile. "That might have been what you were told by the dearly departed benefactress's former attorney, but it simply is not true."

"What do you mean?"

"There's a clause in the trust that you may or may not have read, which states that the board can audit the Farm's use of funds if they felt that there was any misuse in spending. Take the hiring of Dr.

Beeson for example. It has led to some very poor publicity for the Farm, and by extension, the Foundation."

The existence of the clause was news to me, but I did my best not to show it. "Are you saying that hiring Dr. Beeson, a maple sugar expert, is a misuse of funds? There was no way for me to know what was going to happen to him."

"That is at the board's discretion to decide." Henry showed his teeth, reminding me of a wolf. "You do know that Cynthia liked her checks and balances when it came to the estate. She did everything she could so that one person couldn't control everything." There was a hint of bitterness in his voice.

I bristled. "You can't take the trust away from me."

"No, we cannot," he said with regret. "But we can limit the way you spend funds, if we choose."

That was a threat. There was no question about it.

I stood up. "Hiring an expert for a program on the Farm is not a misuse of funds."

"Ms. Cambridge, can you please have a seat?" Henry's voice was mild, but I knew not to trust it.

"I see no reason to," I said. "In fact, I think our meeting is done here." I turned toward the door.

"Is it?" he asked. "It has come to our attention that you added a trailer to the village side of the property so that an employee could live there. Is that not true?"

Slowly, I pivoted back around to face him.

"Is that true, Ms. Cambridge?" he asked.

I took a deep breath. "Yes. My farmhand, Jason Smith, lives on the grounds."

"And wouldn't you consider that a misuse of Farm funds?"

"No, I wouldn't," I said.

"Why are you letting him live on the grounds at all?" Denise asked.

"It's been a great help to me to have another employee living on the site. He needs to care for the animals. He can run to the barn at a moment's notice."

A man in the corner of the room spoke up for the first time. "Have there been concerns in the barn that would warrant a need for this? Sick animals and the like?"

"Not as of yet, but in January, a frozen pipe burst in the visitor center," I said. "Jason was there to help me clean up the mess."

"Have there been other times that Jason has come to your aid in the middle of the night?" Henry asked.

"Of course."

"Such as?"

My mind went blank, completely and utterly blank. I couldn't think of a single instance.

"I see," he said. "So this is the situation. You'll have to ask your employee to move off of the grounds, or the board will exercise its right to audit all the Farm's purchases. Understood?"

My stomach dropped because I knew this was not an idle threat. "Understood," I said.

He smiled. "I'm glad to see that we've come to an agreement. That wasn't so hard, was it?"

I closed my eyes for just for a moment to stop myself from saying anything I would regret. The best chance of that was not to see Henry's smug expression.

"How did you find out about Jason living in the village?" I asked.

He folded his hands on the tabletop. "A concerned Farm employee brought it to our attention."

Shepley. I knew it. I ground my teeth. Why couldn't the gardener realize that he endangered not just Jason but the entire Farm when he tattled to the Foundation.

Denise leaned forward in her chair. "Kelsey, please understand—we aren't saying any of this to upset you, but we are concerned. I think even you would say our concern wasn't unfounded. The events of the last year on the Farm grounds have been alarming."

I tried to unclench my fists at my side, but my knuckles ached with the effort. "I understand that, but I don't understand why you're so against the maple sugaring program and other programs like it. I think you would like to see the Farm be self-sufficient, so that our trust will last far into the future. Barton Farm hosts these events for that purpose."

"The Foundation cannot be associated with anything unseemly, such as this latest business with Dr. Conrad Beeson," Henry said.

"A man is dead. Maybe he wasn't a nice man, but he was still a person. Someone out there is sad today because he's no longer on this earth. She deserves our respect," I said, thinking of Corrie. She and her father might have been estranged, but I knew she was reeling from his death.

Henry sat back in his seat with a smile. "Perhaps."

And I'd thought Maxwell Cherry was bad.

"Was there anything else?" I didn't give them a chance to think of anything. "Thank you for your time," I said, as if it had been a choice for me to come to this meeting. "I'll do my best to have the Farm presented in a warmer light."

"And you'll ask Jason to leave," Henry reminded me.

"I will talk to him," I said evasively, promising no more than a conversation.

Henry looked as if he wanted to say something else, but Denise beat him to it. "Thank you for taking the time to meet with us, Kelsey. We know that you have much to do to prepare for all the events this weekend. You can expect to see some of the board members there. Maybe if we could meet Jason Smith and see where he lives, we can reconsider asking him to leave the grounds."

It was a ray of hope for Jason, and I clung to it. "I'd be happy to show all of you every nook and cranny of the Farm. We have nothing to hide, and we want the Cherry Foundation to be as proud of Barton Farm and what we do there as we are."

Denise smiled. "Very good. We're looking forward to it."

Henry shot her an irritated look but said nothing. I really didn't need to have a translation for his look. I knew when a new enemy was made.

I walked out into the Grecian-inspired corridor and was happy to see that Miles wasn't waiting for me. I wasn't about to let my trip to the Cherry Foundation be a complete waste of time, and the best way to do that was to find Conrad Beeson's wife Sybil.

TWENTY-FOUR

IF THE CHERRY FOUNDATION had still been located in the brick building downtown, I would have known exactly where the administrative office was, but in the rambling Cherry estate, it could be anywhere. I had to find it quickly before the board meeting broke up. The last thing I wanted was for Henry or one of the others to find me creeping around the estate. Miles wouldn't be much better. I knew that he would love to throw me out the door. Cynthia had always stopped him from doing it before.

I knew the general layout of the house, and my best guess for the office was where Maxwell Cherry had kept his office. It made the most sense, and I had to move at once if I didn't want to be caught lurking in the halls.

Maxwell's office had been on the second floor in the west wing of the mansion. Yes, the house was large enough to have wings. To lessen my chance of running into a board member, I went through the kitchen and up the servants' stairs. Although the Foundation had kept Miles on, the rest of the live-in estate staff, such as the cook and housekeeper, had been dismissed soon after Cynthia's death. I wondered again if they kept Miles on out of respect for his advanced age or if they just liked someone else answering the front door for them.

The dark stairway opened onto the second floor. The door that I slipped out of was a barely noticeable break in the floor-to-ceiling wooden paneling in the hallway.

I closed the door behind me and heard laughter coming from the office at the end of the hall. Bingo. I'd picked the right place. As I walked down the corridor, I realized that I might have sent myself on a fool's errand. Would Beeson's wife really be at work the day after her husband's death? I almost turned around right then.

"The snake lied to me. He's been lying to me all this time!" a shrill woman's voice cried. "Here I was, thinking he was making tens of thousands of dollars off of his ridiculous book, and he only made a thousand bucks. All of which he spent on his sugaring operation." Her voice ran up another octave.

It appeared that Sybil Beeson was in. I inched down the hallway. The plush carpet muffled my steps. There was a moment of quiet, and then I heard Sybil say, "I just came into the office today to drop off some files. I'm taking the rest of the day off. I'll call you later."

There was some rustling in the office. This was my chance. I knocked on the doorframe and stepped into the room.

Sybil was a thin woman with a pinched face. She was wearing a sweater dress and knee-high boots. A winter coat hung over her arm, and her cell phone was in her other hand. "Can I help you?" she asked.

I gave her a bright smile. "I hope so. I'm Kelsey Cambridge. I have a meeting with the board today."

She eyed me. "The board is down in the library."

"Oh." I laughed like this was news to me. "I must have taken a wrong turn somewhere. The Cherry estate is so huge."

She sniffed. "I'm surprised the butler didn't tell you where to go. He's always bossing me around."

"I didn't see him on my way up," I said, which was true. I didn't add that I'd purposely avoided him.

She headed toward the door. "Can I show you the way? I was just leaving."

I didn't want Sybil to walk me into the library like I'd just arrived. Henry and the others were suspicious as it was. I didn't need to give them more reason to question me. I saw a nameplate on her desk that read "Sybil Beeson" and knew it was my opportunity to bring up her husband.

"You're Sybil?" I asked.

She arched one eyebrow at me. "I am."

I put on my most sympathetic face. "You're Conrad's wife."

She scowled. "Did you know my husband?"

I nodded. "I'm so sorry about your loss," I said sincerely. "I'm actually here at the Foundation to talk about the accident yesterday."

She pointed at me with a sharp fingernail. "You're the woman from Barton Farm."

"I am."

She sniffed. "Well, I know why the board called you in then. Henry wasn't happy about another incident on the Farm."

That was putting it mildly.

"I'm sorry about your husband," I repeated.

She smoothed her coat over her arm. "You can save your sympathy, unless you feel pity for me for the mess that he's left behind for me to clean up."

I took a step backward. "Pardon?"

"Conrad Beeson was the most selfish human on the face of this earth." She glared at me as if she were daring me to contradict her. "I was doing everything within my power to rid my life of him. It seems someone else felt the same way."

She said this with so little feeling that I shivered. "You were divorcing him."

She eyed me. "I was trying to divorce him. He wasn't interested in a divorce. Apparently, his first one left a sour taste in his mouth. He was stringing the divorce along and using his book as a weapon against me."

"How did he do that?"

"He lied to me," she said, repeating the sentiments I'd overheard her telling the person on the phone. "I thought, since he wrote the book while we were married, that I was entitled to half of whatever he made off of it. He and his lawyer disagree." She gripped her cell phone a little more tightly. "He claimed the book made him rich. He never said numbers, but he hinted at it. I should have known he was lying. He always was a liar. I thought, since he had the decency to die before the divorce was final, that I would receive all that book money he'd been going on and on about. Then what does the accountant tell me? That he made next to nothing on the book. He'd only told me he was making buckets of money so he could draw out the divorce as long as possible. Can you believe that?" She spat the question at me.

I frowned. I could have told her that a small press that printed local history books wasn't making anyone rich, but I thought better than to say that. She might fling her cell phone at my head.

I wondered if Detective Brandon knew about Sybil's motive, because it was a good one.

"I'm sorry." I couldn't think of anything better to say.

"I'm sorry too. So sorry." She straightened her shoulders. "Now, I need to leave. I have an appointment at the funeral home." Her voice caught, showing me a small crack in her tough exterior. She shook her head as if she realized she'd let her guard down just for a millisecond.

"Have you spoken with Corrie?" I asked. "I saw Corrie today at Conrad's sugarhouse."

"I'm glad someone has seen her. I've called her cell phone a dozen times since I saw her at the hospital during her father's surgery. The child took off when the doctor told us Conrad died in surgery. I haven't seen her since. I don't even know where she slept last night." Her voice had its icy edge back, and some of the sympathy I'd had for her a moment before evaporated.

"She was broken up over her father's death. I'm worried about her," I said.

"I'm sure she's devastated. Now she'll never be daddy's little girl, which is all she ever wanted."

"What do you mean?"

"I married Conrad when Corrie was eleven or twelve. Her mother took off for God knows where and left the girl with Conrad. He wasn't interested in raising a child. I tried to do what I could for Corrie." Her voice softened. "But there was nothing I could do. It didn't matter how much I loved or cared about her, she wanted her father's love and approval. As far as I know, she never got it. I finally gave up trying to fill the gap."

"I'm sure Corrie must have appreciated you trying," I said.

She shook her head as if she couldn't believe how dense I was.

"If I see her again," I said, "I'll tell her you're looking for her."

She nodded. "I need to go."

I stepped out of her way.

"Can I show you the way to the library?" she asked, as if just remembering her manners.

"You go ahead," I said. "I know where I went astray."

"Fine." Sybil closed the office door after us and locked it. So much for snooping around in there, not that I knew what I should look for. She hurried down the hallway, leaving me outside the locked door.

I could easily visualize Sybil plunging a drill into her husband's chest. The woman had a lot of rage.

TWENTY-FIVE

It was close to four thirty by the time I got back to the Farm. With my little detour to find Sybil Beeson, I'd been away longer than I'd wanted to be. That was a mistake—a colossally huge mistake, I realized when I saw my ex-husband Eddie's SUV parked in front of the visitor center.

I parked my car behind it and jumped out. I didn't even bother going into the building, just ran through the gated entrance on the side of it and jogged down the pebbled path toward my cottage.

As I drew closer, I forced myself to slow to a walk. *This could be okay. Maybe this was no big deal.* Maybe Eddie was just dropping something off for Hayden. Or maybe it was Krissie who was here. She was known to borrow Eddie's car. I couldn't believe I was hoping to see Krissie instead of Eddie.

There was a break in the trees and I could see the cottage. Chase and Eddie were standing in the middle of my front yard, and neither one of them looked happy. Hayden and Krissie, if she was even there, were nowhere to be seen. This was bad—worse than I'd feared, actually.

Tiffin, on the front steps to the cottage, barked and drew their attention toward me. Thanks, Tiff.

I jogged up what was left of the path. "Hey, guys!"

Eddie scowled at me. "We need to talk."

Chase shoved his hands into his pockets and rocked back on his heels. "Talk away, *Ed.*"

I shot Chase a look. He was so not helping.

Eddie glared at him. "I need to talk to Kelsey alone. This is about *our* child and has nothing to do with you."

Eddie's handsome face had turned bright red. It was a color I recognized on him. I'd seen him about to explode many times during our marriage. It was one of the reasons we'd gotten a divorce—the other being he was fooling around with a married woman who was not his wife. Both marriages were destroyed by that mistake. Eddie, having moved on with someone new, liked to pretend it never happened. It had. I had the emotional scars to prove it.

I closed the gate behind me. "Eddie, calm down. I had an emergency meeting at the Cherry Foundation. Chase was free, and he watched Hayden for me."

"Would that meeting have anything to do with a man dying on the Farm grounds yesterday?" he snapped.

"He didn't die on the Farm grounds," I said for what felt like the hundredth time.

"A mere technicality," he said. "Everyone in town is talking about how the man was murdered, and you're keeping our son here on the Farm where someone was viciously attacked."

I opened my mouth to say something, but Eddie didn't give me the chance. "Furthermore, you have a man I don't know watching Hayden while you're off at a meeting? How is that responsible parenting, Kelsey?"

My face was hot. "Eddie, Chase only watched him for two hours. It's no big deal. I would have asked Benji or Judy, but they had to leave."

"No big deal? You really think it's no big deal to leave *my* son with your boyfriend?" He towered over me. Since Eddie was a good foot taller than me, it wasn't much of a challenge, but I still hated it.

I put my hands on my hips. "Excuse me? First of all, Chase is my *friend*, and after what you pulled with Krissie, you have—"

The rest of my tirade came to an abrupt stop when the door to the cottage opened and Hayden sprang out. "Mom!" he cried at the top of his voice as he raced across the yard to me. He threw his arms around me like he'd never let go. I gave him a squeeze and saw Krissie standing in the doorway.

"Dad said I'm going to his house tonight instead of tomorrow night because Chase is here."

I let out a deep breath and shot Eddie a look. This was not what we'd agreed to for the weekend. Eddie was supposed to pick Hayden up Saturday afternoon so Hayden could attend the pancake breakfast and a half day of the festival. Last night, Chase had managed to convince me not to send Hayden to Eddie today, which hadn't been hard to do. I hated the thought of losing any time with my son.

"I thought it was in Hayden's best interest if he came and stayed with Krissie and me tonight," Eddie said.

"I see," I said, reminding myself to remain civil. I didn't want Hayden to know I was upset over this.

Krissie came down the steps. "If you're worried about Hayden missing the Maple Sugar Festival, Kelsey, we can stop by tomorrow," she offered. "That way he can see everything." She placed a hand on my son's shoulder. "Would you like that, Hayden?"

Hayden beamed up at Krissie, and a little green monster sleeping inside me came to life. I took another deep breath. I wasn't going to fight with Eddie in front of Hayden, and Eddie knew that. "That would be okay," I said. "Hayden, why don't you and Krissie go inside and pack for your dad's house?"

Krissie beamed at me. "Thank you for being so understanding, Kelsey. I knew you'd understand. Eddie thought you'd be upset, but I said you'd have no reason to be."

No reason at all.

Krissie guided Hayden back to the house. Tiffin ran after them, leaving me alone with two men that looked like they wanted to throttle each other. Great.

Chase looked from Eddie to me and back again, and his shoulders relaxed. "I should get going and let you two sort this out."

I placed a hand on his arm. "Chase, wait. I want to talk to you before you go."

Eddie glared at my hand on Chase's arm with such ferocity I was surprised it didn't burst into flames. I dropped my hand to my side.

Chase nodded. "I'll be over by the visitor center."

"Thanks," I murmured and watched him go.

My ex-husband folded his arms over his chest. "I can't believe you did this, Kelsey. If you needed a sitter for Hayden, you could have called Krissie."

"Krissie to the rescue." My voice dripped his sarcasm.

"You shouldn't speak about my future wife in that tone."

I sighed and counted to three. "Eddie, I don't want to fight with you, okay? It's been a very long couple of days."

"Because you found another dead body." He studied me.

"He wasn't dead when I found him," I said through gritted teeth. I didn't know why I kept feeling the need to make that clarification.

Eddie pointed his finger at me. "We promised each other we wouldn't bring another partner into our son's life without telling the other parent first. You broke that promise."

"Of all the hypocritical things to throw in my face! Hayden met Krissie before I even knew about her existence. You told me you were engaged in a mass email to the entire planet." My voice was nearing shriek level, but I didn't care.

Eddie frowned. "That was different. It was unplanned when he met her, and he liked her so much, I couldn't rip her from his life afterward."

"Are you even hearing yourself? What you're saying doesn't make any sense. And for the last time, Chase and I aren't dating."

"You're not *yet*. Remember, Kelsey, I've known you since we were five years old. I know you. You like this guy. It's written all over your face." His jaw twitched.

Was Eddie jealous? The thought ran across my mind and I felt myself grow angry all over again. What right did he have to be jealous?

Before I could think of something to say back, the door to the cottage opened again and Krissie and Hayden bounced out, all smiles.

Hayden skipped over to me and gave me a hug. I hugged him tight and kissed the top of his head. "I'll see you at the Maple Sugar Festival." Tears sprang to my eyes, and I blinked them back.

"Okay, Mom," he said without a care in the world.

Hayden and Krissie headed down the pebbled path.

Eddie started to follow them but stopped, turning to face me again. "My request to change the custody agreement isn't going away, Kel. I can promise you that," he said as a parting shot.

"I don't imagine it ever will," I said to his receding back.

For single parents, the threat was always there. I bit down on my lip. Eddie was a good father. Why was I so reluctant to allow him more time with Hayden? I shook the thoughts from my head.

I took a moment to collect myself before I made the short walk to the visitor center to find Chase. I finally spotted him leaning against the split-rail fence that surrounded the pasture, in the exact location where I'd stood last summer when we'd first met. I'd been breaking up a fight between two reenactors over a missing canteen, and Chase had been lying in the pasture-turned-battlefield, failing miserably at playing dead.

He smiled. "They're gone," he said. "Krissie waved at me when she left."

"She would," I said. "The truth is, Krissie's not so bad. She's a young, sweet girl, and she obviously cares about Hayden, which goes a long way for me. I'd probably like her under different circumstances." I leaned my back against the fence and faced the visitor center.

"Do you remember this spot?" Chase asked.

I cocked my head. "You weren't a very good reenactor. You didn't play dead well."

"How could I with such a beautiful woman telling off two soldiers just inches away from me?" He chuckled.

I tried to hide my smile but failed. If Chase was trying to cheer me up, it was working.

He barked a laugh. "What did you want to talk to me about?"

"I learned some interesting stuff about Beeson today. I'm trying to get it all straight in my head."

"Tell me. Maybe I can help."

"I hope so." I told him about the Sap and Spile meeting, since I hadn't been able to yet, as well as what had happened today, starting with my visit to the horticulture building where I'd met the mysterious Landon. "Buckley is a potential suspect, as is another staff member at the college and I guess everyone at Sap and Spile, including Stroud. And there was something odd about Stroud." I explained how Beeson had had his student call us to trick us so that he could teach the tree tapping class.

Chase listened intently. "Do you have any other suspects?"

I filled him in on meeting Corrie and Sybil Beeson.

Chase wrinkled his nose. "Sybil sounds lovely."

I nodded. "She's definitely not broken up over her husband's death." I rubbed my eyes. "In fact, any of these people could be guilty, but not one of them is sticking out. Sure, I think the wife is the most likely culprit, but I'm sure Detective Brandon already looked into that."

"I can guarantee Candy did," Chase said.

It set my teeth on edge whenever he called her Candy. It only reminded me of their history. Which wasn't something that I wanted to be reminded of.

"If I ask you a question, do you promise you won't get mad?" he asked.

I arched an eyebrow at him.

He held up his hands. "It won't be about Hayden or Eddie. I promise."

"Go ahead," I said. "Hayden and Eddie are off-limits."

"Are you sure Gavin is innocent?" he asked.

I stood up straight. "What do you mean?"

"Are you sure he didn't stab Beeson? He has as much of a motive as any of those other people you mentioned. He's a member of Sap and Spile too, and didn't you say that everyone at Sap and Spile is a suspect?"

"He … he couldn't have killed him. I've known Gavin for two years. He's a great guy and terrific with the kids. You should see how much the school children who visit the Farm love him."

"But he told Beeson that he wanted to kill him." Chase paused. "Over maple sugar. Doesn't that sound a little crazy to you?"

"He was upset. He would never kill anyone over maple sugar. It's—it's just too ridiculous. I can't believe you're even suggesting that."

"Don't you have maple sugar as the motive for the Sap and Spile members? Is there a reason, a good reason, to let Gavin off of the hook?" Chase raised one eyebrow in question.

I pushed off of the fence. "But … there must be." No good reason came to mind.

"And doesn't he have an even better motive than maple sugar? Maybe he was motivated because of his lost love. Didn't he and Corrie break up because of the feuds between their two families? Maybe he blames Beeson for ending his relationship with Corrie."

Chase had a point, not that I would admit that to him.

"I just want you to consider it." He smiled his slow smile again. "I'll wait."

The sun was setting behind the trees. It wouldn't be long, I thought, before the Farm would be cast into a darkness broken only by the few security lights near the visitor center and my cottage. It was true that Gavin had threatened to kill Beeson; he *had* gone missing not long before Beeson died; and he had a motive—a better motive than I'd ever suspected, now that Chase had pointed out his relationship with Beeson's daughter.

Then Chase stepped in front of me, leaving six inches between us. My breath caught, and all thoughts about Gavin and his possible guilt flew from my head. Chase smiled his slow grin again.

"I know what you told Eddie is true, that we aren't a couple, but I know he at least thinks it won't always be that way." Chase lowered his voice. "This might be the one and only time that I hope your ex is right."

"You heard all that?" I squeaked.

"Your voice carries pretty far. Your dad must have taught you how to project."

I frowned, hoping that Hayden hadn't heard any of my fight with his father.

As if he'd read my mind, Chase said, "I don't think they could hear you from inside the cottage."

"That's a relief." I worried my lip.

He chuckled and leaned forward, kissing me on the forehead. "I'll see you tomorrow, Kelsey Cambridge. I'll be the dashing Union medic. Maybe we can reenact our first meeting. I heard you have a thing for reenactors."

"Who told you that?" I managed to say.

"I did," Laura said, and there was laughter in her voice.

I jumped away from Chase like a bullet out of a reenactor's rifle.

TWENTY-SIX

"LAURA!" I YELPED. "WHAT are you doing?"

"I told you I'd stop by after school. I would have been here sooner, but I had a senior having a meltdown over her midterm grade in the middle of my classroom. Worse yet, her mother called to chew me out too." She smiled at Chase. "Nice to see you, Chase."

"I didn't hear you coming," I accused her.

"I could tell." She was grinning from ear to ear. Chase had the same grin on his face. I hated them both for it.

"This isn't what it looks like," I said.

She shrugged. "Whatever you say."

"I'll let you two chat. I'll see you tomorrow, Kelsey." Chase winked and walked toward the gate, leaving me alone with Laura, who still had a silly smile on her face.

I folded my arms. "I don't want to hear it."

"Hear what? I wasn't going to saying anything." She glanced around. "Where's Hayden?"

"Eddie took him," I said.

"I thought he didn't go to Eddie's until Saturday."

"That was the plan." I sighed. "But Eddie's right—it probably is best for Hayden to be with them tonight. Because of the murder."

Laura snorted. "They used that as an excuse. You shouldn't have let him take him."

"It's just one extra night," I said, as much for my own benefit as for Laura's.

Laura ground her right boot into the slush. I suspected that she imagined it to be Eddie's face. I may have forgiven Eddie for everything that had happened in our past, but my best friend had not. She claimed to have a moral obligation to carry a grudge against him until the day she died.

"One night will turn into two, and then it'll be a week. Before you know it, Hayden will be with them more than he will with you."

"It's just one weekend," I insisted. "They can't change the visitation without my agreement or taking me to court."

"Which they will," Laura said.

"I don't want it to come to that. It would be so hard on Hayden. It's not a bad thing that Hayden has two parents that love him so much."

Laura arched her manicured brow. "If this is Eddie's idea—which I doubt."

"Laura," I said. "What do you mean?"

"Mark my words. Krissie is the one behind all of this, not Eddie. She's putting these ideas into his head. Did he ever want to adjust visitation before their engagement?"

"No, but I can't believe that. Krissie is sweet," I said. "And Hayden likes her."

"Hayden likes everyone." Laura ground her boot deeper into the mud. "I don't trust her. There's something calculating about her sweetness. I hope you watch your back where she's concerned."

I sighed. "Laura, I think I'd rather talk about Chase than this." I held up my hand when she opened her mouth to speak. "Please, Laura."

Her shoulders drooped. "Okay. I'll drop it for now. It's Friday night—let's hit the town."

I barked a laugh. New Hartford was tiny. There wasn't much town to hit. "I do have an outing that I'd like you to come with me on."

"What is it?" Her tone was immediately suspicious.

"I need to drop in on Pansy Hooper."

"Are you crazy? Pansy Hooper hates the Farm, and hates you by extension. Why on earth would you want to talk to her?"

"She or one of her sons might have seen something around the time Beeson was attacked."

"Then shouldn't Detective Brandon be the one to drop in on her?" Laura studied me.

"I'll tell the detective, just as soon as I talk to Pansy myself."

"This is a really bad idea," Laura said. "How much do you want to bet Pansy Hooper meets us at the front door with a shotgun?"

I raised my brow. "Are you saying you won't go with me?"

"No, of course I'll go. I can't let you meet the business end of a shotgun on your own. What kind of best friend would I be if I let that happen?"

I snorted and headed to the gate. "We'll take my car."

She blew out a breath. "Good. I was afraid you'd say we were going to trek through the woods there."

"No, I prefer a car." I glanced over my shoulder. "It's better for a fast getaway."

"That's so not funny," she muttered behind me.

The drive to the Hoopers' home took almost as long as it would have taken to walk there by cutting through the woods. But my statement that I wanted to get away from the Hoopers' quickly wasn't said totally in jest. I didn't know how Pansy Hooper would feel about me dropping in on her unannounced like this, although she dropped in on the Farm at all hours with her numerous complaints.

The Hooper home was set off from the road, behind a row of full pine trees. The way they were planted made me think it had been deliberate, to hide the house from passersby. Milton Hooper had been a reclusive man who'd kept to his house. I hadn't met any of the Hoopers until he died and Pansy and her two sons moved into the old homestead. Now I saw them way too much.

I parked in front of the house.

Laura unbuckled her seat belt. "I feel like we should have stopped to buy pepper spray or something to defend ourselves."

I placed my hand on the door handle. "There's no need for any of that."

"If you say so." She got out of the car.

I followed her around the pines trees and up the driveway. The sun was setting, and the tall pines caste an eerie shadow on the two-story house. The house paint was peeling. One of the top shutters hung loosely from the siding, and the front gutter had leaves from last fall spilling over its sides.

Laura inched close to me. "If you're ever looking for a candidate for a haunted house, I think you just found it. This place would be perfect."

"Let me do the talking," I said.

"What?" She gave me a mock-hurt look. "Do you think I'll offend them?"

"Yes." I walked up the porch steps. The porch light was off; there wasn't a light bulb in the fixture. But a light shone through both of the front windows. Out of the corner of my eye, I saw something move around the side of the wraparound porch.

Laura must have seen it too because she jumped. "Someone's there," she hissed. "We're going to die."

"It was probably a raccoon or squirrel," I said with a shaky voice.

"Yeah," she remarked. "If they came in human size."

I shook my head and knocked on the door. There was no answer. I knocked harder. Still nothing. Knock. Knock. Knock. "Mrs. Hooper? It's Kelsey Cambridge from Barton Farm. I was told that you wanted to speak to me."

"I guess she doesn't want to talk to you right now," Laura said. "Let's go."

I shot her a look and knocked again.

Laura clutched my arm in a vise-like grip.

"Maybe you're right," I said, after we waited for what seemed like an hour but was more likely two minutes.

Laura yanked on my arm "Great. Let's roll."

When we were about to leave, the front door was flung open. "What do you want?" Pansy Hooper bellowed.

Laura yelped and almost fell backward down the porch steps. I grabbed her arm and held her up. I cleared my throat. "Mrs. Hooper, I'm Kelsey Cambridge. We've met on several occasions when you visited Barton Farm."

"I know who you are." She opened the door wider. She wore a stained sweatshirt and a paisley peasant skirt. Her hair was twisted into a loose bun on the top her head and she glared at me with watery eyes. From her wrinkled skin, I'd guessed she was over sixty, but she might have been younger and the wrinkles were a byproduct of a hard life. I didn't doubt that Pansy Hooper's life had been hard. I didn't know where she'd lived before her father's passing, but it must have been awful if she chose to leave it for her father's old dilapidated house.

I gave her my most neighborly smile. "I'm sorry to drop in on you on a Friday evening like this, but a member of my staff told me that you stopped by yesterday to talk to me about the activities on the Farm. I apologize for not calling on you earlier."

She sniffed. "It's about time you came over to address the issue. You have no respect for your neighbors. I've tried to be a good neighbor to you, but my patience had worn thin."

Behind me, Laura made an irritated noise.

Pansy's watery eyes zeroed in on her. "Who are you?"

"Pansy," I said, still hoping to sound friendly, "this is Laura Fellow. She works at the Farm as well. I asked her to come with me to speak with you."

"You could have come by yourself." She held onto the doorframe. "I don't bite."

The jury was still out on that one, I thought.

"Do you have a moment to talk now?" I asked. "Maybe we can come to some type of understanding."

She looked me up and down as if giving my question some serious consideration. "You might as well come in."

I looked at Laura and she widened her eyes. An invitation into the Hooper house wasn't what we'd expected.

Pansy glowered at us. "Well, are you coming or not? If you want to talk, I'm not going to stand in the doorway and let in a draft."

"Yes, we're coming," I said quickly and stepped through the doorway.

After a long beat, Laura followed me inside. "Does this feel a little Hansel and Gretel to you? If she eats us, I'll never forgive you."

"If you're eaten, you won't be able to complain," I hissed.

"Not funny, Kel." She held on to my arm as if it were the last life-boat departing from the Titanic.

Pansy led us into the living room. I tried my best not to stare at the surroundings. There were hundreds, maybe thousands, of glass jars all over the room filled with all manners of trinkets, from screws to marbles to buttons.

Apparently I failed in my attempt not to stare, because Pansy said, "My father liked to collect things. I don't know what I'm going to do with all this junk. The boys claim they can sell it online, but neither one of them have done that yet." She sat on the middle of the old sofa, leaving the one stained arm chair for Laura and me.

"I don't mind standing," Laura whispered. "It'll give me a head start when she starts cooking."

I frowned and sat on the edge of the armchair. "What were your concerns about the Farm?" I directed my question to Pansy.

Pansy picked up a coffee mug and sipped from it. "The noise. The racket coming from the Farm is unbearable. My boys and me moved out to my father's house to get away from noise."

"The Farm has had several new events this winter, but winter is generally our off-season. I'm afraid the noise will only become worse in the summer when we're fully operational."

"You need to do something about it, then." She held her mug in her hands. "You need to have better control over the noise."

"That's near to impossible," I said.

"I can't accept that."

I suppressed a sigh. "I understand your concern, but the events on the Farm will continue whether you like them or not. The Farm has all the necessary permits for the programs that we hold on the grounds. I imagine that it isn't that different from living near a school or somewhere else where events are held."

She pointed at me with her coffee mug. "We live here to get away from all of that."

"There's nothing I can do about the noise. Your father was a neighbor to Barton Farm for nearly fifty years, and he never complained about the noise," I said.

"My father was half deaf. He wouldn't have heard cannon fire if you'd shot it into his ear."

I decided it was best not to warn Pansy that there would be cannon fire on the grounds that summer. I would deal with that when the time came. "I see," I said. "I guess we're at an impasse, then."

She curled her mug into her chest. "Don't think I won't complain to the town."

"I wasn't thinking that," I said mildly.

"Though I may not have to be the one to shut you down, if people keep dying on Farm land." She paused to sip from her mug. "I saw police over there yesterday. I heard the sirens and the shouts. It wasn't until later that I found out that a man had died." She clicked her tongue.

"The incident on the Farm yesterday was unfortunate, but I can assure you no one who works for Barton Farm was involved."

"That's not what I heard." Pansy smiled. "I heard one of the people working at your farm was the one to do him in. It's that young teacher you got. The boy that's always leading the children around."

I stiffened. Pansy was surprisingly well informed about all the events on the Farm grounds. I swallowed. "Who told you that?"

"My boys," she said with a satisfied smile. "They tell me about the news in town. I can't get out much myself. Don't like to. I got everything I need right here. I don't have much use for most people." She gave me a pointed look.

"I was wondering if I could talk to your boys while I was here, actually," I said. "Are they home?"

"Why?" she snapped.

"Well," I began, "they might have seen something yesterday that will help the police find out what happened to Dr. Beeson—that's the man who was killed."

"My boys and I didn't see anything." She squinted at me as if trying to come to some sort of decision about me.

"Are you sure?" I asked. "Have your boys been on the Farm grounds recently?" I shifted on the arm of the chair, wishing I'd opted to stand like Laura. I noticed, out of the corner of my eye, that she was inching further and further away from Pansy on the couch.

"They'd have no reason to go there." Pansy set her empty coffee mug on the table between two jars of pennies.

Just because they had no reason to be there doesn't mean that they weren't, I thought, but I didn't come right out and say that. I didn't want to push her too far, at least not yet. "Can I talk to one or both of them? I know they spend a lot of time in the woods. They might be able to help."

"I told you, they didn't see anything. My boys keep to themselves. They have no interest in the history you spout over there at the Farm."

I didn't doubt the Hooper boys' lack of historical interest. "If I—"

"I said no," she snapped. Spittle flew from her mouth.

"One of my staff members," I said, not giving up, "saw them on the grounds, and we had an incident of vandalism in the garden."

"Don't you be accusing my boys of vandalism." She jumped out of her seat.

"I'm not," I said. "But they might have seen something, either at the spot where Dr. Beeson fell or in the garden."

She shook her empty coffee mug at me. "I won't have you coming here accusing my sons of trespassing on the Farm. You have no right. It's time for you to leave."

I stood and followed her to the door. Laura was already outside. So much for backup.

I stepped over the threshold and turned to face Pansy. "Why don't you come to the Maple Sugar Festival tomorrow to see what it's like? No charge. You're welcome to attend free as our neighbor. I think once you see all the good the Farm does and all we have to offer the community, you'll feel differently about it."

"You think wrong," she said and slammed the door in my face.

Laura was halfway to the car by the time I reached the porch steps. I jogged to catch up with her. "I thought you were supposed to be my backup."

"Sure. I have your back, but I prefer to do it ten yards away from that nutcase. The woman is deranged. Did you see all those jars? I bet they weren't her father's at all. My money is on them being hers."

My shoulders drooped. "It doesn't matter. This whole trip was a waste of time. Pansy is madder at the Farm than ever, and I didn't learn anything new."

Laura patted me on the arm. "Cheer up. At least you can prove with all those jars that she's crazy in case she ever takes you to court."

"How can that possibly make me feel better?"

When we were back in the car, Laura buckled her seat belt. "What are you going to do about the Hoopers now?"

"Sic Detective Brandon on them. If Pansy Hooper doesn't like me coming around, she's going to hate Candy Brandon."

Laura grinned. "I'd love to see that match-up."

"Me too." I started the car, and my headlights caught a form standing in the woods.

Laura screamed. "It's a ghost."

The figure dissolved into the trees.

I placed a hand on my heart and willed it back behind my sternum. "That wasn't a ghost. It was one of Pansy's sons."

Laura shivered. "My mind it made up. The Hoopers are behind the murder."

"But why? What would be the motive? They don't even know Dr. Beeson."

"I don't have all the answers, but the fact they give me the creeps is reason enough." Laura leaned back in her seat as if the case were closed.

I sighed and turned the car onto the road.

TWENTY-SEVEN

THAT NIGHT, I WALKED around my little cottage, picking up the toys and books Hayden had left scattered around the house and missing him desperately. The truth was, eighty percent of the time I got him to myself. As the custody arrangement stood now, Eddie got Hayden two weekends a month and two full weeks during the summer, plus alternating major holidays. Since our divorce, the arrangement had always worked for us. Now that he was getting married, Eddie wanted to change that. I still blamed Eddie for the sudden shift. No matter what Laura said, I didn't think Krissie was the villain in this situation. A little voice in the back of my head told me that I shouldn't blame anyone. As long as Hayden was happy and felt settled, that's all that mattered.

Frankie hissed at me from his perch on the arm of the couch. Then he jumped down, picked up one of Hayden's Matchbox cars in his mouth, and sauntered in the direction of the utility room where his cat box was.

"Frankie!" I warned. "Don't you dare put that in your litter box."

He swished his tail and kept going. That wouldn't be fun to fish out later, but I wasn't going to wrestle him for it. I wasn't in the mood for to go four rounds with Frankie tonight. The trip to the Hooper place to reason with Pansy Hooper had been a mistake. All that I'd accomplished was making her more suspicious of the Farm, and I'd practically accused her sons of being the culprits for the vandalism in the garden. Even though I was certain the boys were behind it, my accusations had only deepened the rift between us. I didn't believe Pansy would really take the Farm to court over the noise issues; she didn't have the means. However, that didn't mean she wouldn't try to make things difficult for me and all the Farm employees.

Tiffin jumped up from his dog bed and growled at the front door.

I stared at him. Tiff was usually a mellow corgi. I'd never seen him behave this way. One of the reasons why he was such a good dog to have on the Farm was that he never met a person he didn't like. I couldn't have a dog running loose that would growl and bark every time someone new visited.

Tiffin growled again. This time, the noise came from deep in this throat as if he was pulling it from his very core.

"Tiff, is there someone outside?"

Bang! Something from outside hit the side of the cottage. I jumped.

Tiffin ran to the front door, barking his head off. I threw the door open. "Who's out there?"

Tiffin stood right in front of me.

I blinked under the porch light, wishing that I had something else to see by. "Who's out there?"

There was laughter.

I clenched my teeth. "Scott and Shaun Hooper? I know it's you!"

The Hooper boys materialized out of the trees and moved toward the cottage with a slouching gait. Even though I knew that Scott, at seventeen, was the older of the two by at least a year, the boys could have been twins. They were both over six feet and walked with a slight slump, as if they even found walking to be a chore. I remained on the porch and glared at them. I'd never been so grateful in my life that Hayden was with his father.

"What did you throw at the cottage?" I asked, taking care to keep my voice level.

Now, in the light, I could see Scott's face clearly. "Who said we threw anything?"

"Something hit the side of the cottage," I snapped.

Shaun brushed his long bangs out of his eyes. "Maybe it was some sort of animal, like a deer?"

"I bet it was a raccoon," Scott said. "They're always making a racket over at our place."

"Could be. Or maybe an opossum," Shaun said thoughtfully. He gave me an appraising look. "Those can be vicious."

I gripped the doorknob and willed myself to relax. "What are you two doing here? The Farm is closed. You shouldn't be here."

"This is all part of the park," Scott said. "Aren't we allowed in a public park?"

"Not after dark. The park closes at dusk, not to mention that Barton Farm is no more a part of the park than your home is. It's private property."

"We just thought we'd drop in for a neighborly visit," Shaun said. "We need to chat."

"We can chat in the morning. It's late."

Tiffin, growling at my feet, agreed with me.

Scott took a step back. "Your dog better not bite me."

"Then don't come any closer. He'll take a chunk out of you if he has to," I said, even though I knew Tiffin would never bite anyone.

Shaun glared at me. "We heard that you were on our land today. You can't be coming around upsetting our mom like you did."

His brother nodded. "She told us you said we were causing trouble on Barton Farm."

"Aren't you?" I challenged.

"If we were the ones causing trouble, you wouldn't have to wonder. You'd know it." Scott smirked.

"It's pointless to talk about this," I said. "I know you're the ones who trampled Shepley's garden. Just go home."

Scott laughed. "You're too little to make us do anything that we don't want."

"Get out of here before I call the police," I snapped.

Shaun took a step toward me. "Do you think the police can do anything about it? They'd have to prove we were here, and they can't."

His brother nodded. "You have even more people wandering around your precious Farm when you don't know it. We aren't your problem."

A chill ran down my back. "Like who?"

"A killer," Scott said in a matter-of-fact tone.

I shivered. This was my chance to find out if the boys had seen anything yesterday, which was why I'd gone to their house in the first place. Now I might get an answer if I could tolerate them for a few more minutes.

"Did you see something?" I asked them.

"We always see something," Shaun said. "There's not much that happens around here that we miss. We know all about your maple sugaring and the people coming and going."

"What did you see?" I wanted to get the boys back on track with the murder.

"Just cause we know something doesn't mean we have to tell you. We don't owe you anything," Scott said in a sullen tone.

"If you tell me, I won't press charges for the vandalism."

They laughed as if that was the funniest thing they'd ever heard. Clearly the Hooper boys didn't consider vandalism charges as much of a threat.

"Did you have something to do with Dr. Beeson's death? Is that why you won't say anything?" I asked, refusing to give up.

Scott glared at me. "You aren't going to pin that on us. We don't have anything to do with a murder. We don't do that."

"That's right," his brother agreed.

"Prove it, then, by telling me what you know."

"It's not that easy." Scott punched his brother in the arm.

"Ow." Shaun winced.

"Let's go," Scott said to his brother. "I'm bored with this."

Shaun looked at me. "Stay away from our home. You're not wanted." With that, they both turned to go.

"I would," I called after them, "if you would return the favor!"

The pair disappeared into the trees. I waited under the porch light until I couldn't hear them moving through the forest anymore.

I stepped back into the house and closed the door. I turned the bolt to locked and leaned against the door, taking a few gulping breaths. The Hooper boys were delinquents but harmless. At least I'd always thought so. Now I wasn't as sure.

Tiffin looked up at me with concerned brown eyes. Frankie was even back from burying Hayden's toy in his litter box. He stood on the back of the couch with his striped back arched in Halloween cat pose.

I knew that I needed to call the police. The Hooper boys had seen something the day Beeson was attacked.

There was a pound on the door and I jumped across the room. "Who's there?"

"Kelsey?" a tentative voice said through the door.

Tiffin barked at the door, but the edge he'd had earlier was gone. I unlocked the door and opened it. "Jason?"

Jason stood in front of me. His eyes were twice there normal size. "I heard yelling and came over to make sure you were okay."

I blinked at him. Jason running to my rescue was more than I would expect from my reclusive farmhand. "Come in from the cold." I stepped back.

He shuffled into the cottage and looked around like he wasn't sure what to do with himself now that he was inside my home. It was his first time being there. Although Hayden and I had invited him to dinner many times, he'd always refused.

"Have a seat on the couch." I pointed to the sofa." You're shivering. I'll make some tea to warm you up."

Frankie glared at him with his one good eye and, to my amazement, began to purr. I blinked at the cat. Jason walked over to him and stroked his back. Frankie's purrs increased tenfold.

"If I didn't already know that you have a special way with animals, I would now. Frankie hates everyone except for my son." I paused. "And I guess you."

Jason sat on the edge of the couch. Frankie leapt onto the cushion and sat next to him. He didn't jump into his lap, but he did snuggle up next to Jason's leg. I stood there with my mouth hanging open. Still in wonderment, I turned to make the tea.

I set the kettle to boil and waited. As I did, I mulled over my options. Now that Jason was here, I was less inclined to call the police about what had just happened. If there was a police report about the Hooper boys, it would give Eddie more ammunition to change the custody agreement. He could claim that I didn't have Hayden in a safe environment. Barton Farm had been perfectly safe before Milton Hooper's descendants had moved into his old home.

Jason seemed to be fine with the quiet. Unlike many people, he never felt the need to fill the empty air with idle talk. I usually did, but not when Jason was around. It was too much of a fight to get him to answer back, so I only spoke when I was in need of important information.

The kettle whistled, and I poured the hot water over the tea bags in two waiting mugs. I carried the mugs back to the living room and held one out. Frankie growled deep in his throat as I handed Jason the mug.

Jason made a clicking sound with his tongue and the cat went back to purring. I sat in the armchair across the couch. "You really have a way with animals. How did you do that?"

"I'm not a threat," he said.

"I'm not a threat either." I cradled my mug in my hands. "I feed him and clean his litter box. I would pet him if he let me."

Jason shook his head. "Frankie wants respect. Some cats—just like people—need that. Do you respect Frankie or tolerate him? I bet if you started looking at him differently, he would come around."

I raised my eyebrows. I'd never expected such deep thoughts from my usually silent farmhand. I wished Laura and Benji were around to hear it. Then they would know there was more to Jason than just being a loner.

He changed the subject. "Was someone here?" He held the mug of tea in one hand and scratched Frankie behind the ear with the other.

"Scott and Shaun Hooper. They were just being loud. I don't think they hurt anything."

Jason stared into his tea. "I should have come as soon as I heard the noise. I was in the barn, checking the animals one final time before I went to my trailer for the night, when I heard shouts coming from this side of the street."

It was a miracle that Jason had tried to come to my rescue. When faced with a decision, his inclination had always been flight rather than fight, at least up until now.

He stared into his tea. "I didn't want what happened to that man, Dr. Beeson, to happen to you," he said with an air of embarrassment. "I keep thinking maybe I could have helped him too."

"But you told me that you didn't hear anything the day Dr. Beeson was attacked."

Jason wouldn't meet my eyes. "I know that's what I told you, but it was untrue. I heard some yelling that morning."

"You did?" I asked.

"I was on this side of Maple Grove Lane when the professor fell." His voice was barely above a whisper.

"Were you checking on the oxen?" It was the only reason I could think of why Jason would cross the street while guests were at the Farm.

He shook his head.

"Or the team of horses pulling the sleigh?"

He shook his head again and managed a small "no."

"Then what?" I was trying to be patient, but I felt like I had to pry information out of him with a crowbar.

"I was looking for Scott and Shaun Hooper. I was in the barn and saw them run across the street into the trees north of the pasture. I just knew they were up to no good." He paused. "So I decided to follow them."

"You followed them?" This was hard to believe.

He met my gaze for the first time. "I knew you would be busy with the school visits coming. I never thought they would kill someone."

I grew very still. "You saw them kill Dr. Beeson?"

He shook his head. "No. But right after I stepped into the forest, I heard them come crashing back in my direction. I jumped behind a bush so they wouldn't see me. They were running so fast you would have thought they'd seen one of the Farm's ghosts."

"The Farm doesn't have ghosts," I said automatically, considering everything Jason had said. This had been a long speech for him, so I waited a few moments before asking the questions on the tip of my tongue. "Why didn't you tell me this when I visited you at the barn this morning?"

He wrapped both hands around his mug. He'd yet to take a sip from it. "I wanted to, but I thought the boys would be careful and stay away from the Farm. I never expected them to come back that night. I knew when they trampled Shepley's garden that they must be dumber than anyone thought. Wouldn't they want to lie low if they'd killed someone? I just wanted them to leave the Farm alone."

"Jason, a man is dead. This is a case where the Farm is not more important than finding the person responsible for a murder." Even as I said this, I knew I was guilty of putting the Farm ahead of finding Dr. Beeson's killer. In fact, if I was honest with myself, my entire motivation for trying to find out what happened was the Farm—

not just clearing Gavin's name. I wanted to have someone else to blame so that the Farm wasn't in any way liable.

"I didn't want to talk to the police. Not like last summer."

"The police just want to find out what happened to Dr. Beeson," I said.

"The detective doesn't like me." Jason said this with so much confidence, I didn't have the heart to lie and tell him he was wrong.

"I don't think there are many people that Detective Brandon truly likes. She's just doing her job. She doesn't have to like anyone to do it," I said.

"I don't want to draw attention. Things go bad when I draw attention."

"What do you mean?"

He frowned and started petting Frankie again. The tiger cat kicked up his purring.

Before I'd let Jason move in the trailer on the Farm grounds, I'd told him he had to tell me his story. After some time, he had told me that he'd gone into foster care at the age of seven and bounced around from house to house until he was eighteen. None of the homes had stuck. My heart broke for him. He hadn't been much older than Hayden when he'd entered the system. It made me physically ill to think of my son in that situation. Eddie and I were fighting over our son, and here was Jason, who presumably no one wanted, but who somehow retained a sweet, quiet way that I came to appreciate more every day.

"I didn't want to lose my home," Jason said. "The trailer, the Farm, is my first real home."

My stomach fell down to my shoes as I remembered my conversation that afternoon with Henry and the other Cherry Foundation board members.

Jason stood. "I'm glad you're okay. You and Hayden—you're the only family I have."

His comment was so sincere, it only made me feel worse. I had to find a way to keep the trailer on the grounds. I set my mug on the coffee table, stood, and took Jason's still-full mug and placed it next to mine.

He headed for the front door. "Thank you, Kelsey."

"For what?"

"Everything." He gave Frankie one final pat. "Good night." With that he strode out the front door, tracking mud back across my floor.

As soon as the door closed, Frankie stopped purring and hissed at me.

"I thought you were turning over a new leaf," I commented.

He turned tail and gave me an unpleasant view of his back end before running upstairs to his lair under Hayden's bed.

TWENTY-EIGHT

I CAN'T SAY I slept much that night. I tensed at every noise the old cottage made and every sound from outside. When you live in the woods there are many noises: hoots from owls, deer crashing through the brush, and the late winter wind whistling through the trees. It's easy to be spooked. I'd never been frightened in the cottage before, not even last summer when there'd been a killer on the Farm during the Civil War Reenactment. Now, I was nervous, and I hated it. I hated it that the Hooper boys and whoever killed Dr. Beeson had robbed me of the peace that the cottage had always given me.

I knew I should have called Detective Brandon as soon as Jason left, but it was already late. I soothed my guilt by promising myself that I'd call her in the morning.

At some point, I must have fallen asleep, because I woke up in a jolt when my alarm went off at six. It was Saturday, the first full day of the Maple Sugar Festival, and there was so much to do before the visitors started arriving for our nine a.m. opening time.

Tiffin was asleep on the floor beside my bed as always, but to my surprise, I found Frankie curled up at the foot of the bed. He glared at me with his one good eye.

"Were you protecting me, Frankie?" Maybe the visit from Jason, the cat whisperer, had worked wonders on Frankie after all.

The one-eyed cat hissed and jumped off the bed as if offended by the very idea.

Then again, maybe not.

I didn't have time to worry about Frankie and his poor manners. I had to get going as quickly as possible and check everything over before the visitors arrived. Benji and the rest of the staff would be arriving within the hour. I threw back the covers and headed for the bathroom.

Thirty minutes later, Tiffin and I were out the door. I scanned the yard as I went. The only evidence that anyone had been in the yard the night before were footprints in the thawing ground. I would call Detective Brandon and tell her about the evening's adventure just as soon as I checked the grounds and made sure that everyone was ready for the festival. I knew I was just making excuses, and the longer I put the call off the more annoyed the detective would be with me for not calling earlier.

Tiffin and I headed down the pebbled path through the maple grove to the visitor center. Tiffin placed his nose to the ground like a bloodhound, then suddenly lifted it and took off down the path.

"Now what?" I muttered as I ran after him.

It didn't take me long to realize what Tiffin was worked up over. In the maple grove, it was obvious. All the pails were knocked off the trees. Sap dripped from the spiles in the sugar maple trunks and fell to the thawing ground.

The sugarhouse door swung on its hinges. I ran inside to see that the table had been overturned, and Gavin's vials of maple syrup, which he showed to visitors to illustrate the difference in color among the grades of syrup, were smashed on the floor.

Tiffin tried to get around me to go into the room.

"No, Tiff, back. You could cut your paw on the glass."

He whimpered and stepped back.

I couldn't put off my call to Detective Brandon any longer. Something had to be done about those Hooper brothers, because I knew they were behind this. I removed my cell phone from my pocket and dialed a number that unfortunately I knew by heart.

Despite the early hour, the detective answered her phone on the first ring.

"Detective? It's Kelsey Cambridge."

"I know that from the caller ID. What do you need, Ms. Cambridge?"

If nothing else, the detective had great bedside manner, I thought sarcastically.

"I need to report more vandalism on the Farm, and I know who did it." I went on to tell her about my discovery, my visit from the Hooper boys the night before, and my suspicions about them.

"Why didn't you call me last night with this information?" Her voice was sharp, even sharper than usual.

"I meant to." I knew it wasn't great as far as excuses were, but it was the best that I had.

She snorted. "I'm on my way."

After the detective hung up, I called Benji, Gavin, and a few of the part-time staff and asked them to come in early to help me clean up the mess.

Benji was the first to arrive, even beating Detective Brandon. She'd been on her way to the Farm when I'd called. She immediately joined me at the sugarhouse to assess the damage. It wasn't as bad as I'd first thought. It could be cleaned up quickly before the festival began.

She looked around the sugarhouse. "Who did this?"

"I know who," I said and I told her about my encounter with the Hoopers. "We should start cleaning up."

"Not yet," Detective Brandon said from behind us. "My team and I need to take a look around."

I turned to find her standing in the doorway to the sugarhouse. "Detective, we have to open in two hours for the festival. The sugarhouse must be up and working by nine. We have three hundred people coming to the Farm today to see how maple syrup is made."

"This is a crime scene and may be connected to Conrad Beeson's murder," she said. "I'll decide if and when you can enter the building."

"But—"

"The longer you argue with me, the longer it'll take."

I glared at her, and Benji and I backed off.

Benji scowled. "She's such a pain. You know she's throwing her weight around just because she doesn't like you."

"Maybe that's a tiny part of it, but she's right. She has to make sure there isn't anything that connects this to the murder." The reality of the circumstances settled on my shoulders like an oxen's yoke. A man had been murdered, and the fact that I was alone with two possible culprits last night turned my stomach. Detective Brandon was right. I should have called her last night.

Benji wasn't cutting Detective Brandon any slack. "But you said it was Scott and Shaun Hooper who came to the Farm last night." She watched me. "Do you think they killed Beeson?"

"I don't know, but at the very least, I do believe they saw something." I told her how Laura and I went to the Hooper place late yesterday afternoon.

"No wonder they came over here and trashed the sugarhouse," Benji said.

"That doesn't make me feel any better, Ben."

She sniffed. "In any case, we'll be ready to set up just as soon as the detective gives her blessing. We can have this cleaned up in no time. Alice is already in the kitchen with her staff preparing for the pancake breakfast."

"Good." I smiled, feeling a tiny bit better.

"Did Barn Boy see anything?" Benji asked.

I arched an eyebrow at her.

She rolled her big brown eyes in return. "Fine. Did Jason see anything?"

"No. But he heard the shouts. He came by my cottage, but the Hooper boys were gone by then."

She shook her head. "I still don't understand what the Hooper boys meant by it. Why would they be so stupid as to do this?" She gestured to the pails and spiles on the ground. "I mean, you saw them. You know it was them."

Good question.

"Kelsey!" Chief Duffy's booming voice pulled me away from my conversation with Benji. "I came as quick as I could, but one can't just throw on regimental uniforms." The police chief was in his full Confederate General uniform, all the way down to the ceremonial sword. "Heard about your troubles on the radio. You think it was the Hoopers?"

I nodded. "They were here last night." I started to tell him and Officer Sonders about my encounter.

Detective Brandon must have heard the chief as well, because she came out of the sugarhouse. She wasn't smiling, not that that was unusual.

"We need the sugarhouse today," I said. "The Maple Sugar Festival could be ruined without it."

"'Course you do. 'Course you do. Candy, are you done here? Kelsey and her staff need to get in there and prepare for the festival."

"Chief, I just arrived. I still have to fingerprint the scene."

He held his coat by the lapels. "Officer Sonders can do that while we run over and interview the Hoopers. Seems to me that your time would be much better spent talking to potential witnesses than keeping Kelsey and her staff from preparing for the day."

"But Chief—" the detective protested.

"Officer Sonders will give it the once-over, and then we'll let them clean up. Won't you, Sonders?"

The young officer nodded.

Detective Brandon glared at me, as if the police chief overruling her was somehow my fault. Yes, I wanted her to leave the sugarhouse as soon as possible, but I hadn't told the chief to kick her out.

Detective Brandon cleared her throat. "I'll be at the Hoopers'." With that she stomped away.

TWENTY-NINE

WITH CHIEF DUFFY'S GO-AHEAD, we were able to hang the sap collection pails back on the trees, scrub up the worst of the maple syrup spills, and sweep all the broken glass from the sugarhouse. By the time we were done, it was eight thirty, which gave me just enough time to run back to the cottage to change before the festival. As we cleaned, Laura and the rest of my staff arrived, as well as Chief Duffy's small troupe of reenactors who'd volunteered to come and entertain the visitors.

When I went inside the visitor center, there was a line out the door of people waiting to enter the pancake breakfast. It stretched all the way to the parking lot, and Judy had just unlocked the door.

I couldn't stop smiling. Despite everything that had gone wrong over that last two days, the Maple Sugar Festival was turning into the success I'd known it would be. This was exactly what I'd wanted to see when I'd first had the idea for the Maple Sugar Festival. With three or four more successful events like this every year, I knew that the Farm could not fail, and I wouldn't have to worry about what

Henry Ratcliffe and the other Cherry Foundation board members said about it either.

I winced internally. Here I was, making plans for the future, and Conrad Beeson was dead. He couldn't plot and plan for his own future. I tried to shake the melancholy thoughts from my head and focus on the day.

I watched Abraham Lincoln chatting with people as they waited in line. With the encouragement of Chief Duffy and his regiment, Abe was in residence, and there were a dozen more reenactors there talking about the War and the maple trees. I had yet to see Chase, not that I'd been looking for him.

A boy stared at Lincoln in awe. "Do you eat pancakes?"

Abe bowed to him. "I love pancakes. Would you like to hear my ode to them?"

The boy nodded, and I noticed that others standing in line leaned in to hear the ode. As far as I knew, Lincoln—the real one—never wrote an ode about pancakes, but I wasn't about to correct the historical inaccuracies.

I was relieved to have Honest Abe there to keep the crowd occupied as they waited. My staff and the dozen or so volunteers who'd come in to help were doing a fantastic job in keeping the crowds calm and patient as the line moved slowly forward.

A young man in a Union army uniform collected tickets from the pancake eaters. "Please go in." He gestured to the dining room.

After they'd finished eating their breakfast, they went out into the Farm where my historical interpreters and more Civil War reenactors waited to tell them what it was like to live in Ohio during the Civil War. Since the ground was too wet for the sleigh, the Farm's wagon, with Scarlett and Rhett at the front, waited to give guests rides back and forth to the maple grove. One of my seasonal staffers sat in the driver seat in his period clothing. At least the festival-goers wouldn't be subjected to Shepley as their driver like the school children had been. Another seasonal worker helped guests step into the wagon for the Maple Sugar Festival's inaugural ride.

Laura joined me near the door. "I knew I shouldn't have left you last night. Benji told me what happened."

"I wasn't in any real danger," I said, trying to sound more confident than I really was. "The Hooper boys were just trying to throw their weight around. I'm sure they're sorry now. Detective Brandon went over to their home to talk to them."

"That would make me sorry." Laura patted the bun coiled at the back of her head. "I haven't been in this get-up for a few months. I almost forgot how to tie my corset." She sighed. "It was one of those times it would have been nice to have a man around to help me out."

Laura was always looking for a date. I knew she could have just about any man she wanted with her long blond hair, curvy figure, and beautiful skin. I just didn't think most men deserved her.

She eyed me. "Speaking of men. Have you seen Chase?"

I shook my head and watched as the full wagon rolled into the trees.

She leaned close to me. "Are you looking for him now?"

I rolled my eyes, grateful that Hayden wasn't around to see me. "I'm trying to see if any of the Sap and Spile members came."

"Back to the scene of the crime?"

"Exactly."

She groaned. "You can't possibly think the killer is here."

"I don't know what to believe. I shouldn't count anyone out as a suspect." *Including Gavin*, I mentally added. He was now in the sugarhouse in nineteenth-century costume, talking to tourists about maple syrup's importance in combatting the Rebels.

Laura tapped her index finger to her cheek. "You know, the Kelsey I know doesn't usually ask for anyone's advice or help to solve her problems."

I laughed.

"But after last night, I think you should leave this whole matter to the police. I'm worried about you."

"Don't be. I'm fine."

A man stepped around the line and headed straight onto the grounds. It was Daniel, the college maintenance worker, who I'd first met at the Sap and Spile meeting. I recognized his ponytail.

"There's one now," I said.

"There's what now?" Laura asked.

"Someone from Sap and Spile. I need to talk to him."

Her groan followed me out the door.

By the time I wove through the crowd trying to get out of the building, Daniel had disappeared. I almost gave up, but then I spotted him heading toward the sugarhouse and quietly followed. I should have known. He must be here to check out Gavin's operation.

Daniel stopped outside the door to the sugarhouse and listened to the demonstration.

"We've been increasing our sugar production tenfold since the war began," Gavin said, in character. "Sugar cane and molasses are harder to come by every day. At first we couldn't get it because the south was closed off to us, but even now that we got Old New Orleans back from the Rebs, it's still hard to come by because the farmland has been abandoned or scorched by our own men."

Daniel rubbed his chin, as if he was considering the story that Gavin told the tourists.

I walked up beside him.

He glanced in my direction. "Been snooping around any greenhouses lately, Ms. Cambridge?"

I felt my face heat up. "Not since yesterday."

"Good to know. This is quite an event you have going on here." He nodded toward the trees, where more reenactors and a handful of my interpreters in nineteenth-century dress entertained the crowds. "Everyone seems to be enjoying themselves."

"I'm happy with the turnout," I said.

"As you should be." He rubbed his chin again. "I just think it's strange how so many people come here to learn about maple sugar and the Civil War."

"Why's that?" I asked.

"It just seems odd to me, is all. It was never a topic of conversation at Sap and Spile until after the release of Beeson's book. We all knew, for a long time, that he was writing a book, but he was always hush-hush about the subject matter. Many of us, myself included, just assumed it was some sort of academic work about plants. Imagine our shock when he produced a history book of all things."

"Dr. Beeson wasn't interested in history?" I asked.

"He'd never showed much interest in it. At least none that I was aware of. At Sap and Spile meetings, he was always focused on the science of maple sugaring and methods about boiling and what woods would burn the hottest and the longest, what property the type of wood would give to the maple syrup it created. It was very strange." He shrugged. "I suppose everyone can have a surprising talent or interest."

"What were your feelings about Conrad Beeson?"

His mouth curled into a smile. "Do you mean to ask, did I kill him?"

I swallowed. "Yes."

He laughed at my honesty. It was a low raspy laugh. "No, I did not." He paused. "I can't say I cared much for the man, but I didn't care enough to kill him either. Maple sugaring is a hobby of mine. It's not my life, like it is for many of our members." He held up a hand to me, as if to stop me from saying something. "And before you ask, I was at work when Beeson was attacked. Six fellow employees can vouch for me."

"Oh, all right."

He chuckled. "Don't look so disappointed, Kelsey. You just have to find the person who cared enough to take Conrad's life."

He said it as if it were a simple task.

I changed the subject. "Why is Sap and Spile only for men?"

"It just seemed to fall in that way. No woman has ever asked to join. We've been having meetings since the 1920s. Over time the word got out that it was men only, but there's nothing in the bylaws that specifically says that. Why?" His eyes twinkled. "Are you interested in joining?"

I shook my head. "I think that after this weekend, I'll have had enough of maple sugar to last until next year's festival."

"You plan to do it again?"

I nodded. "As you can see, it's turned out to be a popular event."

"Hope that no one dies next time."

"That would be nice," I agreed.

"Kelsey! There you are!" My father's voice boomed across the Farm even though he was still thirty yards away from the sugarhouse.

I thanked Daniel for speaking to me and went to meet my father.

THIRTY

As was typical when he visited the Farm for special events, Dad had mixed up the centuries. He wore jeans and boots on the bottom and a Union soldier's coat on top, complete with saber. To my relief, I saw it was made out of plastic. He must have picked it up in the stock room at the theater.

He unsheathed his saber and waved it about. "Where's my young soldier, Sir Hayden?"

"Can you put that away?" I asked with a wince. A tourist had crossed the path to walk on the grass to avoid us. "It may be fake, but you're scaring the visitors."

He re-sheathed his sword. "You never let me have any fun."

"Are you supposed to say that to me? I'm the kid in this situation," I said.

"You were born responsible. You take after your beloved mother that way. A crusader and a dependable citizen of the world."

"Thanks, Dad." I smiled. "That's high praise." I knew he couldn't give any higher praise.

"So where is Hayden?" he asked again, scanning the faces around us.

I sighed, and the glow I'd received from being compared to my mother faded. "Eddie came and picked him up last night. He started his weekend a little earlier than I expected. But it makes sense," I added quickly. "I've been so busy with the festival. It would be hard for me to keep a close eye on Hayden if he were here."

Dad scowled. My jovial father wasn't a scowler, unless it was on stage and required for the part. "He did, did he? I always said that you would have trouble with that one."

I snorted. "Dad, when did you always say that? You loved Eddie almost as much as I did once upon a time."

"Well, I thought it," he grumped in return.

"Hayden will be here later. Krissie promised to bring him to the festival today."

"Hmpf," Dad snorted.

"Krissie's nice," I said defending Eddie's fiancée to my father just as I had to Laura the previous night.

"Hmmm," Dad mused. "Nice, maybe, but she's not you. It seems like a serious downgrade after being married to you."

"I need to get back to work," I said.

Dad grabbed the sleeve of my jacket. "Before you go, I have news from campus."

I raised my eyebrows at him.

He lowered his voice. "About Beeson."

"Let's talk over here." I led Dad away from the crowd, to a picnic table near the employees' entrance to the visitor center. "What did you learn?"

"After you dropped by yesterday, I spoke with one of my acting students who I knew was taking a botany lab from Dr. Beeson. The only reason I knew that was because he went on and on in my class about how much he hated botany. He'd thought it would be an easy A to fulfill his science requirement, but he was wrong."

"What did he say?" I scanned the area around the picnic table to make sure no one was close enough to overhear.

Dad leaned in. "My student said that another horticulture professor, Dr. Arnold Buckley, was stealing from the college and that Beeson had caught him."

"What?" I cried.

When visitors stared over at us, I smiled at them and lowered my voice. "What? What do you mean by 'stealing'?"

"Buckley is the chair of the horticulture department, and he was misappropriating funds in order to take some of the budget money himself. Faking receipts and the like, so that he could pocket the difference."

"And Beeson knew this."

Dad nodded. "He figured it out somehow, according to my student."

I tapped my cheek with my index finger. "That's a pretty good motive for murder. If Beeson went to the college administration, it would ruin Buckley's career. He would never be able to find another teaching job."

"*If* Beeson was going to go to the college administration, which he wasn't."

I leaned against the edge of the picnic table. "What do you mean?"

"According to my student, Beeson promised Buckley that he wouldn't tell the college if Buckley put all the money back. Buckley agreed."

I thought about everything I knew about Beeson. "Beeson didn't go to the administration so that he could use what he knew about

Buckley to his advantage later. He might even have planned to blackmail Buckley," I mused.

Dad beamed at me as if I'd just aced an exam. "Those are my thoughts exactly."

"How does the student know all of this?" I asked.

"He heard the two of them arguing about it a few weeks ago." Dad set his plastic saber on the picnic table.

"And he didn't tell anyone? What about the dean or campus security?"

"He didn't want to get involved," Dad said. "He's regretting that now, which is why I think he confessed what he knew to me."

"Detective Brandon will want to talk to your student. You'll have to give me his name."

Dad sighed. "Dan Jacobs. He's a good kid, and one of the students I have high hopes will go on to earn a BFA at a four-year university. I hope Detective Brandon will go easy on him."

I couldn't promise him that; I didn't think Detective Brandon went easy on anyone. "I'm going to need to talk to Buckley again too."

"You've met him?" Dad asked.

I nodded. "He was in the greenhouse when I went over there to look for clues. This just might be the break in the case we were looking for." I couldn't keep my excitement from my voice.

"Mom!" Hayden called from the pebbled path.

"There's my soldier," Dad bellowed. He grabbed his saber from the table and braced himself for Hayden's full-speed approach. "Stop there, you old rogue, or I'll run you through."

Hayden froze as if he were playing Red Light, Green Light.

A little girl nearby screamed and buried her face into her mother's knees.

"I'm sorry," I told the young mother as she picked up her wailing child.

She glared at me. I wouldn't count on her being a repeat customer at the Maple Sugar Festival.

"You may approach," Dad said in his booming voice, and he lowered his saber.

Hayden ran forward and stopped in front of his grandfather. My son widened his stance and held his hands karate-style, ready to strike. "Your sword is no match for my ninja moves."

The pair ran toward the sugar maple grove. I covered my eyes with my hand, hoping they didn't scare any more Farm visitors.

I lowered my hand to find a smiling Krissie standing in front of me. Did she really have to be so pretty? It almost felt insulting. I shook off any animosity and smiled back at the young woman. "Thank you for bringing Hayden today."

She beamed, probably because I'd greeted her nicely instead of with my usual growl. I growled a lot when Eddie was around, and I rarely saw Krissie without my ex-husband. "Kelsey, I'm so glad that I caught you alone. There was something that I wanted to talk to you about woman-to-woman."

"There is?"

She nodded, and her perfect hair bounced on her shoulders. She wore a beret instead of a stocking hat like most visitors did if they wore a hat at all. Grudgingly, I had to admit that she looked adorable in it.

Despite her cuteness, I knew whatever she had to say, I wasn't going to like it.

THIRTY-ONE

Krissie smiled brightly at me. "It's about the wedding."

It just gets better and better.

"The wedding?" I squeaked.

She nodded and smiled happily. "The many times we've visited the Farm, I've fallen in love with the place. I've seen the events that you've done here, Kelsey. You're able to build something wonderful out of nothing. It's truly impressive."

I didn't like where this was going. I managed a small "thank you."

She clasped her hands in front of her chest. "Because of this, I'd like to have my wedding right here on the Farm. Whatever your price, my parents will pay."

I blinked at her. "You want to get married here? At Barton Farm? You want to marry Eddie at *my* Barton Farm?"

She nodded. "Don't you think it would be just perfect for a wedding?"

Of course I did. Barton Farm had been the location of many weddings over the years. The white New England–style church was the perfect place for the ceremony, and there were any number of wedding photo backgrounds to choose from all over the property. The visitor center would be transformed into the reception hall. It had all the key elements for any wedding. But this was *my* Farm. Krissie and Eddie couldn't get married here. It just seemed like too cruel a twist of fate.

"Are you teasing me?" It was the only explanation that made any sense at all.

Her face fell. "No, never. I really do want to have the wedding here. I've already told my parents. They live in Detroit, but I've sent them pictures. My mother would much rather I get married back home in Detroit, but she agreed that if I insisted on having my wedding in Ohio, Barton Farm is the perfect spot. Eddie and I want to marry here in the community we live in, so that everyone we know can come."

"B—but…" I couldn't even get the words out. The idea of Krissie and Eddie's wedding on Barton Farm was too ridiculous.

"I was hoping for a June wedding. Eddie and I don't want to put it off any longer. The sooner we marry, the sooner we can have some stability for Hayden."

"June?" I squeaked. "It's already March." How could this possibly get any worse? Her comment about stability for Hayden put my teeth on edge.

"I already have my gown and my bridesmaids' dresses picked out. You'll just have to worry about venue, the catering, oh, and the flowers. I know you can do it." She waved her arms at the many happy visitors walking around the grounds. "Look at all that you've accomplished here. This must be much more complicated than a wedding." She tilted her head. "Do you think any of the Civil War reenactors would be willing to come to the wedding to be part of the ambiance?"

I was speechless. For the first time in my life, completely speechless. I'd had more to say when I found out about Eddie's affair. Actually, when I learned about the affair, I'd been anything but speechless, and I'd thrown a cooler at Eddie's head. Most of the time, I'm grateful I missed.

When I didn't say anything, she kept going, "I know it must feel strange to you, but it would be little or no work for you. I have a wedding planner all lined up, and she'll work with you to make sure everything runs smoothly. You would only have to worry about coordinating with her on the Farm's schedule and staff that would be needed."

I knew a lie when I heard one. Krissie might be sweet and nice most of the time, but I was pretty sure there was a bridezilla lurking just below the surface of her skin.

My voice returned. "Wow, Krissie, you really took me by surprise with this."

"A good surprise, I hope." She smiled brightly.

Not even close.

I swallowed. "I think under the circumstances that Barton Farm isn't the best place for your wedding. I know you like to think we're one big happy family, and I appreciate that. Don't you think it would be awkward for Eddie to have the wedding here?"

She shook her head. "I've already talked to Eddie, and he's on board with whatever I want to do."

He says that now. I kept my thoughts to myself. Krissie would have to learn Eddie's faults in her own time.

"You told him that you wanted to get married here on the Farm? And he was okay with that?" It was hard to believe.

She sniffed. "I admit he wasn't thrilled with the idea when I first suggested it, but I finally got him to come around. He's been so understanding. You and Eddie have a good relationship. He didn't think you would mind. In fact, he thought that it would be good news for you."

"Good news?" I was incredulous.

"You're always concerned about the Farm's finances. This would help."

I closed my eyes for a moment. As I did, I listened to the sounds of a full Farm: children laughing, the jangle of the horse wagon, the clang of the Civil War reenactors' rifles knocking against their canteens as they walked, and Abraham Lincoln's booming voice. Eddie was right. I worried about the Farm's finances all the time. I fought to keep those sounds from fading away, but I couldn't have his wedding here. Eddie knew that. He'd either lied to Krissie about how I would feel or she was lying to me now about what he'd said. In either case, I didn't like it, not one bit.

She frowned and her lower lip popped out as if she'd just realized that I wasn't doing cartwheels over her offer. "Kelsey, I want to get married in New Hartford, and the Farm is the best option. It's the best place for photographs. I *must* have wonderful photos. They'll last a lifetime."

Unless you get divorced, the jaded divorcee said inside my head.

"I understand, Krissie, but ..."

"I can convince Eddie to give up his plan to change the terms of Hayden's custody." She said it so fast I almost thought I heard her wrong.

"What?"

"I can convince Eddie to leave Hayden's custody arrangements as they are." She said it much slower this time.

I felt like she'd slapped me across the face. "You would use my son as a pawn in your quest for the perfect wedding?"

"He's not a pawn," she said. "I'm just saying that Eddie will listen to me if I say we should leave the custody arrangements as they are. I was the one who encouraged him to make some changes in the first place."

My heart hurt for my son. I'd been wrong about Krissie, so terribly wrong. She wasn't all sunshine and unicorns; there was a calculating woman under that pink exterior. Laura had been right. I'd always wondered how Krissie and Eddie had ended up together—she wasn't Eddie's type, at least I hadn't thought so. But now it seemed clear. It appeared Krissie could make things happen when she really wanted something. She'd wanted Eddie, and now she wanted their wedding on Barton Farm.

"Don't you want Eddie to stop making threats about the custody agreement?" She cocked her head.

"That's blackmail," I said.

"It is?" she asked brightly.

I was beginning to realize that Krissie was a whole lot smarter than anyone gave her credit for, especially me.

She patted my arm. "Why don't you think on it?" She left me on the side of the pebbled path, reeling from her suggestion, and strolled away as if nothing at all happened.

"You look like you've lost your best friend," a voice I recognized said.

I looked up to see Chase standing in front of me. "Oh, hi."

He laughed. "I didn't think you were going to throw your arms around me, but I'd hoped that I would get something better than 'oh, hi.'"

"Sorry. I just got some very unexpected and upsetting news. I'm still processing. I think I'll be for a long time."

Chase's eyebrows knit together in concern. "About the murder?"

I shook my head.

"About the Hoopers?" He clenched his fists at his side for half a second. "My uncle told me they dropped in on you last night."

"In this case, sadly, no." I sighed. "I sort of wish it was."

"Want to talk about it?"

I shook my head, and to my relief, Chase dropped the subject. As promised, he was wearing his Union medic uniform. He looked quite dashing in it. He held his period-appropriate medical bag in his hand. I smiled. "Nice outfit."

"I wore it just for you. Every time I put it on, it reminds me of our first meeting. It's a very happy memory." His flirty tone was back.

I was still reeling from Krissie's wedding nuclear blast, so I couldn't think of a witty response.

He noticed. "Are you sure you're okay?"

I forced a smile. "I'll be fine."

He didn't appear convinced.

"I promise." I tried to lighten the mood. "You know when Laura told you that I had a thing for reenactors, she was kidding, right?"

He made a mock scandalized face. "Laura would never lie."

That got a genuine laugh out of me. It was known throughout the Farm that Laura was loose with her historical details when it came to giving visitors information. If she didn't know a fact or story that a Farm visitor asked about, she wasn't above making it up. It was a habit I wanted to break her of. I feared for the day sometime soon when a tourist came back to the Farm and said that we were wrong about one of our historical facts. Laura promised me she hadn't given wrong information to anyone who looked like they might look into it further. I'd told her that was profiling.

Chase nodded to the wagon driver as the wagon trundled by. "This is quite an event. Not as big as the reenactment, of course, but not a bad showing."

"Nothing will be as big as the reenactment," I said. That huge event had taken an entire year to plan. I closed my eyes for a moment as I contemplated having to deal with it this summer along with Eddie's wedding. But the wedding wasn't going to be on the Farm grounds. There was absolutely no way I was going to allow that to happen. I would fight Hayden's custody arrangements in court. I would not let Krissie use my son as a weapon against me.

Chase leaned forward and studied my face. "Are you going to pass out?"

I blinked. "No." Even to my own ears my answer wasn't that convincing.

"You're lying. Still don't want to talk about it?"

"Definitely not," I said.

"Okay then." He straightened up. "Find your killer yet?"

"I'm working on it," I said. "That's something I'm more equipped to handle. I need to talk to Detective Brandon."

Chase stepped back from me. "Those are words I never expected I'd hear you say."

"I'm full of surprises," I said, and I marched back to the visitor center.

THIRTY-TWO

INSIDE MY OFFICE, I removed my cell phone from my pocket and stared at it.

"Are you going to call her?" Chase asked.

I hadn't realized it, but Chase had followed me into the tiny room. The space was close when I was there alone. With Chase in the room, it seemed to shrink to an eighth of its normal size.

"I know I should. I have new information that could crack open Dr. Beeson's murder, but..."

"But you want to check it out for yourself." He smiled.

"Is it that obvious?"

He nodded. "What do you know?"

I told him what I'd learned from my father about Buckley's misuse of college funds.

He adjusted his medical bag on his shoulder. "That sounds like a pretty good motive to me."

"I know," I agreed. I started to search my phone for Detective Brandon's number.

Chase crossed the tiny room in one stride and wrapped his large hand around my hand holding the phone. "I have an idea. Candy will kill me for saying this, but why don't we run over to the college to talk to Buckley, and we'll call Candy when we get there. It'll give us just enough time to talk to him before she shows. When she does, she can take it from there."

"This could work if Buckley's there. It's Saturday."

"It's worth a shot." Chase wiggled his eyebrows. "I know you want to take a crack at him before Candy digs her claws in. He's not going to say a word when she arrives, but he might talk to you."

I removed my hand from his grasp and looked him up and down. "You're dressed as a Union medic. Don't you think you would stick out on a college campus?"

"College students need a little culture too. I'll leave my musket here." He removed the gun from his shoulder and leaned it again the wall.

"That's a relief. Let's go."

Before we left, I radioed Benji with an excessive number of "overs" to make sure she had everything she needed for the festival. I hated to leave the grounds in the middle of such a big event for the Farm, but this conversation with Buckley might be exactly what I needed to clear Gavin of any wrongdoing.

Chase offered to drive his truck to the college, but as soon as we were on the road, I wished I'd insisted on driving. Maybe it would distract me from my thoughts—not about murder, but about Eddie and Krissie's wedding. Even when Chase called Detective Brandon to tell her where we were going and why, I only half listened because I was so preoccupied by my conversation with Krissie.

"Ready to talk about it yet?" Chase asked after ending the call with the detective.

I sighed. "It's complicated."

"I'm good with complicated." His voice was kind.

Before I could stop myself, it all came out in a rush: Krissie's plans to have the wedding at Barton Farm and Hayden's custody.

"I never liked Krissie," Chase said.

I laughed. "You don't have to say that just for me."

"I mean it. She's fake. I've always thought so. I prefer people who are real." He paused. "Like you. You don't have to run all over town to solve this murder. You're not a suspect. You don't have to do this, but you are, because you care about Gavin." He turned into the parking lot next to the greenhouse.

"You don't have to be doing it either," I said.

"No." He winked at me. "But I enjoy spending time with you, and if you got hurt when I could have been there, I would never forgive myself. I should have been there last night when the Hoopers dropped by."

I was saved from responding, because as Chase shifted the truck into park, Buckley strode out of the building.

"Stay here and call the detective again," I said. "I'll stall him." I didn't give Chase time to argue as I jumped out of the truck. I approached the professor at a fast walk. "Buckley!"

He turned, holding a box of seedlings in his hands. "Ms. Cambridge, I'm surprised to see you here. Don't you have a big event going on at Barton Farm today?"

I forced a smile. "I do."

"Then to what do I owe this visit?"

"I'd like to talk to you."

Behind me, I heard the door of Chase's truck slam closed and the crunch of his footsteps on the gravel lot.

Buckley looked over my shoulder. "Is there a reason you brought a Civil War soldier with you?"

"This is Chase Wyatt. He's a friend of mine, and he was at the Maple Sugar Festival today," I said, as if that justified Chase's presence.

The horticulture professor looked from Chase to me and back again. "That's all very well, but it still doesn't explain why you're here."

"I want to talk to you about Dr. Beeson," I said.

He shook his head. "I don't have any more to say." He started walking in the direction of the only other car in the parking lot besides Chase's truck.

"I know Dr. Beeson found out about you pocketing money from the horticulture department's budget," I called.

He spun around. "Who told you that?"

"A student overheard you and Dr. Beeson arguing about it and told my father, after the murder. Was Beeson going to blackmail you to keep your secret?" I asked.

Buckley gripped the sides of the plastic container holding the plants so tightly the sides bent inward. "I don't have to answer any of your questions. You don't know what you're talking about."

Three cars pulled into the parking lot. The first was a campus security vehicle, the second I recognized as the detective's SUV, and a police cruise brought up the rear.

Buckley's mouth fell open. "You called the police?"

"She didn't," Chase said. "I did."

Detective Brandon was the first person out of the vehicles. "Arnold Buckley, you're under arrest for the murder of Conrad Beeson."

"This is outrageous!" Buckley cried. "I didn't do anything. You have no proof."

"I have enough," the detective said.

Officer Sonders came out of his cruiser holding handcuffs. Detective Brandon gave him a slight nod, and he moved toward Buckley with the handcuffs in his hands.

Still holding the seedlings, Buckley took a big step backward. "I admit that I was stealing from the college, but I didn't kill anyone."

The campus security guard took the box of plants from Buckley. I noticed that Buckley's hands shook as Officer Sonders fastened the cuffs around his wrists. I bit the inside of my lip. Something about this felt wrong. I couldn't put my finger on it ... Buckley had a motive. He might have even had the best motive—Beeson had the power to ruin his career. But doubt nagged at the back of my mind.

Buckley glared at me. "I didn't do it. I'm telling you, I didn't. Wasn't he stabbed? I didn't stab anyone! I only stopped to talk to him. I wanted to talk some sense into him about the money I borrowed from the department. I never touched him. He bent over like he was having a heart attack, and I left. I didn't help him, but I swear that I didn't stab him either."

Officer Sonders grabbed him by the arm and marched him toward the squad car. "This way, please."

After the officer slammed the door closed on Buckley, Detective Brandon walked over to Chase and me. I was sure she noticed Chase's outfit, but she made no comment on it. "Thanks for your help, Ms. Cambridge, but we'd already come to the conclusion that Arnold Buckley was our killer. We were just waiting for the final piece of the puzzle—the motive. You provided that for us." She frowned. "You should have called me as soon as you learned he'd stolen from the department and not tried to talk to him yourself first. You could have ruined everything. Buckley might have gotten away, and it would've been your fault."

Chase folded his arms. "Candy, that's not fair. You wouldn't have arrested Buckley this soon if it hadn't been for Kelsey."

She scowled at him.

"How did you know it was him?" I managed to ask.

"Your friends the Hooper boys."

"They aren't my friends," I said.

"Regardless, they saw Arnold Buckley running through the woods the morning of the murder. He was headed back to the sugarhouse in the middle of the park. They thought it would be funny to follow him for a little while. He'd parked his car on an access to road to the park. He went straight to it and drove away. One of my officers is there now, looking for tracks to compare to Buckley's tires. Contrary to what you might believe, I do know how to do my job."

"So Gavin is no longer a suspect," I said.

"He's not." She said this almost grudgingly.

I blew out a breath. "I knew he couldn't have done it. I knew it."

Detective Brandon glared at me. "You may think you know Gavin Elliot, but he is capable of violent crime."

"H-huh?" I stuttered, surprised by her anger.

"You might want to ask him about his juvenile record then. He was charged and convicted for assault when he was fifteen."

"What?" I demanded.

Chase frowned. "I thought juvenile records are closed."

Her eyes slid in his direction. "I can still get access to them if I talk to the right people."

"What happened?" I asked.

"Since he's no longer part of this case, it's not my place to say." Detective Brandon shook her head. "You'll have to ask Gavin if you want the story. I've already said more than I should. You should know, Kelsey Cambridge, that you can't put blind faith in a man just because you have a feeling he is incapable of a crime. Everyone is capable of the most terrible things."

"I can't believe that," I said.

"Suit yourself, but be warned." She leveled her gaze at Chase. "You'll only be disappointed." She stomped away.

THIRTY-THREE

BACK AT THE FARM, I jumped out of Chase's truck and slammed the door. My head was spinning with everything I'd learned in the last hour.

Chase came around the side of the truck and studied me. "What's wrong? I thought you'd be happy that Gavin's off the hook for the murder?"

I frowned. "I am, but I can't help believing that the police might be wrong. Buckley denied stabbing Dr. Beeson, and he owned up to everything else."

"He's being dragged off to jail. He'd say anything to be let go."

"Maybe…"

"Kelsey!" Benji met me at the door to the visitor center. "I'm so glad that you're back."

"What?" I asked a little too sharply. "Did something happen? Why didn't you call my cell phone?"

"No, no." She shook her head. "It wasn't an emergency. At least I don't think so."

"Benji, what is it?" What remained of my patience had been lost outside of the college's greenhouse.

"Henry and Denise from the Cherry Foundation are here." She said this barely above a whisper. "Henry didn't seem very happy when I told them that you left the Farm."

Terrific.

I followed Benji into the visitor center and found Henry and Denise sitting at one of the round tables eating pancakes drizzled with maple syrup.

Denise smiled at me. "Kelsey, this is truly a lovely event, and these pancakes are marvelous. They remind me of the ones that my grandmother used to make. The maple syrup does too. I don't believe I mentioned before that my grandfather used to tap the sugar maples on his land. I wished that my family had kept that tradition alive."

"The praise for the pancakes goes to Alice, the Farm's head cook. I'll be sure to tell her you liked them." I smiled.

"I'll drop by the kitchen before I leave and tell her myself. They kept us busy while we waited for you. That sweet Benji made sure we had enough to eat."

Henry cleared his throat. "I have to say I was quite surprised to find you absent on such an important day for the Farm."

"I had an errand in town. It didn't take long, and as you can see, my staff has done a wonderful job running things in my absence."

"It seems to be well in hand," he admitted.

"I told Henry there was nothing to worry about where the Farm was concerned," Denise said.

Henry turned his scowl on Denise.

"It looks like you're finished with your pancakes," I said as a teenager came by with a tray and cleared away their empty plates. "Would you like to see the sugarhouse first?"

Denise stood up. "We would. I haven't been inside of one since I was a girl."

Henry wiped his mouth on a napkin. "I believe it's important that we inspect all aspects of your Maple Sugar Festival, including the trailer where your farmhand Jason is living. It's the reason we're here."

I bit the inside of my cheek. "Of course, but the sugarhouse is closer and it's the best introduction to the festival."

Henry looked like he wanted to argue with me, but Denise said, "Sounds like an excellent plan."

"This way." I headed for the doors leading to the Farm. It wasn't until the two board members followed me outside that I realized Chase had slipped away. I glanced around. I really hadn't expected him to stay at my side all day, but it surprised me that he'd left without saying something.

"Is something wrong, Ms. Cambridge?" Henry asked.

"No. Everything's fine." As we walked down the pebbled path to the sugarhouse, I pointed out the pails and spiles hanging from the trees. "We're quite lucky the temperature rose enough for the sap to run. I think the visitors really do like to see the sugaring process in action."

Denise peered through the slim opening between a pail and its lid. "I can see the sap dripping. It looks just like water."

"It's mostly water," I said. "It's boiled to remove excess water and be turned into maple syrup."

"It doesn't seem to be coming very fast," she mused.

"I think patience is the greatest virtue of a tree tapper." I continued down the path.

241

Denise matched my stride. "This is just wonderful, Kelsey. Between this and the Civil War reenactment, I know you would make Cynthia proud. Don't you think so, Henry?"

Henry refrained from comment. Perhaps he was from the school of *if you have nothing nice to say, don't say anything at all.*

We walked in silence, taking in the sights, smells, and sounds of the festival as we headed on the path into the trees.

When the sugarhouse came into view, Henry said, "I question your methods, Ms. Cambridge, but I do see that you're getting results. It appears that the guests at the Farm today are having an enjoyable t—"

"Look out!" A cry from further down the path interrupted him.

Visitors wandering among the trees and inspecting the maple sugar pails jumped out of the way as a ball of fluff raced through the woods.

I jumped in front of the animal. "Tiffin! Stop!"

My dog froze in the middle of the path and panted. Hayden and Gavin stopped a few paces behind him and doubled over to catch their breath. Krissie came down the path at a much slower pace.

"What on earth is going on?" Henry wanted to know.

Of course, my perfectly behaved corgi would misbehave when Henry was visiting the Farm on behalf of the Cherry Foundation.

"I'm sure everything is fine," I said to Henry and Denise.

I walked over to Tiffin. He looked up at me with his soulful brown eyes. A thick layer of maple syrup covered his head and back. It ran down his long nose.

"I'm so sorry about this, Kelsey," Gavin said, panting almost as much as Tiffin. "It's my fault. Tiffin ran into the sugarhouse and I wasn't watching where I was going as I was moving a gallon bucket of maple syrup. I tripped over him and doused the poor guy."

I knelt next to the dog. "Was it hot? He could be burnt."

"No," Gavin said quickly. "It was the batch I made yesterday during the school visit. It was cool." He frowned. "Just really sticky."

That was an understatement. Tiffin's thick fur was matted into clumps, and dirt, sticks, and leaves, which he must have picked up during his sprint through the forest, clung to him like Velcro. "I can see that."

"I'm sorry, Mom." Hayden worried his lip. "I know Tiff isn't supposed to go inside the old buildings. You tell me that. All the time."

A giggle bubbled up inside me and before I knew it I was bent over trying to catch my breath from laughing so hard. Compared to what else I'd dealt with that week, Tiffin's predicament seemed so incredibly funny.

The corgi gave me a hurt expression. I knelt next to him on the forest floor. "I'm sorry, boy." I patted the part of his head free of maple syrup. "All he needs is a warm bath."

"I can do it," Gavin said. "This is my fault, really. I should be the one to give him a bath."

"What about the sugarhouse?" I asked.

"A couple of the reenactors are there now. They'll be fine until I get back."

I glanced back at Henry and Denise, who were speaking in hushed tones under the trees. "Okay." I removed my keys from my pocket and detached my cottage key from the ring. "You can use the bathroom in the cottage. Try not to make a huge mess." My bathroom was doomed.

"I can help!" Hayden shouted with an enthusiasm I found suspicious.

"We need to get going, Hayden," Krissie said. "You can give Tiffin a bath another day. Your father's waiting for us."

Hayden frowned. "But he's my dog. He's my responsibility."

"Hayden, it's time that we went home." Krissie smiled, but it didn't reach her eyes.

My chest tightened when she said "home." It was Hayden's home, but I felt his real home was here on Barton Farm with me.

"Remember what we talked about." Krissie smiled brightly at me.

I glanced over at Henry and Denise to see that they were still engrossed in their own conversation. "I've thought about it, and the answer is no."

Her mouth fell open. "But the custody."

I shook my head and cut her off. "That's between Eddie and me. I'll talk with him about it in court if need be."

She put her hands on her narrow hips. "You aren't going to stop me. I always get my way."

"Not this time." I stepped around her. "Now, if you'll excuse me, I need to get back to work."

She wrapped her arm around Hayden and steered him away. It took everything in me not to run after them and take my son back.

I smiled brightly at the members of the Cherry Foundation. "Are you ready to continue the tour?"

THIRTY-FOUR

"Since the sugarhouse appears to be occupied, Ms. Cambridge, why don't you just take us over to see the trailer now," Henry said.

"But you've hardly seen the festival," I protested.

"I saw enough, and despite your dog's run-in with a gallon of maple syrup, everything seems to be running brilliantly."

Was this praise from Henry? I wasn't sure if I could believe it.

Denise patted my arm and leaned close. "The sooner Henry sees the trailer, the sooner we will be out of your hair."

"The trailer is on the village side of the property," I said so that they both could hear.

The two board members followed me out of the maple grove and down the pebbled path past the oxen's pasture and a line of reenactors chatting with visitors. We reached Maple Grove Lane, where the noise was considerably less, and when we crossed the street, the noise from the festival was a only a soft murmur. The village was quiet, since it was still closed until the summer.

Puddles of melting snow and ice of every size lined the path to the green.

"I don't see the trailer," Henry said when we reached the green.

I smiled at him for the first time. "That's the idea." I pointed to the barn. "It's in the woods behind the barn, out of sight of any visitors. We wouldn't want a modern building marring the ambiance of the village."

"I see," Henry said, but not with his usual disapproval.

Denise gave me a thumbs-up sign behind Henry's back as if I'd passed some type of test.

I walked them to the trailer well-hidden in the trees. I knocked on the door and called for Jason.

"Can we see inside?" Henry asked.

I hesitated. The trailer was Jason's home, and I hated to invade my employee's personal space. On the other hand, Henry seeing the trailer and what good condition Jason kept it in might be the only way to keep Jason living on Barton Farm.

I knocked on the door again and called Jason's name. No answer. I opened the door. It was unlocked. I wasn't surprised.

I stepped in. The trailer was neat and tidy, as I expected. The pull-out couch that served as his bed was made. There were a few clean dishes on the minuscule kitchen counter sitting in a dry rack.

Henry stepped in after me. Denise didn't come in. I was grateful for that. The trailer was tiny, and three people in there at one time would be tight.

Henry glanced around. "Everything seems to be in order."

"Jason is a good kid," I said. "And a hard worker. His living here helps the Farm and me. It doesn't harm it in any way."

Henry nodded and walked to the door. I stepped out of the trailer to see Jason coming up the dirt path from the barn. He froze when he saw me in his doorway. He started to turn.

"Jason, wait!"

Denise gave him a big smile. "Hello, Jason. Kelsey was just showing us your lovely home."

Jason looked like he wanted to bolt.

I jumped down the last step from the trailer. "Jason, this is Henry and Denise from the Cherry Foundation. They wanted to see the trailer and how we keep it out of view from the visitors."

Jason nodded.

Henry watched him. "You care for the animals on the Farm?"

Jason nodded again.

"Why don't you show us the barn?"

Jason gave me a panicked look.

"That's a wonderful idea." I walked to Jason's side. "I think it would be helpful for the Foundation to know how much you do for the Farm."

Jason started walking toward the barn without a word.

When we reached the barn, Jason relaxed some. He was always calmer when he was around his animals. The dairy cow and the sheep were outside of the barn, in the small yard along Maple Grove Lane. From that vantage point, we had a clear view of the large pasture across the street where the oxen grazed on the dead grass revealed by the melting snow.

Jason showed Denise and Henry everything in the barn and introduced them to all the animals with as few words as possible. Miss Muffins oversaw the proceedings from her hay bale with a small smile curved on her lips. I believed I had the same expression.

Outside the barn, when Jason listed off the names of all the sheep, Henry said, "I believe we've seen everything we need. You've taken good care of these animals, my boy."

I gave a huge sigh of relief.

"We should be going, Kelsey, so you can get back to your regular duties," Denise said.

Denise and Henry headed toward the path. I was about to follow them when Jason stopped me. "Kelsey?"

I turned to face him.

"Thank you."

I shook my head. "There's nothing to thank me for," I said and joined the board members heading toward the pebbled path.

After we crossed Maple Grove Lane and reached the door of the visitor center, I said, "As you can see, Jason is a good addition to the Farm."

Henry turned to face me. "I can see that, but there's still a question of whether he should be living here."

"But everything with the trailer is in order. I thought you approved."

Henry frowned. "I admit it's not as bad as we were led to believe, but the board will have to discuss it. We have a meeting on Monday. You'll have our decision in the afternoon." He walked into the visitor center.

"But—"

Denise shook her head. "It's no use arguing with Henry when he gets this way. Don't worry. The board will consider everything, and I came along. I can speak on your behalf at the meeting."

"Denise, Jason has nowhere to go," I said.

She patted my arm. "I'll do my best, dear. You know that I will."

I watched as Henry and then Denise disappeared through the automatic doors. My shoulders drooped. It had been an impossibly long day. Other than Chief Duffy stomping around the grounds with his regiment, I hadn't seen any police at the Farm since Buckley's arrest. A small part of me still didn't believe that Buckley killed Beeson, but I couldn't even explain to myself why.

The Farm would close at three, and we had only an hour of the festival left. Many of the visitors were already leaving. I was about to start my rounds to make sure everyone had what they needed for the remainder of the day when Corrie Beeson stumbled out of the visitor center's doors. Tears streamed down her face, and festival-goers gave her a lot of space.

I hurried over to the girl. "Corrie?"

She looked at me with red-rimmed eyes.

"I'm Kelsey. I met you at the sugarhouse yesterday with Gavin."

"I remember," she murmured.

"What are you doing here?"

She played with the end of her scarf. "Is Gavin here?"

"He is."

"I want to see him to tell him the police made an arrest in my father's murder."

"I know," I said.

She wiped at her cheek. "Does Gavin know?"

I shook my head. "I don't think so. At least, I haven't had a chance to tell him." I placed a hand on her elbow and steered her toward the side of the visitor center. "Why don't you wait in my office while I go find him?"

"Are you sure? I know this festival is really important to Gavin. He's been talking about it for a while. He was so happy when you came up with the idea for the Maple Sugar Festival." She paused. "I was happy for him until I learned that my father would be involved in it." Her face clouded over.

"It's not a problem." I placed a hand on her arm and guided her to the employee entrance. I took a detour through our bustling industrial kitchen, where farm staffers and volunteers still zoomed back and forth in an effort to keep up with the demand for pancakes. By the looks of it, they had the task well in hand, passing along plates of pancakes assembly-line style.

I took one of the plates from a staffer with a wink, along with a cup of milk and a small container of pure maple syrup before ushering Corrie from the kitchen.

Outside the kitchen, I turned down a short hallway. My tiny office was at the end of it. The office was actually in decent shape. There were only a few stacks of books and museum catalogs on the floor. I'd spent much of January trying to make sense of the mess.

"Have a seat at my desk," I said, nodding to my office chair. I set the pancakes, syrup, and milk in front of her. Then I walked around the desk and sat in one of the two wooden chairs facing her. "Now eat."

She looked down at the plate. "I'm not hungry."

I folded my arms and used my best mom voice. "When was the last time you ate?"

She seemed to consider the question. "Thursday, I think."

"Since it's Saturday, that's not going to work. You have to eat something or you're going to keel over. You need your strength to face everything in the next couple of days."

"You mean for the funeral."

"Among other things, I'm sure."

She picked up a fork and pointed at the small container of maple syrup. "I don't like maple syrup." Her eyes held a challenge.

"Plain pancakes will do, then. Now eat."

She set her fork down and tore off a tiny piece of pancake and put it in her mouth. It was better than nothing, I supposed.

THIRTY-FIVE

"I DON'T HAVE TO worry about the funeral," Corrie said between bites of pancakes. "My stepmother is in her glory planning it. She's so mad at dad since he was fighting the divorce. She's probably happy he's dead."

"I saw your stepmother yesterday."

She tore off another piece of the pancake. This time I was happy to see the piece was bigger. "How? Why?"

"I was at the Cherry Foundation for a meeting. The Cherry Foundation sponsors the Farm, so I go there often."

"Oh, that's right," she said as if it made perfect sense. "I'm not sure what I'm going to do now. Sybil's going to throw me out on the street now that Dad is gone."

"She said that you didn't come home the night before."

"Home? Why would I go there? The house is all hers now. I crashed with friends."

"Maybe you should go to the house and talk to her. You're Conrad's daughter. You must be entitled to something."

The girl shook her head. "I'll go over and get my stuff when she's at work one day, but that's it. I don't want any of his things. Sybil should have them, not me."

I opened my mouth to argue but closed it. Conrad's attorney would have to contact her if she inherited anything, and I hoped that she did. I hated to think of the girl bereft in the world.

Corrie stared at Beeson's book on the corner of my desk. "I hate that book. It was my father's obsession. It ruined two marriages and my childhood. I don't even know why my dad got married or had children. All he seemed to love was maple sugar."

"Was he writing the book when he was married to your mother?"

"I don't know, but he was crazy about maple sugar. I can't remember a time that he wasn't. I think my father would rather have sugar maples than a daughter."

"You can't mean that." I picked up the book and flipped it over to read the back.

"Believe me. I do." She ripped off another piece of pancake and popped it into her mouth. "At least they arrested Buckley. Soon this will all be a bad dream."

It seemed to me that it would be more than a bad dream for Corrie for a long time to come. "They did arrest Buckley," I said. "But ... "

Her head snapped up from her plate. "What is it?"

"I'm not sure this is over. I don't think they got the right person."

"But the police arrested him," she protested.

"Sometimes the police make mistakes."

She frowned and forked another piece of pancake.

I stood. "You keep eating, and I'll see if I can find Gavin."

She nodded and concentrated on her food. I made a mental note to refill her pancake plate when I got back.

I left the building through the employee entrance again and headed for the sugarhouse. Visitors strolled away from the sugarhouse and lined up against the split-rail fence to watch the reenactors.

In the pasture, the police chief stood with the few members of the regiment that had come to the Farm that day. He walked up and down the line checking over their uniforms and making sure they stood up straight. There wouldn't be a battle during the Maple Sugar Festival, but Chief Duffy still wanted to run some drills to entertain the crowds.

"About face," yelled Chief Duffy in his Confederate General uniform. "March!"

The line of men in both blue and gray advanced forward in perfect synchronization.

There were a few people milling around the sugarhouse still, but they were watching the pasture too. This was the perfect time to pull Gavin away—if he wasn't at my cottage giving Tiffin a bath—to talk with Corrie.

Inside the dimly lit sugarhouse, I found Gavin in his nineteenth-century trousers and blue work shirt stirring the boiling maple sugar. John, one of my seasonal employees, poured maple syrup into the hydrometer to see how many brix the syrup had.

"Gavin?" I said.

"You just missed the big crowd I had in here. They cleared out when the regiment's drills began." He smiled. "By the way, Tiffin is fine. He's taking a nap back at your place. Your bathroom, on the other hand, is a little …" He searched for the right word. "Damp."

I grimaced.

"How's the syrup coming?" I asked as I peered into the basin at the finished product.

"Good. I plan to go to the sugarhouse in the park after I leave here to finish boiling off that batch. I volunteered to do it at the Sap and Spile meeting last night."

"That was nice of you." I stepped back from the hot basin. "I wondered if I could pull you away for a moment."

Gavin frowned. "Why? The drill won't last that long, and the visitors will come back to see my presentation."

"I know that, but it's important."

Gavin stirred the maple sugar.

"Sixty-six brix," John declared.

Gavin gave him a thumbs-up. "Great."

"Corrie is here," I said, trying to regain his attention.

He dropped his paddle into the boiling maple sugar. "Oh."

"Dude," John said. "That paddle's a goner."

"There's an extra one leaning against the wall there." I pointed.

John picked it up and handed it to Gavin.

Gavin shook his head. "Can you watch the sugarhouse until I get back?"

John's eyes widened. "What if a visitor comes in? I don't know what to say. What if I have to talk to someone?"

I shook my head. "Ask one of the reenactors to come step in. You can watch the sugar while he does the talking."

John still looked uncertain as Gavin and I left him in the sugarhouse alone.

"He'll be all right," I told Gavin as we walked back to the visitor center.

"I know." He increased his pace, and I had to half-jog, half-walk to keep up. "What did Corrie want? Why is she here?"

"She wanted to talk to you."

That was all Gavin needed to hear, and he took off toward the visitor center at a run.

I continued to the visitor center at a much slower pace. Once inside, I stuck my head in the kitchen and grabbed another plate of pancakes before I walked the rest of the way to my office.

When I reached it, Gavin stood in the hallway. With as fast as he'd taken off, I thought he'd have been inside of my office by now talking to Corrie.

"What are you doing out here?" I asked.

He glanced at me. "I can't make myself go in."

"Here, take this. Food is always a good peace offering, and she really likes the pancakes." I handed him the plates.

"With no syrup," Gavin said.

I smiled. "That's right."

He took a deep breath and stepped into the office. There was a yelp and a bang. Afraid that Corrie had knocked him to the floor, I peered in.

Gavin stood with his arms outstretched, holding the plates of pancakes. Corrie's arms were wrapped around his torso, and her face was buried in his chest.

He inched forward, Corrie still clinging to him, and set the plates on my desk, then wrapped his arms around the crying girl. Through blubbering tears I heard her tell him about Buckley's arrest. "I'm sorry. I'm sorry. A little part of me thought you'd killed him. It was just a small part, but I'm so sorry."

Gavin shushed her and rested his cheek on the top of her head.

I backed away. Maybe the murder investigation was really over. Detective Brandon believed it. Corrie believed it. Why didn't I believe it?

I headed back outside to watch the regiment's drills with the visitors.

"This is quite an event that you have here. I'm happy I was able to be a part of it." Robert Stroud stood at my side in a Confederate soldier's uniform.

"Thank you. Everyone at the class yesterday seemed to enjoy it."

"I would be happy to teach it next year," he said, a little too eagerly.

"I—I don't know what our plans will be for next year, or if we will even host another tree tapping class like that one."

"I think you should. I'm glad that sugaring during the Civil War is getting some attention. It's an important piece of history."

The sun popped out from behind a cloud, and I shielded my eyes. "Have you read Dr. Beeson's book, then? I've only read snippets of it myself, but it appears to be very well-researched."

"Of course it's well researched," he snapped.

I took a step back.

"I apologize. I only say that because Beeson got the best research that he could find." His smile was strained and he cleared his throat. "I haven't read it. But I know what it says better than anyone." He marched away, his back rigid like a man facing his fate on the front line.

A few feet away, a Confederate and a Union soldier argued with each other in front of a couple with forced smiles. Obviously, they felt caught by the two men.

"You see," the Union soldier told them, "maple sugaring is a way to preserve the Union, and one doesn't need sugar cane for sugar. We have no need of anything that the South has. We're far superior in our farms and our industrial production."

"Who wants cookies or cakes with no real sugar?" the Confederate asked. "It's a travesty, I tell you, an absolute travesty that you fine

Northern ladies"—he directed his comment to the woman—"don't have access to real sugar because the Yankees will not recognize that we're our own free country. We would happily trade with the North all the bounty of the South if they would give us that."

"Those Rebs are delusional if they think they can walk away from the great United States of America without ramifications. We beat the British Empire. A few traitorous states will not stop us."

The confederate soldier glowered at him. "You beat the empire with our help."

"And you should remember that you were part of something great once upon a time."

I was about to go over and break the argument up when the radio on my hip crackled. "Kelsey, come in, over!" Benji's voice came over the radio.

"Yes, Benji." After a beat, I said, "Over."

"Kel, you need to come over to the village, we have a situation. Over."

"What kind of situation?" I asked. "Over."

There was no response.

"Benji, answer me. I said 'over,' for Pete's sake."

Still no answer.

THIRTY-SIX

I HEADED TOWARD THE village at a fast trot. A power walker didn't have anything on me. I didn't run because I didn't want to attract visitors' attention to the possibility that something might be amiss on the Farm. In truth, I didn't know how my erratic walking was any less obvious than running.

Chase came up alongside of me. "What's wrong?"

"Where have you been?" I snapped.

"Hello to you too."

"I'm sorry," I said, not breaking my stride. "Benji radioed me. Something's wrong at the village. She asked me to go there right away. It seems to be one crisis after another around here."

"What happened?"

I increased my pace. "She didn't say. She broke radio contact."

We crossed Maple Grove Lane. As soon I reached the other side, I broke into a run.

Chase kept pace. He was over a head taller than me, so my flat-out run was only a light jog for him.

The green came into view, but I couldn't see anything out of place, and there was no sign of Benji either.

"Did she say where she would be?" Chase asked.

The village side of the Farm wasn't that big, but it could take a lot of time to search all the buildings for Benji.

I ripped the radio from my belt. "Benji, come in. Where are you? Over."

There was a pause. I was about to repeat my question when the radio crackled to life. "I'm in the barn. It's Ba—I mean Jason."

I sprinted in the direction of the barn. This time, Chase had to keep up with me.

I ran to the barn door, which was wide open. "Benji!" I could hear Chase behind me but I didn't turn around. "Benji!"

"We're in here!" She stepped out from one of the stalls.

I hurried over to Scarlett's horse stall and found Jason sitting on the floor holding a bloody rag to his head.

"What happened?"

Jason didn't answer.

I looked at Benji. "How did you find him?" I asked.

Benji gripped her radio. "I was just walking the grounds to make sure none of the visitors had wandered over here because we're closing. I made my loop and was about to leave when Jason stumbled out of the woods with his head bleeding."

Chase walked over to Jason. "Let me take a look."

Jason shrunk back and pressed the piece of cloth down on his head.

"I'm an EMT, remember?" Chase said, in a calm even voice that I knew he'd mastered on the job.

Jason relaxed just a little.

Chase knelt in front of him and opened his medical bag. He removed a pair of latex gloves.

"Those aren't historically accurate for a Civil War medic," Benji said.

Chase laughed. "I'll be sure to hide them from the visitors."

"You have real medical supplies in there?" I asked.

"You never know if you'll need them, and I learned at the reenactment last summer that reenactors hurt themselves all the time. It's best to be prepared." Chase reached for the cloth that Jason held so tightly to his head. Finally, Jason relented and let Chase remove the rag. It was saturated with blood. The wound was gruesome, but only a few beads of fresh blood had appeared when Chase removed the cloth. It appeared that the worst of the bleeding had stopped.

As Chase cleaned the wound, I began to pace. "Jason, you have to tell me what happened. What were you doing in the woods?"

"Following someone," he said barely over a whisper.

I froze. Benji and I stared at him. The idea of reclusive Jason once again voluntarily running after another person was baffling. Chase was unfazed by the announcement and dabbed at Jason's cut with antiseptic. With each dab, the cut was beginning to look less and less gruesome.

"You followed someone?" Benji asked.

Jason licked his lips. "After you left my trailer earlier, Kelsey, I saw someone moving through the woods. I thought it was the Hooper boys again. I know they must be angry that the police questioned them."

I stared at him. I hadn't realized he knew what was going on around the Farm.

Jason's Adam's apple bobbed up and down. "I wanted to make sure they weren't making any trouble, so I followed who I thought was them."

Benji wrinkled her nose.

"It wasn't them?" I asked.

He shook his head. "No, and whoever it was wasn't coming to the village. He was just moving through the trees toward Maple Grove Lane. I saw him cross the road out of view of anyone at the Farm. It was like he crossed there for that reason. He was headed into the park."

"Wow, B—Jason, you're downright chatty," Benji mused.

I shot her a look to be quiet. I didn't want Jason to freeze up again.

Chase placed a piece of gauze on Jason's forehead and held it there as he tore off a piece of cloth tape one-handed.

"Why did you follow him?" I asked.

"I thought the person wanted to cause trouble. I know Shepley is mad about me living here, and h-he told me he'd tell the Cherry Foundation board and they'd make me move. When I saw you and those two board members coming out of my trailer I knew it was true. I thought if I could protect the Farm, I would prove my worth."

"Oh, Jason," I said.

"How did you get hurt?" Benji asked.

Jason frowned. "After the guy left the Farm grounds, I headed back to the barn through the woods." His face flushed. "I tripped over a tree root and fell. I knocked my head on a rock."

"You were lucky that you weren't knocked out cold," Chase said as he smoothed the last piece of tape onto Jason's wound and started packing up his kit. "That cut wasn't so bad. It doesn't even need stitches. You might have a nice scar over your right eye, but it's a battle scar." He winked at Jason. "Girls like battle scars."

Benji snorted, and I had to agree.

"Thank you," Jason murmured.

Benji tapped her finger to her cheek. "Jason, what did this man look like? Did you recognize him?"

Jason tentatively touched the bandage over his eyebrow. "I've seen him this week at the Farm on the edge of the red maple grove, but I'm not sure who he is."

"What did he look like?" I repeated Benji's question.

"He was short, bald, and wore glasses."

"Robert Stroud?" I asked. "He taught the tree tapping class yesterday."

Jason nodded and then winced as if it pained him. "I guess. I first saw him the day before, on Thursday."

Chase and I shared a look.

"You saw him the day Dr. Beeson was murdered?" Benji yelped.

THIRTY-SEVEN

CHASE, BENJI, AND I headed back to the visitor center. Jason remained at the barn. Chase said that there was no need for him to go to the hospital.

Chase and Benji increased their pace to keep up with me. "Kelsey, what are you going to do?" Benji asked.

"I have to talk to Chief Duffy. He needs to talk to Stroud."

She ran in front of me and started walking backward. "Don't you think you should talk to Detective Brandon? It's her case."

I shook my head. "She's already made up her mind who the killer is."

"Buckley still could be," Chase said. "The Hooper boys saw him in the woods, and he even admitted to being there and witnessing the start of Beeson's heart attack. He could have easily taken the drill and finished him off."

I grimaced as the visitor center came into view. All the festival-goers were gone by this point, and the Civil War reenactors were making their way to the exit while my employees walked the grounds picking up the litter left behind. John from the sugarhouse had unharnessed

Scarlett and Rhett from the wagon and led them into the pasture for some peace and quiet.

"I know that," I said. "But it doesn't change the fact that Robert Stroud was on Farm land when the murder happened. He never told us that. There has to be a reason."

"Maybe he just didn't want to get involved," Benji said.

I ignored Benji's last comment and marched to the visitor center. Judy stood just outside the door, waving to the reenactors as they left, reminding me of Civil War photographs I'd seen of Southern ladies waving to bedraggled soldiers as they tramped by in a line.

"Judy, have you seen the chief?"

"Chief Duffy?" She dropped her hand in mid-wave.

I nodded.

"He left about a half hour ago. He said duty called him to leave early. He had to get to the police station. It seems that Detective Brandon found the person who killed the maple sugar professor."

"I know." I frowned. "Is Gavin around?" I thought I might ask Gavin what he knew about Stroud before I took this much further. Maybe I was wrong.

"He and a girl—I suppose it was his girlfriend by the way she was hanging on him, not that I've ever seen her before. Anyway, they left not long after the chief. Gavin said they were headed to the sugarhouse in the park. They took off across the pasture toward the red maples." She pointed in the direction Dr. Beeson had walked on the day he died.

A shiver ran down my spine. It was too similar to what had happened with Beeson. Just like before, Judy was telling me that someone had wandered off toward the red maples.

"I have to go after them," I said.

"But why?" Benji asked. She and Chase were behind me now and must have heard at least most of what Judy had said.

"Stroud could still be in the woods," I told her. "Something is off about his story. I can't rest until I know that Gavin and Corrie are okay."

"Stroud is a shrimp." Was Benji still trying to talk me out of it? "What could he possibly do to Gavin? Gavin is twice his size."

"If he stabbed Dr. Beeson, there's no telling."

Judy gasped. "But I thought the police already arrested the murderer."

"They think they did," I said. "I'm not nearly as certain. I may be wrong, but…"

"You're right," Chase said. "If you really think something is off with Stroud, we have to find those kids. If you're going, I'm going with you."

"Me too," Benji agreed. "Even though I think this is a waste of time."

I shook my head. "Benji, you stay here and call the police. Tell them everything Jason told us and that Stroud is in the woods with Corrie and Gavin. Tell them to meet us at the sugarhouse in the park."

With that, I headed for the pasture, just as I had two days before. Had it really only been two days? So much had happened in a short amount of time. There was Beeson's murder, the Hoopers' vandalism, Henry's threat, and finally Krissie's wedding plans. It was almost too much to take.

Chase squeezed my hand briefly after we climbed over the fence. "They'll be fine. We're worrying for no reason. Really."

"I hope you're right." But even as I said it, I knew that he wasn't.

We ran the half mile between the edge of the Farm grounds and the park's sugarhouse. Neither of us said a word, even when we passed the place where Beeson had been attacked. The crime scene tape tied around the trees to mark the spot looked as if it had been chewed on. I wondered if one of the squirrels who'd been wreaking havoc on Beeson's sugaring tubes was responsible.

When the sugarhouse came into view, the heady scent of maple sugar filled the air. Gavin must have been in the middle of production. The tubing was still attached to all of the trees, and I felt like I'd brought both Chase and myself on a fool's errand.

I slowed my pace. Chase was about ten paces behind me, looking at the tubing. "Everything seems to be—"

Thwack! A sickening sound interrupted Chase in midsentence. I spun around to see him on his knees, holding his forehead. He crawled to the closest tree and leaned on it. He closed his eyes. I thought he was passing out.

"Chase!" I screeched. I knelt on the damp earth in front of him. There was a large red welt forming in the middle of his forehead. "Chase! Wake up!"

My attention was so focused on Chase that I didn't see Corrie Beeson step out of the trees holding a shovel in her hands.

"He's out cold. You should be more worried about yourself," Corrie said, adjusting her shovel. "Get up!" she ordered.

I didn't move.

"Get up or I'll hit him again. This time I'll make it count." She glared at me.

Slowly, I stood. "Corrie, where's Gavin? Where's Robert Stroud?"

"Let's chat about it in the sugarhouse."

I looked at the tiny building with the smoke billowing out. "I don't think so."

She raised the shovel over Chase.

I waved my hands. "Okay! Okay!"

Corrie smiled and gestured to the sugarhouse. "Why don't we go in and check on our syrup?"

I looked around for Stroud and Gavin, but I didn't see them. It was possible they'd never been there at all.

"Go inside." She poked me with the shovel's blade, just enough that I knew she meant business.

There was no way I was going into the sugarhouse with Corrie.

When I didn't move, she raised the shovel over Chase's head again.

"Okay," I snapped. "Just don't hurt him."

Guilt washed over me. I'd been an idiot to run to this sugarhouse with Chase instead of waiting for the police. I knew they'd be here any minute, though. Benji would have called them by now. I just had to stall for time.

I walked the few feet to the sugarhouse. I stepped into the dimly lit building and blinked. "Where's Gavin?"

She sniffed.

"Corrie, where's Gavin? Is he okay?"

She pointed to a heap in the corner behind the table. Gavin lay there, unconscious. "I didn't want to hit him. I love him, but he gave me no choice."

I took a step toward him.

She pointed the shovel at me. "Don't move."

I inched back. I prayed that Gavin was still breathing. "Where's Stroud?" I asked in the calmest voice I could muster.

"You mean the person who was supposed to be blamed for my father's death?" she asked.

My eyes widened. "What do you mean?

"Stroud was the one who was supposed to get the blame, but everyone ignored him. Even you ignored him. He was the perfect suspect. I don't know why you couldn't see that."

"Buckley was arrested, not Stroud," I said.

"Yes." She nodded. "And that's fine with me too, especially since everyone seems to be happy about it. But you said you think the police arrested the wrong person. That's when I knew this would never be over, not as long as you kept asking questions. I need this to end."

I swallowed.

There was a dog-eared copy of *Maple Sugar and the Civil War* on a rickety wooden table in the corner of the room. The book had only been out a month or two, and I was surprised to see a new book in such poor condition.

"I see you have your father's book," I said, trying to stall.

"His book?" She snorted. "He didn't research that book. Robert Stroud did. Dad stole his notes, and I helped him. It's just another example of what I did for my father to prove I was worthy to be his daughter, but did he care? No. He never cared about me."

A chill ran down my spine, as it all made sense. Stroud had tensed up every time the book was mentioned because it was *his book*. He knew that Beeson had stolen his notes.

Something Corrie's stepmother had said came back to me—something about Corrie just wanting her father's approval and never getting it. I stared at the angry girl, who wasn't more than twenty-four years old. She had her whole life ahead of her. What life would it be now?

"And that's why you killed your father, isn't it?" I asked. "Because he wouldn't say he was proud of you."

"You don't know what you're talking about." She shook the shovel at me and I jumped back.

"Where's Stroud now?" I asked, almost afraid to hear the answer. She'd already hit Gavin and Chase over the head. Who knew what she'd done to Stroud?

"He was here when Gavin and I arrived. He was checking on the maple sugar. He left almost immediately."

I gave a sigh of relief that at least one person had gotten away from the sugarhouse without meeting the business end of Corrie's shovel.

"Buckley was there when your father had the heart attack. Were you two in this together?" I asked.

"Buckley was a coward. He had an argument with my father in the woods and upset the overweight monster so much that Dad keeled over from a heart attack. Buckley fled." Corrie snorted. "He's thought all this time that he was responsible for Dad's death. Maybe he is, in a way."

"Why were you even there?" I asked.

"Because I was helping him with the sugaring in the park. I knew he'd be busy getting ready for the tree tapping class, so I offered to check our trees. I was heading to the Farm to tell him I'd finished when I saw him arguing with Buckley. After Buckley left, I went to Dad and tried to help him. He pushed me away and told me I was making his chest pain worse. He said I made everything worse."

She was crying now. Large tears rolled down her cheeks. "Even when the man was dying, he criticized me and put me down. By taking his side in that argument over the sugarhouse, I'd given up Gavin, who I loved and who loved me, for my father, who didn't care for me at all. I saw the drill on the ground and picked it up. I don't know what happened. Something in me snapped. Every horrible thing my father ever said to me rang in my head in a rush. The next thing I knew, I was standing over him and the drill was sticking out of his chest with my hand on the handle."

My stomach clenched. "Why didn't you just run away when you realized what you'd done? Why didn't you leave New Hartford?"

"I couldn't leave Gavin. I love him."

I glanced over at Gavin again. "But you hit him."

"He figured out what happened," Corrie said mournfully. "I couldn't have him telling the police."

"Then go now. I'll take care of Gavin. Just go." I stepped away from the doorway to give her a clean getaway.

She stared at Gavin, who didn't stir.

"It's too late for that. The police will always be looking for me." She smacked the handle of the shovel against her hand. "I can't let you go. You know that. You know what I did."

"You think I'm the only one?" I thought quickly. "Chase Wyatt is outside. He's the police chief's nephew, and the police are on their way. My assistant already called them."

"You're lying."

Before I could answer, I heard noise from outside. "Kelsey!" someone called.

"See, they're already here," I said.

"Then I'll have to make this quick." Corrie took a step toward me with determination in her eyes. I didn't have much time.

The handle of the sugaring paddle stuck out of the boiling trough of sap.

I grabbed it, boiling drops of maple sugar falling onto the floor and onto my hand. Ignoring the burning, I whacked Corrie in the shoulder with the blade of the paddle in one sweeping motion. She cried out and dropped the shovel.

She didn't fall, so I whacked her again, this time on the other side. As she fell to the concrete floor, she reached out and grabbed the spigot on the maple sugar basin. A boiling hot stream of maple syrup poured onto her hands. Corrie screamed as it spilled onto the floor.

I jumped over her and turned off the spigot. My boots stuck to the floor and made a sickening sticky sound when I tried to lift them.

"Corrie?" I asked.

The girl moaned and cradled her hands. I didn't know how badly she was burned, but I had to get her some relief.

I put my hands under her armpits and half-lifted, half-dragged her through the open door of the sugarhouse.

Much of the snow in the woods had melted over the last two days, but there was still plenty in the places shaded by the trees. I dragged Corrie to a snowy patch and dropped her there. Then I made a snow pack and placed it on her hands, which were already red and blistering. She moaned.

Detective Brandon, Officer Sonders, and Benji came crashing through the woods just as I was packing more snow on Corrie's hands.

"Step back, Ms. Cambridge," the detective said.

I did as I was told. "Gavin is in the sugarhouse. She hit him over the head."

Officer Sonders took off for the sugarhouse at a run.

"Kelsey!" a weak voice called.

I ran to Chase, who was still at the tree where I'd left him. He was trying unsuccessfully to stand up. I put his arm around my shoulder and helped him.

He touched the welt on his forehead and winced. "I have a headache."

"You might have one for a few days." I rubbed his arm.

"Corrie hit me … with a shovel."

"I know. She killed Beeson."

"Why?" Chase wobbled.

"You're going to fall over. I'll tell you everything later."

He tried to focus on my face. "Did she hurt you?"

"No." I glanced over at the girl who was pressing snow to her hands while Benji and the police looked on. "I don't think we have to worry about her anymore."

Detective Brandon was talking on her cell phone. "I need an ambulance here ASAP. We have a burn victim and two head injuries."

"One head injury is me," Chase said, wincing.

"I know. Gavin's the other. Corrie really liked that shovel." I brushed Chase's hair out of his eyes to check if they were dilated. "You need to go to the hospital, and I'll take care of you until you're one hundred percent."

"That's sounds nice." Chase squinted. "Paramedics make terrible patients. I thought you should know that. We're kind of like doctors in that way."

I smiled at his attempt at a joke. "I'll take that under advisement."

EPILOGUE

By Monday, I'd come to a decision about Chase. I would give him a chance, a real chance.

It was time to stop controlling every little event in my life and see what would happened. I'd ended up marrying Eddie because it was planned and what was expected. Maybe it was time to face the world embracing the unexpected.

It turned out to be a good thing that Hayden was staying with Eddie that weekend, because as soon as Chase was released from the hospital, I'd trundled him to my cottage and parked him on the couch with Tiffin standing guard. Chase claimed he didn't need all the attention, but he said it with that teasing smile on his lips that I found equal parts infuriating and adorable.

The festivities on Sunday had gone off without a hitch. On Monday, I went to my office to do paperwork and called Henry several times, hoping for an answer about Jason and his trailer. Henry wasn't answering my calls. I figured I'd think about it later, and in the early afternoon I headed home. I knew Chase was preparing to leave—he was well enough to take care of himself, and we'd both agreed that he should head out before Hayden got home from school. I still wanted to take things slowly for my son's sake.

Chase was waiting for me outside the cottage, and he stood up when I walked through the gate. "There's my guardian angel."

I rolled my eyes. "Hardly. How's your head?"

"Fine. I've been fine for a while." He grinned as he walked toward me. "But I thought if I let on, you'd make me leave."

I suspected as much.

"I heard from one of my buddies at the hospital," he said. "Gavin is fine too. He was discharged yesterday."

I gave a sigh of relief. I wished the same could be said for Corrie. Her physical wounds would heal, but I didn't know if her emotional wounds ever would. Thinking of her made me terribly sad.

In three strides, Chase reached me. He placed his hand under my chin and tilted my face up.

I knew he was going to kiss me. It would be our first kiss. But then my cell phone rang. I checked the readout.

"Ignore it," Chase said.

I stepped back. "I can't. It's from the Cherry Foundation. It must be about Jason." I put the phone to my ear. "Hello?"

"Ms. Cambridge, this is Henry Ratcliffe from the Cherry Foundation."

"Yes, Henry. Have you come to a decision about the trailer?" I made a face at Chase, and he smiled.

"We have. You have all the appropriate permits, and after being to the Farm myself, I can vouch that everything is in order. We have no reason to force you to ask him to leave."

"That's wonderful news! Thank you!" I grinned at Chase.

Henry took a breath. "I have more good news."

"More good news?" I asked. Warning bells went off in my head.

"Yes. The Pumpernickle family has made a very generous donation to the Foundation."

"The Pumpernickle family?" There was only one person I knew with that last name.

"Yes. The only stipulation of the gift was that Barton Farm host their daughter Krissie's wedding to her betrothed, Edward Cambridge. Is he any relation to you?"

I couldn't answer.

"Ms. Cambridge, are you there?"

All the blood drained from my face. "I'm here."

"In any case, I told the family you would be happy to accommodate them. I'll be emailing you the wedding dates and requests for Barton Farm staff. It's a June wedding, so I know you'll want to start working on it right away."

"Okay." It was all I could manage. I thought it was pretty good under the circumstances.

"This is a wonderful development for the Foundation and for Barton Farm."

"Okay," I repeated. Now I knew what it felt like to be shell-shocked. I didn't like it.

Henry sniffed, perhaps at my lack of enthusiasm. "Well, I won't keep you. Have a good day, Ms. Cambridge."

"Good day." That was two words. A good sign that my vocabulary might recover.

Chase put a hand under my elbow. "What happened? You look like you've just been fired."

"It's not that." I swallowed hard. "You know that problem with Krissie that I didn't want to deal with?"

He nodded.

"It just got a whole lot worse."

He took my hands in his. "How?"

I studied him. "Are you sure you want to hear it? Are you ready for all the baggage that comes with me? A kid? An ex-husband and his future wife? Not to mention my father. And then there's this Farm and all its strings. It's a lot to take on. If you run away now, I'll understand."

Chase's face softened. "And my ex-fiancée is a police detective who hates you. I'd say we both come with some serious baggage."

I slipped my arm through his. "I guess we do."

ACKNOWLEDGMENTS

Thanks to my readers who enjoyed *The Final Reveille*. I hope you will love *The Final Tap* even more, and that Kelsey and her friends will make you laugh.

As always, thanks to my superstar agent Nicole Resciniti, who understands my quirky voice better than anyone else, and to my editors Terri Bischoff and Sandy Sullivan for giving this series a home.

Thank you to my assistant Molly Carroll-Syracuse and the Cozy Club for their endless publicity support of this and all my mysteries. Thank you also to my dear friend Mariellyn Grace for reading the manuscript in its early and somewhat convoluted stage.

Very special thanks to those who helped me research this novel, including Allegra Waldron for answering my countless questions about tapping trees, maple sugaring, and Ohio maple syrup, and Andy, Isabella, and Andrew for our undercover research trip and pancake breakfast taste test. Any mistakes about maple sugaring practices found in the novel are my own.

Finally, gratitude to the Heavenly Father for creating so many of the earth's wonders, including maple trees.

© Sara E. Smith

ABOUT THE AUTHOR

Amanda Flower, a multiple Agatha Award–nominated mystery author, started her writing career in elementary school when she read a story she'd written to her sixth grade class and had the class in stitches with her description of being stuck on the top of a Ferris wheel. She knew at that moment she'd found her calling: making people laugh with her words. She also writes mysteries as *USA Today* bestselling author Isabella Alan. In addition to being a writer, Amanda is a public librarian in Northeast Ohio.

www.amandaflower.com